HAMMERHEAD

A NOVEL BY

JASON ANDREW BOND

ISBN-10: 1463571917
ISBN-13: 978-1463571917

For more about the author, future novels, and events please visit:

www.JasonAndrewBond.com

ACKNOWLEDGMENTS

I want to offer sincere thanks to all those who helped me make my first novel a reality and have continued to support me as I move forward on new projects. I am grateful to my wife for her support and sincere honesty. I offer my mother thanks for all the flights in small airplanes and showing me how to "go for it" in life. My father's medical expertise was invaluable for this novel, as was his overall review. To my sister Jennifer, I extend my sincerest thanks for all the hours she put into reviewing my work. The technical expertise and insight she afforded me was invaluable. Sincere thanks is also due to Pat Johnson for her equally helpful review and editing. I must also thank Dennis 'Mac' McElroy for his invaluable fighter jet and flight expertise. There are many more who answered questions related to guns, drugs, etc. Their assistance is greatly appreciated. *Hammerhead* is a far better novel thanks to all these people's wisdom and support.

The talent and selfless effort Todd Krummenacher put into the cover art has brought a beauty and presence to *Hammerhead* well beyond my expectations. I am in his debt for it. I owe my extended family thanks as well for all their help during the many hundreds of hours Hammerhead took to write and edit. I want to offer special thanks to Eli for allowing me to tag along with him to Comic-Con and for putting up with all my short stories. Also, thanks is due to my writing instructors from Baldwin to Lyons. Without their mentorship, I never could have started down this long road.

Final thanks goes to my son for helping me wake up from my trance and chase my dreams. When I think of his future, my highest hope is that he will be brave enough to listen to his heart; in that hope, I have learned to listen to mine.

Convention dictates that I should select one person to dedicate this novel to. With so many wonderful people in my life, this is difficult. In the end, I have decided on someone who did not have a great deal to do with the creation of Hammerhead itself. His influence on my life goes back to younger days. I have often wondered where I would be now without his friendship...

For Jay

Thanks for loaning me the Interceptor.

TO THE READER

Before you begin reading *Hammerhead,* I would like to offer you sincerest thanks. I appreciate your time as a reader more than I can express. It is my ambition to create something of quality that is entertaining and satisfying. In pursuit of that goal, I have focused on Elmore Leonard's advice, "to leave out all the parts that readers skip."

It has been five years since I had my initial vision for this novel: a man standing on a mountain ridge watching a ship crash into the desert. Since that moment, I have spent hundreds of hours writing and editing. Now, the time has come to save the file one last time and let the story stand on its own. New projects are calling. Letting go is more difficult than I could have believed. I must trust that, in my hours of work, I have created something that you will enjoy. But, of course, I must let you be the final judge.

I do have one request. As I am currently a self-published writer, word of mouth is the main engine I must rely on. In light of this, I humbly ask that, if you should find *Hammerhead* to your liking, please tell others about it.

For my part, I will continue to strive to create the best stories I am capable of.

PROLOGUE

Stacy Zack sat in the freighter's command chair, her arms and legs strapped down and her head lashed to the headrest. Her hands and feet had gone numb from the tightness of the restraints, and crusts of blood rimmed the straps at her wrists where she had wrenched at them. To her right, blurring at the edge of her vision, she could see legs with a dark pool extending around the boots. Behind her someone choked on wetness every few breaths.

"David? Matt?" she said into the dark expanse of the bridge.

As before, she heard only the resonant vibration from the heart of the ship.

Looking over the control panel, she saw all the decades of the freighter's service worn into the switches and bezels. A cracked display continued its countdown with only a few seconds remaining. She pulled at the straps again, and pain burned into her shoulders.

"I can't die here," she said, "not now."

She looked above the console, out the bridge windows, to where the curved Earth filled the lower half of the long bank of glass. The sunlight glowing off the Pacific Ocean washed out the stars, leaving only blackness hanging above the planet. The blue ocean, laced with white storms, reminded her of the stained-glass windows of her father's church.

That's where they'll have my funeral.

She envisioned her coffin sitting at the head of the sanctuary, blades of colored sunlight falling across the polished black lid and brass fittings. Her father, mother, and sister would sit in the front pew, beyond the sunlight. But there would be no body. She would be reduced to ash in the atmosphere above their heads. They would have no proof she had died, and might live for years with false hope. Tears welled in her eyes and ran down her face. She did not sob, but allowed her grief out in silence.

The numbers ran out on the display and retro rockets fired. The freighter thrummed and lurched. Her restraints pressed on her as the ship slowed.

A feminine voice came through the bridge speakers: "Crash landing procedure initiated. Atmospheric contact is imminent. Please make your way to the nearest evacuation pod."

Stacy gripped the command chair's armrests.

The Earth tilted up in the windows and began to expand. Then, as the ship prepared to go belly in on the atmosphere, the rockets kicked the nose up. The Earth fell out of the windows, and Stacy had one final view of the stars.

After a few moments, individual gas molecules began tinking and popping on the hull. These increased in frequency until they grew to a roar, and the windows burned in orange fire.

CHAPTER 1

In the darkness before dawn, Jeffrey Holt walked across the tarmac of Las Vegas International Airport carrying a cooler and a stainless steel coffee mug. His transport sat out on the tarmac, a gunmetal tadpole of a ship, heavy in the center with large windows, high stubby wings, and a long rear stabilizer. A breeze trailed in from the west, and the fading stars spanned the mountain ridges, uninterrupted. It all meant one thing to Jeffrey: a good morning to fly.

Someone had propped a ladder up against the transport. As Jeffrey approached he saw a maintenance tech on top of the transport, head first in the jet intake. The tech slid out of the intake, stood, and came down the ladder. He had his back to Jeffrey as he folded some tools into a pouch.

"Working early this morning?" Jeffrey asked, bending over and setting his lunch cooler down.

The tech's arm jerked and his eyes targeted Jeffrey. "Jeez old man, you scared the hell out of me."

Old man is it?

Jeffrey stood up. At six foot six, his shoulders came even with the bridge of the tech's nose. The tech dropped his eyes to Jeffrey's chest and then back up.

A peppering of gray in the tech's hair and the lines around his eyes suggested experience, but his gaze flicked from one thing to the next like a sparrow searching for grubs. A good mechanic should have a hawkish stare. This one didn't. Unfocused mechanics made stupid mistakes, such as leaving a loose screw in an intake or improperly securing a wiring harness. Jeffrey looked up to where the tech had been standing on his transport.

"Who are you?" he asked the tech.

"I'm with Huntington Aircraft."

"What are you doing?"

"The guys in the office told me you leave pretty early, and I had some PM's I didn't want to leave for the weekend. Boss told me you're gone pretty much all day, every day."

Jeffrey looked the tech over. His jumpsuit had creases across the arms, chest, and legs from the original packaging, the "Huntington Aircraft" shoulder patch, and a name badge, which read "Arlo".

"Just start with Huntington?"

The tech looked at the creases in his jumpsuit and then back to Jeffrey.

Had there been a flash of hostility in his eyes just then?

"Yeah, just started, but I've got a lot of experience."

"Nothing personal, but I only want Javier Martinez working on my transport. I've made that clear to the folks in the office."

"They told me you might be upset," Arlo said, "but I only greased some Zerks. I'm a good tech you know."

"I don't know," Jeffrey said. "I want my transport handled right."

"Pal," Arlo said, picking up his tool pouch, "I'm good at my job. If you have a problem with something, tell the boss." He tilted the ladder off the side of the transport and hefted it under his arm. Then he turned and walked away, saying, "Thing's a pile of crap anyway."

Jeffrey picked up his lunch cooler and looked at the transport. Dents and scrapes marred its aluminum surface. A hairline crack ran down the side window. Below the window, worn lettering read:

US D par me t of Orb tal Reclam tion.

"It's definitely a pile of crap, Arlo," Jeffrey said to himself, "but it still gets me to work." He pressed his thumb on a plate, and a green bar of light scanned it. The rear ramp popped open and lowered to the tarmac.

He set his cooler and mug on the ramp and looked up to the top of the transport.

Zerk greasing?

He took his sat-phone out of his pocket, scrolled through the contacts, and tapped the number for Huntington Aircraft. The phone went to voicemail after several rings, and he said, "This is Jeffrey Holt. What's the story on this 'Arlo' you've got working for you? I've said before, I only want Javier working on my transport. Call me."

He hung up the phone, pocketed it, and looked back up.

I don't have time for this.

Picking up his cooler and mug, he walked up the ramp and bent to enter the cockpit. He toggled a switch on the bulkhead, and the ramp lifted and closed.

Placing his cooler to the side, he settled into the pilot's seat and pressed a button. The seat shifted forward, bringing him up to the controls and instruments. He balanced his coffee mug on the console, fired up the engines, and went through his preflight.

Everything seems to be running well, so maybe Arlo's okay.

Jeffrey had his doubts though. He had known very few good mechanics.

Pulling back on the controls, he lifted the transport off the tarmac and aimed it at the northern desert. He slid the throttle forward, and the transport accelerated, pushing him back into the seat. When he reached his cruising altitude, he looked over the panel of circular gauges. They all read within range, yet something felt wrong. He tapped on the air intake pressure gauge. It read a few ticks lower than usual, but everything else appeared to be normal.

Just let it go.

As he looked out on the morning sky, cold and blue over the mountains, he couldn't let it go. He closed his eyes and listened to the transport. He tapped his finger with the rhythm of the twin engines. Then he realized what was bothering him. Somewhere above the rhythm ran a thin whine. Jeffrey turned, reached up, and smacked the roofline with the palm of his hand. The whine remained. He tilted his head aiming his ears at the sound.

Looking out the windows, he considered what to do. Turn around and have it looked at, or just head on? To his left, the night's last star—Jupiter—hung over the western horizon. To his right, the rising sun caught chips in the windshield causing them to sparkle a deep orange. He had already flown over halfway to the landing strip, and he had to be on-site this morning. He'd have the whine dealt with later.

Careful not to bump the flight yoke, he shifted his weight, trying to relieve the ache in his lower back. He lifted his coffee mug from its balanced place on the console and watched steam rise from its vent. He sipped from the cup, trying to forget the whine, but it did seem to be getting louder.

Was it? Or was he just reading into it too much?

Damn Arlo and his Zerks.

Jeffrey's wife had often complained that he overanalyzed life. At times, during their thirty five years of marriage, she had half joked that she should leave him because he could not simply accept things as they were. She finally had left him the previous winter for the great hereafter. The memory welled up a sad burn in his chest, and he forced it back down where it seemed to exist permanently, in the center of his rib cage, tucked up under his heart.

As he closed in on thirty miles to his destination, he set his mug aside and took hold of the steering yoke. The engines hummed along and he reached out and switched off the autopilot. A bang like a gunshot overwhelmed the sound of the engines followed by a piercing shriek. Then the engines fell silent. Warning indicators lit up across the console, and Jeffrey felt the flipping sensation of weightlessness. The transport tipped down and fell toward a mountain ridge.

His harness held his weightless body to the seat as he watched the mountain rise up at him. He froze. As a Marine he had served six years of heavy combat. During those years, even when he had to wipe his hand across the inside of his windscreen to clear it of blood and bits of bone and fly without a navigator, he had never frozen. Now he had. The void of his mind took in the ridge filling the windscreen and the feeling of weightlessness tickling his guts and throat. A pocket of air shook the ship, and his mug launched weightless off the console. It clipped a corner, popping the lid off, and hot coffee splattered across Jeffrey's face and chest.

Jeffrey's body jolted with the heat of the coffee, and he came to life, reaching out and hitting a switch, which purged the fuel system. He pulled back on the stick, but without thrust the stubby wings wouldn't generate lift. The transport stalled, and the nose dropped again. The mountains came at him faster now, and he could make out detail in the shadows of boulders. He waited for the light to indicate a primed fuel system. When it blinked green, he thumbed the 'engine on' toggle hard enough to crack the clear plastic stem. The mountainside filled the transport's window now. He would pin in halfway down the slope. He jammed his finger on the firing button. The engine razzed hard and shuddered. He jammed his thumb on the firing button again, and the engine roared. The transport launched at full acceleration toward the mountain, shoving Jeffrey into his seat. He yanked the throttle back.

Too close and too steep to pull up over the mountain, Jeffrey stamped on the foot pedals, slipping the transport onto its side. Then he wrenched the flight yoke back. The transport's frame groaned. Jeffrey gritted his teeth and growled under the G force, but the transport pulled true and, with only a few hundred feet to spare, the mountain slid away. He leveled off and brought the transport down to fly slow and close to the desert floor.

He wiped the coffee off his face with the palm of his hand.

"What the hell," he said, looking back up to the rear ceiling. The twin engine design used bulletproof turbines. Failures were unheard of. With two... having both shut off at once should be impossible. Jeffrey remembered that touch of hostility on Arlo's face.

He thought about landing at the base of the mountain and radioing for help. The transport sputtered, but seemed to want to keep going. He didn't feel like spending eight hours in the desert waiting for help when in ten minutes he could be sitting at his desk. He still had work to do. Pushing the throttle forward, he brought the transport up over the mountain he had almost crashed into. The engine hesitated a moment and then accelerated. He continued on across the desert. He kept his attention focused on the transport now, ready to land if he sensed any trouble from the engines.

He flew over another ridge of mountains, and the landing strip came into view: a one-time inland sea between two ranges of craggy mountains. The valley floor, a flat sheet of salt-encrusted dirt, ran east to west ten miles wide and roughly fifty miles long. The eastern side of the valley floor still lay in shadow. Beginning in the shadows and running out into the sunlight lay long, ripped craters made by the crash landings of hundreds of ships. Thanks to Jeffrey's long hours of work, no wreckage remained.

The transport, now showing no signs of trouble, crossed the width of the strip in minutes. When Jeffrey flew over the northern ridge of mountains and into the next steep valley, he turned hard right. On any other day he would have turned left, brought the transport down into the valley, and flown over the scrap yard surveying the cut pieces of wreckage set in stacks and rows. Today he flew straight toward the squat bunker on the eastern end of the valley. High, thin window slits broke the smooth surface of the bunker's gray walls. He aimed the transport at the white landing pad next to the bunker.

Smacking a toggle, he felt the landing skids thump into place. He stabilized the transport over the black X on the landing pad, jets firing down, and–without ceremony–dropped it to the ground. He reached up and yanked the yellow and black emergency stop handle. The engines went silent and all the lights on the console fluttered off. He exhaled and sat for a moment, feeling adrenaline still glowing in his arms and legs.

"Not today, you pile," he said.

He had some trouble unbuckling his harness as his hands and arms felt weak and trembled slightly. Looking to his left, he saw coffee spattered across the cockpit glass. He took a rag from his pocket, wiped the window, and then the console between the instruments, then pocketed the rag and scowled at the smeared glass. He pressed a switch, and the seat pulled away from the controls. Stooping, he stepped around the seat and picked up his cooler. He found the coffee mug and its lid lying in the back corner. Opening the cooler, he put the mug in it. Then he flipped the manual ramp release and the ramp popped open, its weight pulling it to the tarmac. Turning his shoulders to fit through the doorway, he made his way down the ramp and into the desert's warming morning.

He looked up at the exhaust ports and saw white dust coating the carbon-stained metal.

That's not good.

He reached up and held his hand near the metal. Heat radiated from it. He'd have to let it cool down and give it a look later, after the freighter crash. Stepping around the side of the transport, he set the cooler down and stuffed a hand and a foot into spring loaded panels and pulled himself up. He lay down on top of the transport, feeling the cold metal against his stomach and chest. He peered into a vent grid, but the sunlight glinting on the aluminum slats prevented him from seeing into the darkness. He took a penlight from a thigh pocket and shined it into the vent. Shielding his eyes with his hand, he could only make out a few dim shapes of wire bundles and pipes. He put the penlight back in his pocket and slid down to the hand holds.

As he walked toward the bunker, dust lifted around his worn, steel-toed boots. He passed a weathered sign which read, "United States Government Orbital Reclamation Facility. No unauthorized personnel allowed."

Jeffrey made his way into the shade of the bunker, up the cement stairs, and into the cool doorway. He typed a code into the keypad, and the magnetic lock gave way with a thump. He pushed the door open.

Stepping into the large one-room bunker, the door shut behind him, and he said, "How the hell did you get in here?"

CHAPTER 2

A tarantula the size of his hand walked across the center of the room. Jeffrey moved sideways around the edge of the room, keeping the spider in sight. He bumped into a table, and the spider turned and skittered towards him. He grabbed an empty box from the table and threw it onto the spider. Two hairy legs stuck out under the edge of the box and then rasped back.

Jeffrey realized he was holding his breath and let it out, his spine tingling. He took another sheet of cardboard, slid it gently under the box and then picked the entire container up. The spider skittered around, dry feet on paper fibers. Goose flesh rose on Jeffrey's arms. He took the container outside and tossed it off to the side of the bunker. He walked back inside, twitching once more as the door shut behind him.

He walked to the desk near the center of the room and sat down. A computer monitor, keyboard, phone, and legal pad sat on the desk. Beside the monitor, a titanium cup that had once been part of a ship's instrument console held two pens and one pencil. Jeffrey straightened the pens in the cup. Next to the cup sat a plain, black frame with a photo of his wife, young and pretty. A photo of his son lay over the lower corner of the frame, covering his wife's shoulder. His son wore BDU's and posed kneeling with his rifle. It had been taken the year before. The two photos complimented each other. His son was physically more his mother's son, shorter and thin. The similar smiles hinted at broad senses of humor. Jeffrey smiled at his son's photo, a living part of his wife still with him.

Jeffrey tapped the screen with his finger. It glowed dark blue, booted, and brought up the operating system with a flick of light. He took a folded red cloth from the desk drawer and wiped the already clean screen.

He brought up a Las Vegas news station on the computer and set it to run in the background. Opening his e-mail client, he typed:

"Transport 1534-AF experienced trouble this morning. Engines lost power approximately 25 miles from work site. Repair crew requested. Note work done in AM by tech named 'Arlo' with Huntington Aircraft." He tapped the send icon on the screen.

Standing, he walked toward the kitchen area and looked back at where the tarantula had been on the floor. The bunker was sealed. He looked at the half-inch steel grates over the air vents. It could only have entered the bunker by hanging on his leg last Friday when he had come in the door from the yard. The thought made his shoulders twitch again and gooseflesh rise, so he put it out of his mind.

"…protests of the new military spending budget met with greater public support over the weekend…," the news program from his computer went on, as he stepped into the small kitchen area and took the stained carafe from the coffee maker. He reached into the cabinet above him and brought down a rumpled bag of sugar, a plastic container of creamer, and a mug with 'Hoover Dam' printed on the side. "…was quoted as saying that without an external threat there is no need for the new weapons systems…"

He looked into the small mirror and saw coffee soaked in across his shirt. He turned on the faucet and washed his face and then, picking up a clean towel, scrubbed the water out of his trimmed white beard. He looked back in the mirror. He looked older every day. His white hair with shocks of gray had not one strand of its once jet black color. Even his eyebrows had gone silver. At least the smile lines in the corners of his eyes made him look younger, and he supposed he had held up well over the years, more distinguished than worn out. Looking down at the coffee stain on his shirt, he set the carafe aside. He'd had enough coffee for one day. He walked back to his desk, and began reviewing his work files.

The transport's engine failure kept coming back into his mind. He took out his sat-phone.

"In local news the 'landing strip' will be active today."

Jeffrey's eyebrows went up. He set his phone down and brought up the video to see a young, female reporter standing next to the image of a man positioned for effect on the bridge of a battle cruiser. The man wore a Naval Officer's uniform. Behind him, the Earth floated at geosynchronous distance. The man's evenly toned hair did not quite match the age of his face.

Not six months earlier, that man had held a cup of coffee poured from the old carafe on the counter and sat in the chair across from Jeffrey's desk.

The woman said, "The 40-year-old freighter Jules Verne will be entering the Earth's atmosphere at 11AM and touching down shortly after. So, if you feel a thump, just be glad we're 175 miles away."

"I think I'll get slightly more than a 'thump' here," Jeffrey said to the screen.

The reporter continued, "We have with us, via live feed, Admiral Sam Cantwell to give us some more information on the process." She turned to the Admiral. "What is the purpose of landing the freighter here?"

"Let's start off with the fact that this is not a landing," the Admiral said in his smooth, political voice. "This is a controlled crash. After the Jules Verne is 'landed' there will probably be no pieces bigger than a living room."

The reporter said, "That's quite an impact for a freighter that is nearly 1,500 feet long."

"Yes it is. But it is all well controlled. Safety is our highest priority. We will 'land' the ship far out in the desert away from population centers. This is more for the limitation of noise than for safety's sake as we have the ability to autopilot these ships down out of orbit into a very precise area."

"Why don't you just land them carefully and then dismantle them?" the reporter asked.

"That's a good question. First let's touch on what is happening with these ships. They are being decommissioned. We would like to retain as much of the materials in the ships as possible, but dismantling in orbit is far too costly and dangerous. We cannot bring them in for a polite landing as they were never designed to come down out of orbit. Just the reentry tears them up badly. We add re-entry shielding, but it is only enough to prevent premature break up, not preserve the structure. Also, these ships have no landing gear, no method of safely touching down. Not to mention that the 'landing' starts the demolition process for us very nicely."

"That's easy enough for you to say," Jeffrey said to the screen. "Just make sure your folks land this one square so I don't have to walk ten miles hunting hull fragments."

"What about any environmental impact from the burning of the hull on reentry? Some groups claim…"

Jeffrey brought up his work files. He viewed a message reminding him that the Jules Verne would be coming in today. He had been waiting for the freighter for weeks. Over a month ago he had finished up his work out on the landing strip cleaning up a retired asteroid mining ship and was left organizing the scrap yard and coordinating shipments of materials out. This 'new' ship, the Jules Verne, was a Kappa class freighter built by the General Electric Corporation, a steel cage of a ship. Some ships came in and exploded into two inch strips of aluminum and powdered glass. With those he was left to sift through the wreck with magnets to separate the metals. A Kappa class freighter would leave him with a lot of demolition work, the best part of the job.

He looked at his watch. It was getting up on 9AM. If he wanted to see the ship come in, he'd have to start walking soon.

· · ·

The footpath switchbacked up the ridge. As Jeffrey hiked along the narrow trail, his back loosened up and the ache went out of his knees. He breathed in the now warm air, smelling the iron dust of lava rock and the faintly floral mark of the desert spring. By 10:45 he stood on the crest of the ridge. The heat of the day and the exertion of his hike brought out sweat on his forehead. Sweat also soaked the armpits of his shirt and the fabric between his shoulder blades. He wiped his face with his hand and looked out on the landing strip stretching away west, shimmering with heat waves. As he stood, the dull ache returned to his knees and the small of his back. He thought how he had not heard back from Huntington Aircraft yet, and he reached for his phone, realizing only then that he had left it on his desk.

Oh well, soon enough.

At 11AM Jeffrey held his hand up to shade his eyes and searched the eastern sky. The sun overhead blinded his eyes and he took his cap from his back pocket and put it on. Searching again, he caught a glowing point between two gauzy clouds. The point grew, and a faint trail of smoke rose behind it. He knew an arc of fire traced across the sky behind the ship, but he could not see it. Where he stood, the freighter was coming in, give or take, straight at him.

The point became a ball, then a small sun, then a hulk searing the atmosphere at well over the speed of sound. Then the thing looked too close. It wasn't coming down square into the valley. It appeared to be coming straight for the mountain ridge Jeffrey stood on. He shouldn't have been on the ridge. When a ship came in, protocol directed him to stay in the bunker until he heard it hit, and then go to work. For years however, he had climbed the mountain and watched the spectacle of the ships slamming into the valley.

As the fireball came closer, it took on the shape of the freighter. Small bits tore off and vaporized in streaks of smoke.

The freighter cleared the mountain range, pelting the rocks with burning chunks and flashed past him no more than a quarter mile away. It hammered into the valley floor close to the base of the mountain range.

He realized at the last moment that he had not put in ear protection, and he clapped his hands over his ears just as the sonic boom punched him in the chest. Then the shock wave from the ship's impact, passing up through the ridge of rock, vibrated the ground. Dust and smoke wrapped over the freighter and accelerated outward, billowing up the mountainside. Jeffrey lowered his hands, his ears ringing.

Well, I'm not getting any smarter apparently.

He massaged the small of his back. The dust and smoke rolled up the ridge, and the wind caught it and brought it up and over. The blue sky hazed to brown as the clean acid smell of burning metal washed over him. Down below, the wind thinned the dust and smoke enough to expose debris glinting along the foot of the mountain.

Great, what a mess.

...

An hour later, he sat in the bunker on the phone with the Commander of the re-entry team.

"This is Holt."

"Holt?"

"Yes, Holt with demolition."

"Oh yes, the breaker, good to hear from you. I assume everything is fine on your end then?"

"We got a bit more of a bump than usual down here," Jeffrey said, fishing for an admission that the ship had come in off-course.

"Yes, we were close to you on that one; however, from here it looks like we hit the valley floor just fine. We're calling the landing successful and handing responsibility of the Jules Verne over to you."

"What's left of it anyway."

"That's affirmative."

No sense of humor, those guys.

Hanging up the phone, he pressed his hands on the tops of his thighs as he stood, walked over to a steel cabinet, and opened it. The inside smelled of gun oil. He took a jumpsuit from its hangar. The tough green fabric of the jumpsuit had thin metal bands mounted at the ankles, knees, elbows, and wrists. Stripping down to his boxers, he stepped into the suit's legs, shuffled his arms into the sleeves, and zipped it up from crotch to neck. He put his boots back on and snapped a metal band around the arch of each foot. Reaching back into the cabinet, he pulled out gloves with similar metal bands around each finger joint and put them in a thigh pocket.

A faint ticking sound caught his attention. He looked over at the door. The twig-on-glass tapping sound stood out in the silence of the bunker. Jeffrey walked to the door and pushed it open, shoving the tarantula aside.

"What the hell are you doing back?"

The tarantula ran at him, and Jeffrey stomped down on it. In that moment, he knew that his transport's engine failure had not been accidental; someone was trying to kill him. Despite his best efforts to stay clear of them, he had stepped on tarantulas before, crushing one now and again as he walked around the scrap yard. For someone naturally troubled by spiders, crushing one the size of an apple was traumatic. The thin, woody crunch of the exoskeleton and the following sliding sensation, as the spider's gutty smear filled his boot tread, made Jeffrey's skin crawl for days after.

He had failed to crush this spider. Instead, the abdomen of the spider still pressed into the sole of his boot. He lifted his boot, and the spider ran at his other foot. Jeffrey jumped back and brought his heel down hard. He heard a pop, and smoke puffed out one side of his boot tread.

He lifted his heel and watched the legs. They did not move. He pulled his foot away, ready to bring it down again, and saw where a break in the abdomen of the spider revealed a circuit board. Jeffrey walked over to his workbench and brought back a pair of pliers. He picked the spider up with the pliers and took it back to the workbench, set it down, and looked it over. The outside had a natural appearance. The 'skin' had been torn away in a few places revealing the glossy grid of carbon fiber. He gripped one leg with the pliers and turned the spider over. The bottom appeared to be a normal tarantula aside from a bevel cut hypodermic needle extending from the jaws.

He touched the belly of the spider and his hand reflexively pulled away. He put his hands on the workbench, his right arm twitching.

Damn thing's too real.

He took leather work gloves from a hook and put them on. Picking the spider up, he squeezed the thorax. The needle extended farther out of the mouth, a drop of clear liquid emerging on the tip.

"I don't know what you had for me there, but I hope you're the only one."

He turned around and scanned the floor, his back and arms crawling with gooseflesh and his lower legs feeling exposed. Nothing moved in the bunker. Jeffrey walked across the room. He had been lucky. If he hadn't come in just when he did, while the spider was crossing the room, it probably would have had him. He wondered if its programming had gone haywire causing it not to hide and wait for its target. As he walked, he stayed well clear of areas that had low lying shelves and boxes. He took an old ammo box from a shelf and returned to the workbench. He set the spider into the box, clamped it shut, took a black bag from under the work bench, placed the box into the bag, and set it aside.

Pulling the work gloves off, he put a specialized screwdriver in his pocket, and walked out of the bunker. The sun felt warm on Jeffrey's face and arms as it chased the morning's coolness out of the shadows. When he reached the transport, he stepped into the shade of the tail section and looked up at the engine exhaust. A White layer coated the burned-in carbon of the exhaust. He ran his finger over the white material, and it cracked under his touch, falling away in chalky flakes. He caught a large flake and, holding it in the palm of his hand, jabbed it with his index finger. It crushed to powder. He smacked his hands together, knocking the powder off. Then, moving around to the side of the transport, he climbed up.

The metal rings on his jumpsuit clicked on the hot aluminum surface. Sitting on his knees, he took the screwdriver out of his pocket and loosened the fasteners on a vented inspection panel. He pulled the panel open and looked over the fuel and coolant pipes and heavy looms of multicolored wire. He ran his hand along the wire looms, smooth and solid. Moving to the other side of the engine intake, he pulled a similar panel. There he found the same thing: nothing wrong. He rubbed the back of his neck and clicked his teeth together.

He traded the screwdriver for his flashlight, turned it on, and put it in his mouth. Then he got down on his belly and slid head first into the engine intake, the metal rings on his jumpsuit scraping.

Waist-deep in the intake, he found a box glued down with a blue smear of epoxy. The sun had heated the intake enough that sweat began to run into Jeffrey's eyes. He took the flashlight out of his mouth and wiped his forehead with the back of his arm. He inspected the box. It was about the size of a kid's lunchpail and had a curled antenna sticking out one side. On the front, an LCD readout flashed dashes.

Along the top edges of the box hung ragged strips of what appeared to be canvas. He gripped one, ripped it off, and held it up to the light. By the shape of the strips, Jeffrey guessed the canvas had been some kind of containment bag. The pattern of the strips suggested it had been blown open with small explosive cords. He ran his fingers inside the top of the box and found the same white powder as on the exhaust port, but here it was fresh and loose. He touched the tip of his finger to his tongue.

"Sodium bicarbonate," he said, "Nice trick. Well Arlo, you certainly don't care about leaving evidence behind."

He took the screwdriver from his pocket, jammed it under the box, and yanked up. The box cracked free from its place. He pushed himself out of the intake with his elbows. Outside, a breeze blew on his damp face. His transport had nothing permanently wrong with it, and he had successfully evaded two attempts on his life. He looked up at the mountains around him. Thinking of these positive points did not improve his mood.

Jeffrey looked back at the box and thought on what to do.

Why would someone want me dead?

He had done nothing important for over thirty years. During the war he had killed, but there was never a face-to-face interaction. In the end they had killed the invaders entirely. No one of any consequence should know him, and he had no current conflicts. He looked out at the smoke rising up over the southern ridge from the crash site and considered that his answer might lie in the wreckage of the Jules Verne.

He slid off the transport and jogged to the bunker, carrying the box. As he opened the door, his sat-phone rang. He took it out.

"Hello?"

"Jeffrey?"

"Yep."

"This is Sal over at Huntington Aircraft. You called about a tech named Arlo?"

"Yeah. Does he work for you?"

"No. You sure he said he was working with me?"

"Yes."

"That's not possible—"

Jeffrey cut him off, saying, "Sal, watch your back. Something's very wrong."

"Are you all right?"

"For now, but don't tell anyone you spoke to me. If anyone comes asking about me, treat them like a rattlesnake: be nice and keep your distance."

"Is your transport okay? Do you need a lift? I can be there in less than an hour to pick you up."

"No. I'm okay, for now," Jeffrey said, looking back to the smoke over the hill. "But I need to do a bit of research before I head out of here."

"I don't know what the hell is going on, but be careful."

"Will do, Sal."

Jeffrey ended the call and stepped inside the bunker. He walked to the workbench and opened the bag with the spider in it. Setting the box from the air intake into the bag, he folded the top over. He went to the cabinet where his jumpsuit had hung and opened a drawer. He took out two boxes of ammunition and two loaded magazines. He put the boxes and magazines into the cargo pockets of his jumpsuit. Then he took an angular .45-caliber Colt 1911 pistol from the drawer. The gun had nicks and wear along the surface, but when he thumbed the magazine release, it drew smoothly out. Setting the magazine down, he pulled the slide back. A round flipped out. He caught it in the air and then inspected the gun's chamber and barrel. Picking up the magazine, he pushed the round into it, slid the magazine into the gun's handle, and thumbed the slide release, chambering the round. He walked to the workbench, picked up the bag containing the box and the spider, and stepped out of the bunker. Without ceremony, he test fired the gun up into the mountain. He pocketed the gun and walked out into the scrap yard making his way toward the Gorilla.

CHAPTER 3

Jeffrey walked toward what appeared to be a stack of scrap metal among several other stacks. This stack was more compact and unified than the others: a pile of metal angles, hydraulic hoses, and scratched black paint. He stepped through a gap in the side of the stack and into the shade. In the dim light underneath, he climbed up a ladder and opened the cab of the Gorilla. He strapped the bag containing the box and the spider in the corner, leaned against the back rest, pulled a five-point harness over his shoulders, and buckled it in the center. Then he reached between his legs, pulled the final strap up, and buckled it in. Flipping up a cracked plastic cover, he pressed the green power button. A whine and vibration rose up from the machine. He pressed the 'CAB CLOSE' toggle, and the steel plate doors swung shut leaving him with only the green glow of the power button. In the darkness, he found the gloves in his pocket and put them on. Then, reaching up, he took the VR goggles from a hook and pulled them over his head. In the goggles he could see, so close it was difficult to focus on, the outside surface of the Gorilla. He pushed the ear pieces into his ears.

"Activate controls, code: Delta Oscar Romeo India Sierra."

A female voice said, "Activation Code accepted."

The Gorilla unfolded in a slow arc to stand twenty feet tall, squat legs and long arms, heavy shoulders, and no head. Jeffrey went through his pre-op check moving the fingers of one hand and then the other. He closed the fist and inspected the armored knuckle plates. Aside from a slight glitch now and again, the stereo HD image from the VR goggles soon fooled the mind into perceiving the large metal arms as physically part of the operator.

Jeffrey held his left hand up in the black space of the cab, and the gorilla's arm mimicked him.

"Gorilla, cutter," he said. The left hand folded open at the wrist, lay back on the forearm, and a metal bar extended from the opening. He pulled his index finger in a trigger motion, and a blue arc sparked along the edge of the bar.

"Gorilla, hand." The cutter retracted, and the hand flipped back into place. Jeffrey took a step. The cab's floor panels shifted, imitating the sensation of ground moving underfoot. The Gorilla stepped forward.

"Let's get to it then," Jeffrey said. The Gorilla, mimicking his motions, slapped its metal hands together and walked off through the scrap yard to a tunnel in the side of the mountain.

Entering the tunnel, Jeffrey said, "Gorilla, lights," and spotlights on the Gorilla's shoulders flashed on, illuminating the shot-creted walls.

As Jeffrey walked the Gorilla down the tunnel, more and more dust floated in the beams of the spotlights. When he should have seen sunlight glowing at the end of the tunnel, only dust and darkness surrounded him. Where the tunnel should have opened into the desert, Jeffrey found the way blocked by a section of the freighter. Brilliant pinpricks of sunlight shone through breaks in the structure. Jeffrey reached out, and the Gorilla gripped the obstruction, the metal folding in the hydraulic hands. Jeffrey pushed on it. The section of hull shifted but would not move.

Jeffrey pulled at the structure. Two large pieces ripped free. He threw the pieces aside and pulled two more chunks of metal off the structure. He did this again and again, and larger beams of light broke through.

When he had ripped out a hole as large as the Gorilla's shoulders, he kicked at the lower section. The metal petalled out with each kick. He stomped the metal down and walked out onto the flat sheet of the landing zone. There, the lakebed ranged away from the mountains, its horizon a liquid blur in the heat. Wreckage lay strewn along the side of the mountain and out across the dry lakebed. A few hundred meters away, the freighter's bridge, windows shattered, sat half-buried at the end of a long gouge in the dirt.

He walked the Gorilla over to the bridge and looked it over. The Gorilla's hands moved to its hips. "What a mess," he said, and poked out the last unbroken window.

"Gorilla, thermal," he said, and his vision switched to a three-dimensional field of oranges and reds. The hull still showed some signs of heat, but had cooled significantly since atmospheric entry.

"Gorilla, visible spectrum," he said, and his view returned to normal.

"Now let's see if you can shed some light on what's going on."

"Gorilla, cutter," he said, and the left hand flipped back and the cutter extended. He held the cutter to the first window support and curled his finger. The blue arc sparked, and metal splattered away, leaving a gap as wide as the cutter. When he had cut all the window supports, he gripped the roof and folded the entire section back. The metal whined and hoses cracked. As he bent the roof back, sunlight filled the bridge, and he saw the internals had not fared well. All the seats had ripped free, and they—as well as other debris—had destroyed most of the instrumentation at the flight consoles. Shattered glass, metal housings, and insulation lay across the floor. He reached in and lifted out one of the broken chairs, exposing a human leg.

"Gorilla, power down," Jeffrey shouted. Heart pounding, he flipped the CLOSE CAB toggle, unbuckled his harness, and slid down the ladder even as the Gorilla finished crouching down. He dropped off the end of the ladder and ran out into the desert sun. He ran up the berm of dirt and climbed over the cut-open window frames. The ship smelled of burnt oil and baked paint. He began throwing debris away from the leg. He grabbed hold of the ankle, and the leg slid out of the pile. A gray pant leg covered the skin, but just above the knee the leg ended in a cracked femur that protruded from the meat of the thigh. He tossed the leg aside and felt his stomach flip.

He took a moment to settle himself and then turned over a panel exposing the rest of the body, both arms dismembered from the torso. Blood soaked the surrounding debris. He felt his head spin, and bile rose in his throat. He knelt down, put his hands on the deck, and drew in a breath. The cool of the metal deck soaked through his knees and palms.

God, I've gotten old.

Sitting back on his heels, he drew another breath, spit into the debris, and pressed his palms to his forehead. Feeling the metal rings of his gloves on his face, he pulled the gloves off and folded them into his back pocket.

The flipping in his stomach faded. He stood, favoring his stiff back, and began moving more debris. He found a second body stuffed under a console. The head had been sheared off across the bridge of the nose. Under the exposed bone of the sinus cavity, the mouth hung slack. As with the first, the body had bled out in the final resting position.

He found a third body, a young woman, lying face down under another console. He pulled off a few more pieces of debris and turned the body over. Her impact with the controls had stamped the word 'Ion' backwards on her forehead, and a deep cut exposed the white of her cheekbone. Even in death she was pretty; however, Jeffrey could see from her athletic shoulders and arms that she had been tough. Her short brown hair, which was still pixie cute, appeared more 'efficient' in uniform.

He turned, and something gripped his ankle. Jeffrey shouted out and jumped, yanking his leg away. He stared at the woman, his heart hammering at his ribs. She now lay with her arm extended toward him. Her eyes fluttered, and she grimaced. Lifting her arm, she brought the shadow of her hand over her eyes. Her arm began to tremble, and she let it drop to her belly. Jeffrey stepped around and crouched over her, blocking the sun from her face.

Her eyes opened, hazel and glassy, one pupil larger than the other.

"Can you hear me?" he asked.

The woman's eyes tracked to him. The larger pupil constricted somewhat but still did not match the other. She

29

reached out, and her fingers closed on his forearm. She whispered, "Did we survive the crash?"

Jeffrey looked back to the bodies and then put the palm of his hand on her forehead. "You're safe now, at least for the time being. Just relax."

"They're trying to kill me."

"They already tried, sister."

The woman muttered and lost consciousness.

"Hey," Jeffrey shouted at her, patting her uninjured cheek, "you have to wake up. You can't go to sleep. Can you hear me?" But she had lost consciousness. He sat back on his heels and looked out at the desert sky and then to the two bodies and the woman.

Before today's over, someone else is probably going to die.

"I'll be damned if it's going to be me," Jeffrey said to the desert. He looked back down at the young woman. "Right now I need to get you stable and then get us the hell out of here."

CHAPTER 4

Stacy Zack heard shouting nearby, but darkness surrounded her. She tried to remember where she was. She had been on a ship. The memory materialized into a dream, and she found herself sprinting down a ship's corridor, jumping through each hatch. As she ran, footfalls landed close behind her.

"Wake up," a deep voice said. "You have to wake up." It boomed through the metal in the walls of the ship and shook the deck. The hallway seemed to grow confused and too small, then unfocused, and then it disappeared. A bright redness grew all around her, and she opened her eyes to a splitting-white light. She saw blue sky and a wisp of cloud. She tried to sit up, and the sky shifted sickeningly sideways. Her stomach turned. She lay back down and gagged. A shadow leaned over her.

"You back with me?" the voice asked.

She held her hand up over the sun and made out the figure of a large, fit, gray-haired man with a neatly trimmed beard. He wore a green jumpsuit. Her hand felt heavy and trembled as she held it up. She let it drop. The sun blasted back into her eyes. The man moved away. A rasping sound came near her, and then something large and rectangular blocked the sun over her.

"Where am I?" she asked. As her eyes adjusted to the light, she found herself in the shade of a chair.

"You've crash-landed in the desert, very near the center of Nevada," the man said.

She tried to sit up again. Her vision blurred, and she felt the man's hands grasp her shoulders, pressing her back down.

"Be careful now," the man said. "I think you should just lay flat until we figure out how bad off you are. You hit your head very hard."

"Am I alone?"

...

Jeffrey wished she would just lay back and stop asking questions. He looked over to the blue tarp he had draped over the other bodies. A breeze tugged at the tarp exposing the open sinus cavity. He thought to ignore the question, but sooner or later it would have to come out.

"You were with two others, but they didn't survive," he said.

The woman laid her arm on her belly. A trail of blood ran from the cut on her cheekbone, across her ear, to the back of her hair.

"What's your name?" he asked.

"What?"

"Your name, what's your name? I'm Jeffrey."

The woman lifted her hands and stared at them. "Um, I…" She scowled and then said, "My name." She looked off to the

32

right and then back at Jeffrey. "It's Stacy Zack." She reached up, touched her cheek where the blood flow had almost stopped. Her finger slipped into the cut and across the bone and she yelped. Her eyes rolled up in their sockets, and she lost consciousness again.

"Damn it," Jeffrey said. He went to the cracked wall of the cab, ripped some insulation foam-rubber from it, and carefully placed it under her head, bracing the sides of her neck. "You're lucky to be alive. What the hell were you doing on this freighter?"

He patted the good side of her face again and shouted at her, "You can't sleep now. You have to stay awake." But she remained still.

Jeffrey gave up trying to wake her and found a first aid kit bolted on the back wall of the bridge. He brought back several supplies. He laid out a sterile cloth and then set out some swabs, a packet of suture, a needle driver, bandages, and tape. He scrubbed his hands with hand sanitizer and then put on a pair of nitrile gloves. He tore the end off a paper pouch, exposing a swab that dripped with an iodine solution. He swabbed out the cut on her cheekbone, going up under the skin and across the bone.

"It's probably good you're unconscious for this."

He opened the packet of suture and grasped the curved needle with the needle driver. As he pulled the needle away, the attached suture drew out of its plastic holder. Stabbing the needle into the skin at the edge of the cut, he threaded the suture through. He tied a small knot to fix the end of the suture and pulled the wound closed with ten stitches.

Tying off the suture at the other end, he clipped away the extra, and set the needle driver down. After he had coated the area with more iodine and then a light greasing of antibiotic ointment, he looked over his work and said, "That will get you through for today anyway." He laid a rectangle of dressing over the area and taped the edges down. Then he sat down in the debris beside her.

Every so often the woman muttered a few quiet sounds and shifted. He looked around the cabin, thinking about how to build a stretcher for her. He took up her wrist to check her pulse, and she pulled her arm away. Her eyes opened, and she sat up fast. She winced and held the small of her back.

"You should stay on your back," he said. "You probably have a pretty bad concussion."

Stacy looked to the wreckage around her, and then to the mountains over the severed window frames. Holding up her arm, she inspected the remnants of a strap on her wrist, loosened it, and tossed it into the debris. Jeffrey saw that straps had made raw marks on both of her wrists. One of her ankles still had a section of torn strap wrapped around it as well. Jeffrey undid the strap and threw it aside.

"I have to get out of here," she said.

"You pretty much covered that before you passed out again."

"How long was I out?"

"You lost consciousness again for about 10 minutes. I was about to try and rig a backboard and get you out of here."

She looked left and then right, her eyes a bit wide, on the edge of frantic.

"No, don't move your neck so much." He reached out and took hold of the sides of her face, stopping her head from swiveling. She pushed his hands away.

"Don't worry about it, my neck is fine. I'm just sore." She rubbed the back of her neck and then touched the bandage on her face.

"Holy Mother that hurts," she said.

Jeffrey took her hand away from the bandage. "Yeah, you may have cracked your cheekbone. Try and leave that alone, and it might heal right. Now tell me, what were you doing on a ship that was being intentionally crashed?"

Stacy looked at her hands and then shook her head, "I don't really remember. I was running down a hallway with two other SO's, running for our lives. But I don't remember why." She scowled at her hands. "Why would that be? We were on a training run." She looked up at Jeffrey. "I remember it was a training run."

"It'll come back," Jeffrey said. "But right now, as you said, we have to get out of here. Someone has already tried to kill me twice today and you at least once. I think we can safely assume it's somehow related. Can you stand up?"

Jeffrey helped Stacy to her feet. She took a step, a chunk of metal under her foot shifted, and she stumbled.

"How you doing?" Jeffrey asked.

"Not really myself yet. The sky's spinning on me."

Jeffrey kicked the command chair he had shaded her with, and it flipped upright.

"Sit there for a moment. We need to get going, but we can take a few minutes to let you get your bearings."

"So how did they try to kill you?" Stacy sat down. "You seem well enough."

"This is going to sound strange, but a poison robotic spider."

"Really? You're not messing around? A robotic spider? Poison?"

"I don't know that it was poison, but I can assume as much as I like here."

"Maybe it was just a sedative, you know, to put you to sleep?"

"Perhaps, but I don't think so. My transport had a bomb in the intake filled with what I'm pretty sure was sodium bicarbonate. It blew when I turned off my autopilot."

"A baking soda bomb? A robotic spider and a baking soda bomb?"

"You think I'm loose a few screws." Jeffrey said.

"Yes."

"How do you put out a grease fire?" he asked.

"You throw... baking soda on it."

"So if you tossed a thick enough cloud of it into the intake of a jet engine?"

"You smother the burn, kill the motor."

"Yeah, the plane just falls out of the sky. They recover their device, and maybe no one is the wiser. It's certainly easier to cover up than a large explosive device."

"It would have to be a lot of baking soda to smother a turbine."

"It was."

"The spider's not very subtle. Suspicions would be raised if someone found you dead with a robotic spider stuck in your leg."

"Yes. I'm guessing they planned on recovering the spider. If that's true, they'll be close. But both methods feel overdone, arrogant. If I wanted someone dead, I'd walk up and shoot him in the face."

Stacy stared at Jeffrey for a moment and then said, "You have to admit it's harder to cover up a guy with his head blown off."

Jeffrey nodded at that. "I think they were in a rush to implement and planned on having time to clean up their mess.

I'm definitely not going to stay around with a target on my back." He motioned for her to stand. "Do you think you can walk to my Gorilla?"

"Your what?" she asked, but Jeffrey held up his hand to silence her.

He heard the faint whistle of turbines. Looking over the ruined edge of the bridge windows, he watched a gunship hop over the northern mountains.

CHAPTER 5

The gunship, serious special ops gear with black paint absorbing the sunlight, flew directly at them. It had the look of a predatorial insect with wings like long blades, and a cockpit turned down, aggressive. A larger section behind the cockpit probably accommodated a small number of troops. A long stabilization tail extended out the back.

"That was fast," Jeffrey said.

"What was fast?" Stacy said, shifting her weight to stand up.

"No, no, no," he said, pushing her back into the chair.

"You told me to get up! What the hell is wrong with you?"

"There's a gunship coming in, looks like a new generation Kiowa."

"You don't think they're here to help."

"I haven't called for help, and I know you haven't. I'd bet my two front teeth these folks are the cleaners." He looked back at Stacy sitting in the chair. "You're dead, you understand me?"

"I do not understand you."

Jeffrey looked at her position relative to the cockpit and then turned her chair.

"Do you have a gun?" he asked.

She patted her hip holster, unsnapped it, and drew her gun. She checked the magazine and slid it back in.

"Loaded?"

"Yes."

"You take loaded weapons on training runs?"

"We're Special Warfare, not children."

"Well, if they left your gun on your hip, they definitely didn't plan on you surviving the crash. Take it out and sit on your arm like this," Jeffrey held his hand just behind his hip.

He gripped the sleeve of her jumpsuit below the arm patch and tore it open. "This will be a bit ugly, but what can you do?" He turned and walked over to the blue tarp, crouched down, and lifted it up. He looked back to Stacy. "How do you feel about bodies? Are you squeamish?"

"I have only seen one body before this, my grandmother at her funeral," she said.

He pulled one of the severed arms, which ended above the elbow in bloody shreds of upper arm muscles. "Well, we'll just have to toss you in the deep end."

A gray sleeve, splattered with black blood, covered most of the dark hair of the man's forearm.

The illusion might work.

Jeffrey walked back and set the arm on Stacy's lap, tilting the torn end onto the arm rest. He looked over his work and pulled the shred of bicep to the side, exposing the cracked, white end of the humerus. Then he smeared blood on her torn sleeve.

Seeing Stacy turn a lighter shade of white, he said, "You'll do fine. Just tell yourself it's made of wax."

"Won't they be able to see my shoulder isn't damaged?"

"I'm betting these non-combatant training squids–" He paused and then said, "No offense of course."

"Yeah, well, some taken."

He waved his hand in the air, dismissing the slight. "I'm betting their minds will lock on that bone and won't see anything beyond it." He looked at her, noticing her color had improved. "How are you holding up?"

"I suppose bodies don't bother me that much," she said, patting the arm with her free hand.

"Good, so you're with me right?"

"Like I have a choice."

"You always have a choice. Right now it's live or die."

"I'll go with live."

"Good, now here's how we pull that off…"

...

The gunship circled around the wreck. Jeffrey looked out at it, contemplating its size.

"We'll probably be dealing with six to eight troops," he said, not taking his eyes off the gunship.

It turned around the wreckage one more time and then touched down raising a cloud of dust. The landing ramp lowered from under the ship's tail and several troops ran out dressed in desert pattern body armor. As they ran off in different directions, each one shimmered and vanished.

"Oh that is not good," Jeffrey said. He stared into the dusty air, not allowing himself to blink. His eyes watered in the warm breeze.

Stacy sat with her eyes closed and her head to one side. "Can you specify 'not good' please?"

"These guys have active camouflage. But–" and he went silent.

Stacy said through her teeth, "But what?"

"But there are only four so far."

A man came down the ramp dressed in basic black fatigues. He wore sunglasses. The breeze flicked at his mop of white-blonde hair.

"That's all," Jeffrey said and looked around the cabin. He saw a panel with a picture of a fire extinguisher on it. He walked to the panel, metal debris clattering under his feet. He opened it, pulled the extinguisher out, and fired it back and forth until a fine powder floated throughout the cabin.

"Watch for the shoulders," he said. "The powder will settle on the shoulders." He threw the extinguisher down and looked back out over the broken windows through the cloud of powder.

Halfway to the wreck, the man with the blonde hair saw Jeffrey and shouted up to him, "You must be the demolitions specialist. The breaker."

A hint of a smile twitched at the corner of Jeffrey's mouth.

You have no idea.

He felt a calm electricity glowing in his heart, glittering out to his fingertips.

"Yes, that's me," Jeffrey shouted. "I'm the demolition 'team' out here." He held up his fingers and curled them in apostrphes to highlight 'team' and grinned. "I assume you folks know there was a bit of a problem and that's why you've come. There's bodies up here! Just got a fire out as well."

Walking up the dirt berm, the man stepped over the ruined window frames and dropped into the bridge, saying, "Yes, that's why we've come." The man waved his hand through the floating powder as he walked over to Jeffrey. He scanned the area, looking over the tarp and then Stacy in the chair. A scar ran from his upper lip, up over his left ear. It brought his lip up into a slight snarl. The man's gaze stayed on Stacy, so Jeffrey reached out and grabbed the man by the back of the arm.

The man pulled his arm away and put his hand on Jeffrey's chest. "Let's just keep our hands to ourselves."

He thinks he knows his way around a fight. That's good. You're big, bad black-ops, and I'm just a worn-down old man who's no threat at all.

Jeffrey heard the thud of boots, and debris shifted on the floor by the windows. There were more boot-falls to the right and left. A gun clicked.

This new camouflage is good; there's no halo, no shimmer, no distortion at all.

The blonde man tracked Jeffrey's gaze. "Now it's time for you to answer some questions for me."

Where's the fourth soldier?

Jeffrey could begin to make out floating panels of dust settling on the three soldiers' shoulders. Faint outlines of their guns and forearms came into view as well. The soldiers did not train their guns on Jeffrey, but lazily on the floor.

Where the hell is the fourth soldier?

The blonde man looked down at Stacy. "Are they all dead?"

"Definitely dead. They came in at probably 800 to 900 miles an hour. There was no chance for them."

The blonde man looked at the arm in Stacy's lap again.

Jeffrey reached out and grabbed his shoulder. "Who do you suppose they were?"

The blonde man stepped close to Jeffrey, making an effort to get into his face, but his having to look up at Jeffrey diminished the effect. "You will stop making physical contact with me, is—that—clear?" He jabbed Jeffrey in the chest with his finger with each of the last three words.

But Jeffrey was not looking at him. He was looking up at the fourth soldier, who had just stepped into view on the roof of the bridge, where the Gorilla had folded the metal back. The soldier had his back to the sun, and his outline shimmered against the sky as the armor failed to fully process the brilliance of the sun.

Just the kind of mistake someone who had never seen combat would make. I can't blame the guy though. Some things are just not obvious until you figure them out by watching a friend die.

"Oh, yes sir," Jeffrey said, holding up his hands in submission. "You're all right by me. You see, my boy's in the service and I always say, take the one at three o'clock, MARK."

The blonde man looked at Jeffrey as though he were an idiot. Jeffrey grabbed the man's arm and yanked, spinning him so he faced out toward the desert. Wrapping his arm around the man's neck, Jeffrey side stepped, putting the man between him and the soldier by the center windows. At the same time, Jeffrey reached down with his right hand and pulled the pistol from his pocket. He lifted the pistol and fired up into the soldier on the roof, the only one smart enough to have his gun on Jeffrey. The slug found its mark in the soldier's face. A bright red mist and whipping cap of skull sprayed away from the crystalline figure. The soldier pulled his trigger in a death spasm and bullets ran across the floor of the bridge.

Jeffrey turned his gun on the soldier on the right side of the bridge and heard Stacy's gun fire behind him. He aimed directly over the two dusty shoulders and again, fired a slug into the face. A thick, red oval of blood and brain spattered across the wall. The third soldier, the one by the broken center windows, fired his weapon. Jeffrey felt a bullet slam into the blonde man, hammering the man's torso into Jeffrey. Jeffrey turned his gun on the dusty silhouette of the third soldier. But as he turned, he heard three quick shots, and the invisible soldier's head and neck exploded out over the broken windows into the desert.

Jeffrey aimed his gun at the last soldier, the one to his left, but there was no need. The body had fallen to the ground, disappearing as the camouflage still did its job. On the wall, about head high, an angular spray of blood told him that Stacy had shot sure and true.

He spun the blonde man around and looked at him. The man's eyes searched Jeffrey's face for the answer to the question Jeffrey knew all too well: 'What the hell just happened?' Jeffrey looked down and saw blood blooming around a hole in the man's shirt. The bullet had ricocheted off something inside, blowing out the side of his ribcage, which hung open.

Jeffrey looked back at the man's face. "Who sent you?"

The blonde man's hands gripped Jeffrey's shirt and his mouth opened and closed. His wrecked chest could no longer drive enough air to his mouth to speak.

"I am sorry," Jeffrey said to the man. He let go of the man, who slid off Jeffrey to the right, landing on the debris. He came to rest on his side, one elbow up. His chest sucked with each breath. When Jeffrey realized the man was not going to die right away, he reached down and unsnapped the man's holster, pulled his gun, and threw it out over the broken window frames into the desert.

"Do we kill him?" Stacy stood and absently handed Jeffrey the arm. Jeffrey scowled at it and threw it down.

"No." Jeffrey crouched down and, taking hold of the blond man's face, turned his head. The man looked at him, his eyes wide and searching.

"He'll probably die," Jeffrey said, still looking into the man's eyes, "but he's no longer a threat, so we leave him be."

Jeffrey looked to Stacy and asked, "Do you have an emergency med kit, like you might carry in combat?"

"Sure, here," she said and pulled a hand-sized black case from her right cargo pocket. Jeffrey took the case from her, opened it, and took out a sealed vial of heavy pain killer. He took out the vial and the plastic wrapped syringe and filled the syringe.

"Hey, if I don't turn that in…," and she stopped herself.

Jeffrey leaned over the man, making eye contact with him. "Blink if you can hear me."

The blond man closed his eyes and then popped them open. His eyes went hazy for a moment.

"Do you want this?" Jeffrey held out the syringe. "To cut the pain? Blink if you do."

The blond man closed his eyes and pulled them open again. Tears welled in them. Jeffrey pulled the knife from the blond man's hip and slashed the fabric of his pants. He pocketed the knife and tore at the slash, exposing the man's thigh. He slid the needle into the muscle of the thigh and injected the liquid. In a moment the man's eyes closed and his face went slack.

Jeffrey stood up. "We have a gunship to heist."

"Sounds fine to me, but where do we go?"

"Right now, 'where' is very simply 'not here'." He patted her on the back. "You did all right there, shot straight." Jeffrey's genuine smile made Stacy smile, but then she looked back at the gore around the cabin and the man at their feet, air sucking wet in the hole in his chest.

45

"Doesn't this bother you at all?" she asked.

"Yes." He intended to say nothing more, but the expression on Stacy's face made him go on, "But now's not the time. Stuff it down until you have a time and place to deal with it. It's important that you look at it then, not now." He put his hands on either side of her head, a gesture a father might make. "It will keep trying to get under your skin right now. Don't let it. You have to be sharp."

"I won't, sir."

"Don't call me, 'sir'," Jeffrey said, walking away from her and picking up one of the soldiers' rifles. "Just call me Jeffrey."

Stacy picked up another rifle and wiped blood off the stock. She clicked the safety, and slung it over her shoulder. Jeffrey looked over to her.

"Where's the safety on this thing?" he asked.

Stacy walked over and pointed at the small thumb button under the stock. "I thought you said you were a military guy."

"I didn't say. But if I was in the military, it was before this rifle was used."

"That rifle has been standard issue for over 20 years."

"You're getting the idea."

"So what branch were you in?"

"Marines."

Stacy's eyes scanned the mountain ridge just as two more gunships jumped up over the northern ridge.

"We have to go," she said, "now."

CHAPTER 6

The gunships came at the wreck fast. Jeffrey looked out to where the first gunship stood on its landing gear. He and Stacy would be caught out in the open if they tried to run for it. The Gorilla was closer.

"Follow me," Jeffrey said and pulled himself up over the broken windows and ran to the Gorilla. He wondered if Stacy would be able to keep up. When he looked over his shoulder, he saw her hop over the window frames and run down the berm with a limp.

Jeffrey ran underneath the Gorilla, waited for Stacy, and then pointed up the rungs to the cab. Stacy climbed up.

Standing in the cab, Stacy set the rifle aside. "There's only a place for one person."

Jeffrey came up the ladder behind her. "This is going to be uncomfortable, but it's our only choice. Lean up against the backrest there." Stacy put her back against the backrest and Jeffrey turned around and backed into her.

"Hey, wait," Stacy said, pushing on him. She turned her face to the side. "I need to keep you off my cheekbone."

"You good?"

"Yes."

Jeffrey looked down at the rifles sitting loose on the side and kicked them out of the cab.

He extended the straps of the harness to make room for both of them and strapped himself in front of her, pinning her securely between him and the backrest.

"Move your feet back, out of the way," Jeffrey said.

Her feet slid backward.

Jeffrey heard the ships circling the site. He closed the cab and darkness sealed around them.

"This is going to be pretty blind for you, so you'll just have to trust me."

"Again, I find myself without a choice," she said, her voice muffled, "but so far you're working out for me." She wrapped her arms around his waist and grabbed her own wrist. He reached into his back pocket, pulled out his gloves, and put them on. Then he pulled the VR goggles over his eyes. Shaded, dry lakebed blinked into view with a roll and stabilization of the image. He pushed the earpieces in, and the sounds of the ships clarified, loud and circling.

He gave the activation command and code, and the feminine voice responded, "Activation Code accepted."

The Gorilla unfolded, and Jeffrey stood still watching the ships circle around.

Had the gunships seen the Gorilla stand upright?

The next few seconds would tell him. The ships continued to circle.

"What are you doing?" Stacy asked.

"Waiting."

"I am aware of that, but why? Why not get out of here?"

"There's no way the Gorilla can run from those ships. Their main guns alone would tear it apart, and God knows what other ordnance they have."

"So what good does getting into this do? Why don't they just shoot at us now?"

"I'm gambling they didn't see us get into it. If they didn't, they might land and do reconnaissance on foot. Then I'll try to put them on the defensive long enough to trash their gunships and take the third out of here."

"Do you think they'll both land?"

"No. Well, I wouldn't. I'd leave one ship up for air coverage, but these guys don't think they are dealing with a very big threat. I'm hoping that they feel very safe and will saunter in here."

"Safe? Their friends were just killed," Stacy said.

"Odds are they don't know that yet."

"What if you're wrong?"

"Then we die."

"What about small-arms fire?" Stacy asked, her voice calm considering her situation.

"That should be no problem. The Gorilla is constructed to crush and tear apart armored ships. It's covered in thick enough metal for small arms."

"So, you're going to take on gunships and soldiers with a dump truck?"

"Heavy is heavy."

"But this doesn't have any weapons, right?"

Just then the gunships each turned in reducing circles, their landing gear extending.

"Now we're in business," Jeffrey said.

Dust billowed around the gunships as they settled onto the lakebed. They now stood in a line, the two new ships closest, and the blond man's, farther beyond. The ramps opened and four soldiers came out of each, crouched and running. One at a time, they shimmered into invisibility. The pilots of each ship came out on the ramps armed with rifles. More cautious than the blonde man had been, they looked around before moving off the platforms and vanishing as well.

"Gorilla, thermal," Jeffrey said, and his vision of the desert swirled into brilliant reds and oranges. Jeffrey scanned the area, but could see no sign of the camouflaged soldiers.

"That's some good armor," Jeffrey said to Stacy. "It doesn't even throw a heat signature."

"The new generation covers heat signature. The soldier wears a respirator that cools breath to the ambient temperature."

"Good work, Stacy."

"What did I say?"

"Breath," Jeffrey said. "Gorilla, Visible light." The desert flickered, and the white salt and blue sky returned.

"Gorilla, layer over imaging for significant CO2 density." In Jeffrey's vision, dark blue puffs formed up about head high here and there around the wreck site.

"You know the best thing about newbie special forces?" Jeffrey asked.

"Again, I might take this personally."

"No matter how hard you try to beat it out of them, training at that level runs the risk of developing arrogance. When you're told you're the best of the best, and you train ruthlessly to get there, you tend to actually believe it."

"So why shouldn't they?"

"There is no best, only luckiest. Skill's important, but it only keeps you alive by the grace of blind luck."

"You learn that in the war?"

"I didn't say I was in the war."

"Please."

A puffing line of CO_2 made its way toward the Gorilla. It came right next to the leg, the soldier apparently using it for cover from the wreckage. Jeffrey noted that all of the blue clouds of CO_2 had moved far enough away from the gunships.

"I guess that makes you first," Jeffrey said. He moved and the Gorilla lifted its foot and stomped the soldier into the dirt. The Gorilla reached down and picked up a section of hull, close to a ton of metal. It turned and tossed the hull section at the first gunship. The section of hull hammered into the side of the cockpit, shearing halfway through the pilot's seat.

Bullets began to crack and clink off the Gorilla. Jeffrey saw sparks flicking all over the Gorilla's surface, but none of the bullets left appreciable damage.

A trail of blue puffs approached right up in front of the Gorilla, and an electric bolt jumped out at Jeffrey. He had not expected the bolt, and the Gorilla's hands came up in a shielding motion mimicking Jeffrey. When he realized the Gorilla had withstood the shock, he gritted his teeth, stepped forward, and punted the soldier a few hundred feet across the lakebed.

He walked the Gorilla toward the gunships. Bullets clicked on the metal plating. Under the pressure, Jeffrey moved his legs too quickly. This caused the Gorilla to stop and rematch his legs. If one of the remaining two gunships got in the air, he and Stacy would die. He had to be patient and move his legs at a rate the Gorilla could keep up with.

He had to disable the second gunship and get the third airborne. He walked past the nose of the first gunship and, confirming that the hull plate had made it unflyable, walked on toward the second. The second gunship stood farther away than Jeffrey had estimated. A trail of blue exhalations moved toward it at a full run. The Gorilla walked just about as fast as a person could run, but the soldier was closer. As the blue puffs of gas coming from the soldier disappeared into the gunship, the Gorilla had only crossed half the distance. Jeffrey looked around for a section of hull to throw, but found none.

Jeffrey saw the soldier, now uncamouflaged, in the cockpit, jerking at his seat restraints and throwing switches. Jeffrey continued his steady walking pace. The engines fired and dust blew out, blinding Jeffrey's cameras. Inside the cab of the Gorilla, the sound of the gunship's turbines rose to a scream. Only a few more steps. Jeffrey felt Stacy's bear hug tighten around his waist. Small-arms fire continued to crack across the Gorilla's surface. The silhouette of the gunship lifted out of the dust and Jeffrey reached up for the ship.

He caught the ship on its side, near the bottom. The Gorilla's armored hand sank deep, and Jeffrey–gripping his fist in the empty black of the cab–prayed that he would catch some significant part of the frame. The ship lurched, and the Gorilla's hand stayed solid, wrist deep in the side of the ship. The Gorilla weighed much more than the gunship despite its being significantly smaller. Jeffrey pulled the ship back down into the dust cloud and punched into the nearest engine housing. The engine blew apart. Fan blades, pipes, hoses, and sheet metal slammed into the Gorilla, shaking the cab. The ship lifted to one side, but the Gorilla held it steady and Jeffrey pulled the ship down, aiming his cameras at the pilot. The pilot looked at the Gorilla with terror.

Swinging the Gorilla's forearm down, Jeffrey smashed the cockpit flat. He then pushed the ship to the ground, reached over the top, and hammered the other engine's air intake shut. The engine died. Jeffrey tore large sections of the wing off. He stuffed a section under the left arm of the Gorilla and then tore off another section and passed it to the left hand. He tore off a third and walked around the ship toward the final gunship.

Three trails of blue exhalations huffed toward the third ship. He took aim at the one closest to the gunship and tossed the section of wing in the Gorilla's right hand with a blistering overhand pitch. The section of wing connected perfectly with the running soldier, spraying chunks of metal and an arm.

"Gorilla," Jeffrey said, "External speakers. High volume."

"I see you," Jeffrey said. His amplified voice boomed out over the lakebed and echoed off the distant hills. The tink and clack of small arms fire halted. The two traces of CO_2, which had been trailing toward the ship, stopped and pooled, gusts jetting out from the panting soldier's mouths. Jeffrey took the chunk of scrap out from under the Gorilla's armpit so each hand held a ragged piece of wing.

"Forty years of throwing scrap with this thing," Jeffrey said, holding up the chunk of scrap in his pitching arm, "has made me ready for the majors, folks. If you want to live, back off."

One of the soldiers ran at the gunship, while the other remained frozen out on the lakebed. Jeffrey pitched the section of wing at the running figure. The scrap caught the wind and spun, cutting the soldier in half. A set of legs appeared out in the desert and fell to the salt, blood gushing from them.

"Don't be stupid folks. You've lost this time. Live or die with it. You choose." No one else moved toward the gunship, but the one last soldier still stood out in the open, halfway to the gunship, breathing. Jeffrey turned and walked straight at him.

"That gunship is mine, squid. Run, NOW!" Jeffrey's shout distorted in the speakers making it a metalized growl. The soldier's blue exhalations turned and trailed away in a line toward the wrecked freighter.

Jeffrey said, "Gorilla. External speakers off."

"How are we doing?" Stacy asked.

"We're doing great." But he knew a lot could still go wrong. "Here's how this works," he said. "I'm going to get us set so, when we come out of the Gorilla, the gunship will be on our right. It's going to happen fast, and we'll be blind from dust so just run. When you get in the ship, you close the ramp and get strapped in fast. Any questions?"

"None."

"Excellent."

The Gorilla walked up to the gunship, turned sideways, and Jeffrey said, "Gorilla, blower, left." A pipe extended from the left forearm, and Jeffrey closed his left fist turning the blower on full. He aimed the blower at the lakebed and moved it back and forth raising a billowing cloud. After doing this for several seconds, he said, "Gorilla, power down."

The blower shut off, the Gorilla crouched over, and the air began to clear. Jeffrey smacked the Cab-Open switch. He tore off the VR goggles, and his hands scrambled at the straps of his harness. He pulled away from Stacy and felt cool air on his sweat-soaked back. He spun and climbed down the rungs as the Gorilla finished hunkering down. Then the bullets came in, cracking off the Gorilla's legs. Stacy came hopping down the rungs, slipped off the last one, and fell. She grunted, push-upped off the ground, and ran out from under the Gorilla into the dust. Jeffrey remembered the spider and box. He lifted himself up, reached into the cab, unstrapped the bag, and dragged it out of the corner. He dropped back down to the lakebed, throwing the strap over his shoulder, and ran after Stacy. Gunfire clacked off the looming silhouette of the gunship. A round licked at the dirt near Jeffrey's feet. Stacy jumped onto the ramp. Jeffrey jumped on right after her. As his feet touched metal, the ramp began to close.

He tossed the bag down and ran to the cockpit, shifted around the seat arm, and hit his head. He cursed, rubbing his scalp as he looked over the controls. The basic setup hadn't changed since his time. He flipped the Engine-On switch.

"Please let them not have locked the console."

Stacy came up behind him and reached over him, pulling at his five-point harness. He looked over to her.

"Don't worry about me. You just get this damn thing in the air." She pulled the shoulder harnesses over his arm as he fired the compressors. The compressed air whined in the engines, spinning them up, and they blasted to life. In the back of the ship, the ramp clamped shut. The roar of the engines reduced to a vibration, smooth and quiet. The gauges for operating temperature both flicked to green as the desert sun and recent use had left the turbines still hot. All the while, bullets sparked off the cockpit glass.

Stacy moved into the back. Jeffrey looked into a small, curved mirror, placed for the pilot to see the navigator, and saw Stacy, surrounded by instrumentation, strapping herself into the seat behind him.

"Are you good?" Jeffrey asked.

Stacy shouted, too loud for the new quiet in the cockpit, "Yes. Go."

Jeffrey yanked the gunship off the ground, spun it around, hammered the throttle forward, and shot out across the long distance of the lakebed.

"Holy God," Stacy said, "how far off the deck are you?"

Jeffrey looked at the instruments. "Thirty feet."

"You have to fly higher."

Jeffrey looked at her in the mirror. She continued looking at the back of his head. He reached up and tapped the mirror. Her eyes snapped up to it.

"Would you keep your hands on the controls?"

"You don't need to shout."

"I'm sorry, but you really need more altitude."

Jeffrey looked back out on the lakebed blurring by, turned the ship a bit, and then said, "Have a little faith."

She did not reply.

The gunship flew sharp and clean. The lightness and precision of the thing filled Jeffrey's heart with gladness, and a grin cracked across his face.

"Great," Stacy said, looking into the mirror, "you're nuts. Can you please fly higher?"

"I'll take it up another five feet, how's that?" Jeffrey said.

Stacy groaned in resignation.

...

As the soldiers sat hunkered in and around the freighter wreckage, their last gunship flew away with professional precision. It appeared after a few seconds to be still touching the ground, and then the rooster tail of dust and warping heat waves obscured it entirely. The soldiers verified there were no other people in the vicinity and then powered down each of their camouflage units. Out of fifteen soldiers, only five still stood and had nothing to show for it.

One of the soldiers threw down his helmet. "What the hell just happened?"

Another soldier, kneeling on the ground near him, said in a quiet voice, "We got our pants torn off and stuffed in our mouths is what happened."

A soldier in the freighter's bridge shouted out, "There's four dead up here, but Sergeant Morgan is still alive. Barely."

CHAPTER 7

The mountains bordering the western edge of the lakebed ran up on the gunship with an unreal sense of speed. Jeffrey throttled back just a bit and lifted the nose of the gunship. As it rose, G-Forces pulled him down into his seat. He instinctively tensed his leg and stomach muscles to keep blood in his head. The mountain ridge passed beneath the gunship's belly. Jeffrey nosed the ship down and went weightless in his gut. Beyond the mountain ridge, a desert floor, scarred with shallow canyons and washes, ran out to the next mountain range. As he brought the gunship down over the canyon floor and leveled it off, the canyons and washes seemed to weave and snap as the ship ripped past only a few spare feet above the ground.

"Are you supersonic?" Stacy asked, her voice tense.

"Yes, we have to move fast and low."

"What about the IFF transponder?"

"Dammit!" Jeffrey said, hitting his leg with a fist.

"What?" Stacy asked, "What's wrong?"

"I forgot about the damn IFF transponder." Jeffrey looked over the navigation and flight computers, "Is there a way to shut it off?"

"I don't know."

"Are you rated to fly?"

"No," Stacy said. "I specialized as an ordnance engineer. Explosives."

"Not exactly what I would expect," Jeffrey said, looking at Stacy in the mirror.

She shrugged her shoulders.

Jeffrey curved the ship to the left.

Stacy asked, "Where are we going?"

"San Diego. Do you have a personal sat-phone on you?"

"No."

"I'll keep it smooth, go ahead and dig around in back. See if you can find any duffel bags or other personal items. Look for a sat-phone. I need to make a call." Jeffrey increased his altitude to 400 feet to allow him to fly straight away so Stacy could walk around. With the IFF transponder blasting a big, electronic floodlight on them there was probably no benefit in running lower anyway. Whoever might come after them would still take time to launch more gunships, and if this was really a black-op, then it would take even longer to launch without triggering too much attention. That was all well and good, as long as they didn't already have more gunships in pursuit.

"I found one," Stacy said as she came back into the cockpit. She held the phone out beside Jeffrey.

"Dial for me."

"Finally some caution? Thank God for that," she said, strapping back into her seat.

Jeffrey gave Stacy the number. She entered into the phone's screen. When the phone began to ring, she reached forward and tapped it on Jeffrey's shoulder. He took it from her.

"Hello, Leif?" Jeffrey said into the phone.

"Dad?"

"Yeah, it's me. Thank God you're off duty."

"Is there a problem?" Leif asked.

Jeffrey paused, considering what he was about to get his son into. Options were limited.

"You there? Dad?"

Jeffrey said, "Yes, sorry. First, let me apologize. By calling you I'm involving you in something fairly ugly, but I need your help... badly. Do you know how to disable the IFF transponder on a new generation Kiowa gunship?"

"What the hell kind of question is that?"

"Just answer it."

"Yes. Definitely. But why?"

"You're going to have to roll with me on this one."

"Tampering with transponders is serious stuff, Dad."

"Leif, I don't have time for this, I..."

Leif cut him off, "Are you in some kind of trouble?"

"Unfortunately, yes. Long story short, we've had an attempt on our lives and..."

"We?"

"Yes. There are two of us."

"Two? Who?"

"That's not important right now."

"Look dad, this is bizarre. Are you feeling all right?"

"I'm fine, I just need your help."

"Sorry, but this is just way too out in left field."

"What do you want from me?" Jeffrey asked, now angry. "I need your help, and I don't have a lot of options. I would have gone to someone else, but—"

"Relax, relax. I just… Look, I'm sorry, I just didn't expect this. You know I'll do what I can."

Jeffrey lowered the phone down and looked back at Stacy. "He's going to help us." He put the phone back to his ear.

Leif had continued talking. "…could try and walk you through it, but it will take some time."

"Time is a luxury we don't have."

"I thought as much. I assume you are in a Kiowa then?"

"Yes."

"Heading this way?"

"Yes, and broadcasting my location the whole way."

"Don't be so sure of it," Leif said. "Those transponders get dodgy at low altitude and high speed. Can you get it low and fast?"

"Do you need to ask?"

"Look, no war stories, just get it low. 500 feet might be enough. Don't go any lower than that though. You need to get here in one piece."

"You telling me how to fly now?" Jeffrey looked back at Stacy. "He says we shouldn't fly lower than 500 feet for safety. You two already have something in common."

Leif asked, "Who are you talking to?"

"That's the other one. You should meet her; she's pretty as hell, and could probably kick your butt."

Stacy scowled up at him through the mirror and made a motion with her thumb across her neck, 'cut it off'. Jeffrey felt a smile pulling at his face, but suppressed it. She pointed at her eyes and then pointed in an angry jab out the front window to the ground rushing by.

Jeffrey asked Leif, "Can you get to the ball field where you did little league?"

"Yes, how long?"

"At this speed I can make it there in just under an hour," Jeffrey said.

"I can do that. Is there anything else?"

"Yes, the people we are dealing with have a lot of firepower and are shooting to kill. Watch your back."

"Yes, sir."

"One last thing."

"What's that?"

"Thank you."

"Don't give it a second thought," Leif said, and hung up the phone.

"You know someone named, Leaf?" Stacy asked.

"My son."

"Your son's name is Leaf?"

"Something wrong with that?"

"It's a little 'moonbeam' for a Marine's son isn't it?"

"It's not 'leaf' like on a tree." Jeffrey turned the ship right, curving around a large mesa. "It's spelled L-E-I-F. I pronounce it 'leaf', which I've been told is wrong, but…" Jeffrey shrugged to complete his point. "It's an old Norse name which, depending on who you ask, means 'loved'. That's the meaning I chose to give it. It made sense to me. From the day my wife told me she was pregnant I knew he was Leif."

"Jeez," Stacy said. "That's really… sweet." She was quiet for a moment, and then asked, "So he can help us with the transponder?"

"Says he can. He's Army. Electronic counterintelligence."

They flew on in silence for some time. Glancing back, Jeffrey saw Stacy's head leaning forward, and he thought she might be drifting off to sleep after everything she'd been through. Then she looked up at him, her eyes red with tears.

In an angry, low tone she said, "What?" and then louder, "What?" She glared at him, daring him to keep looking at her crying.

"I make no judgments, Stacy. I've been there. It's safe now. You can let it out a little."

Stacy sighed and rubbed the tears out of her eyes, "I'm sorry, Jeffrey. Thanks." She looked down. "I still can't believe I'm alive." She held up her hand and curled her fingers. "At this point just having hands and feet feels miraculous." She continued looking at her hand for a moment. "Thanks, for saving my life."

"The same to you," Jeffrey said. "I couldn't have gotten through that without your help."

Jeffrey looked back in the mirror for a moment and saw Stacy's face tighten and her lower lip tremble. Her hands came up to her mouth, and she sobbed with big, wet gasps, her whole body shaking. Jeffrey put his attention back on the desert, feeling terribly bad for her.

"I'm sorry, Stacy. Like I said, it's very difficult the first time round. No one should have to experience it."

"Oh," Stacy said, the crying turning her voice like a little girl's, "it's not so much that I just killed someone." Jeffrey glanced back at her as she wiped her eyes and rubbed her nose on her sleeve. Then anger came into her voice, "I know those bastards had it coming, but," a sob stopped her short and she drew a deep breath. Her chin quivered as she said, "They were U.S. soldiers, weren't they? Oh God, Jeffrey, what does that mean? We just killed something like eight or nine U.S. soldiers.

They had families, right? They signed up and had the same dream we had, didn't they? Serve the country?" She looked down.

Her crying filled the quiet space of the gunship's cab, and Jeffrey felt an old sorrow weigh down on his chest. He gave her some time in silence.

When Stacy's crying quieted, and she wiped at her tears again, he said, "I honestly don't know what it means. Who's serving the greater good is a complicated question, which very often goes unanswered. Sometimes we understand the big picture, and sometimes we only fight for our own hides."

Stacy looked out at the mountains and said, quiet and calm now, "But what if we were wrong? What if they weren't there to kill us? They didn't fire a shot until we started killing them."

"I can't say with certainty if we just survived our own death or made the biggest mistake of our combined lives, but would an honest military solution involve killing an old man and strapping three Special Warfare trainees into a crashing ship?"

"No, it doesn't make sense to me either."

Jeffrey said, "My instincts are telling me that we have played our cards right so far."

"Well that's not much," Stacy said, finally smiling, "but it's something at least."

"What are your instincts telling you?" Jeffrey asked.

"Something's very wrong." Stacy went quiet, looking out the side window. Jeffrey followed her eyes to a mountainside covered in pine trees.

She asked, "Do you think we'll get out of this?"

"You want my true opinion?"

"What do you think?" Stacy said, and her scowl told Jeffrey 'no B.S.' At that moment, Jeffrey saw the fire in her returning.

She would never be the same bright-eyed recruit she had been, but she appeared strong enough to keep going.

"Most likely this is going to end up with us dead or in prison. We have a slim margin to come out in a good way."

"So why involve your son in such a slim margin?"

"Because with him involved, the margin gets a lot wider."

CHAPTER 8

In the hills east of San Diego, boulders extend out of the green vegetation like bones from a carcass. The gunship came over those hills low and quick and crossed the town of Ramona. Jeffrey spotted the ball field just west of town, and he turned around it. He saw several cars slamming on their brakes in the surrounding streets. The neighborhood had grown smaller in the years since he had lived here. He saw where old houses had been recycled and the desert had returned. The houses that did remain were pleasant with palm fronds shading decorative gravel and small patches of grass. People walking on the sidewalks pointed up at the Kiowa.

He looked over the ball field. Beyond the first baseline fence he saw Leif's car, but no Leif. He would not put down until he saw him. He turned the ship around, the jet wash blasting clouds of dust across the outfield. Third base flipped up and tumbled into the dugout. Jeffrey rotated the gunship around again and saw a police car come to a stop on the far side of the fence.

"Easy buddy," Jeffrey said, "just see that it is outside of your ability to deal with and report it in. Stay in your car."

Jeffrey saw Stacy straining to look and he turned the ship so she could see the cop getting out of his car.

"Oh great," Stacy said.

"If he's smart, he'll do the right thing," Jeffrey said, "just get back in his car and report it. A military gunship is out of his jurisdiction."

Then Jeffrey saw Leif walking from the dugout. Leif held his arms straight out in front of him and pulsed his palms downward, telling Jeffrey to 'land.' He wore tan cargo pants and a dark green Army issue t-shirt and had a canvas bag slung over his shoulder. The t-shirt whipped over his skinny frame. Jeffrey turned the back of the ship toward Leif. Stacy unstrapped, and Jeffrey felt the air inside the ship bluster as the ramp opened. He set the ship down and looked at the rear camera monitor. Leif sprinted across the infield as the cop yelled at some kids, motioning with his arms for them to get back.

Stacy shouted from the back, "He's on."

Jeffrey looked to the monitor and saw the ramp closing. He lifted the gunship and cleared the old hills just as the ramp sealed, shutting out the blast of air and returning them to the quiet of the cockpit.

Stacy strapped herself back into the seat behind Jeffrey, and Leif leaned forward, patting Jeffrey on the shoulder with the palm of his hand.

"Hey dad, been up to much?" Leif's blonde hair had gone nearly pure white in the Southern California sun and his face was tanned.

"Are you getting enough to eat?" Jeffrey asked.

Leif scowled at his father. "I'm not so much worried about that at this minute. What the hell is going on?"

"I'll make you a deal," Jeffrey said. "After you shut that transponder off, I'll give you the whole story."

"Consider it done. The IFF transponder control board is beside your foot controls, can you find a place to land so I can take it out?"

"I would prefer if we could keep going."

"I'll do what I can," Leif said, and backed away. Jeffrey heard the muted clinking of a fabric tool bag being set on the deck, and then Leif–lying on his side–shoved himself between the seats and the bulkhead, the textured floor panels dragging on his Army t-shirt. He held a metal punch and a hammer.

Wedging his thin frame up beside the seats, Leif aimed the punch at the rivets on a small cover. Drawing the hammer back, Leif bumped Jeffrey's leg. Jeffrey moved his legs out of the way. Leif punched out a rivet and then bumped the rudder pedal, and the gunship turned to the left. He shifted his weight and punched out another rivet, and another. With the last rivet still in place, he rotated the cover, exposing a hole with blinking green and orange lights deep inside. He reached elbow deep into the hole, and his shoulder twisted as he searched.

"If I pull the wrong board we fall out of the sky."

"Maybe I should land."

"No, I have it by feel. It's a board with three large resistors and a… there." Leif drew out his arm and opened his hand, exposing a circuit board the size of his palm.

A warning indicator appeared on the gunship's proximity screen. Something was in range and coming in fast, over Mach 2. Jeffrey tapped the green-on-white screen to enlarge the area, and the point grew to three ships in formation. In a few moments they would be in weapons range.

"They found us," Jeffrey said. "Hurry up."

"It's done," Leif said, holding up the board.

"That's it?" Stacy asked.

"The secret isn't in how to disable the system, it's where the board is." Leif shimmied out of the space between the seat and the console. He leaned back over the seats and pointed at a monochrome screen that had various frequencies displayed on it. "You see that screen there? Just press the 'silent' link on it. That will shut off all civilian transmissions of position as well. You do that, and we disappear off the map."

Jeffrey tapped the button, and the list of frequencies disappeared.

"What about the navigation system?" Jeffrey asked.

"When running silent, it goes passive, only taking in information from the satellites, not sending anything back out."

"You and Stacy need to get back to the seats in the back where you can strap in fully, heads against the seat restraints as well," Jeffrey said.

"I'm good here, Jeffrey," Stacy said. "I can help you—"

"No," Jeffrey said. "We don't have any flight helmets, so you need to be fully strapped in. Only the seats in the back have head and arm straps."

She stared at Jeffrey in the mirror for a moment.

Jeffrey said, "I don't have time to—"

Stacy flipped her hand up in resignation. "Okay."

...

As Stacy unstrapped herself from the navigator's seat and followed Leif into the back, she felt angry at being sent off like a child. But she reminded herself that Jeffrey must have his reasons, so she tried to put her anger out of her mind. In the back, there were four seats on each side with full restraints. Green padded canvas covered the seats' aluminum frames.

Leif and Stacy sat down and pulled the five-point harnesses on. Leif reached down and strapped his ankles to the lower seat frame and then pulled a head strap over his forehead and tightened it. Then he slipped his wrists through straps and thumbed a button. An electric motor whirred and the straps pulled snug. Stacy stared at him; she only had the five point harness on.

"Are you secure yet?" Jeffrey shouted from the cockpit.

"Almost," Leif shouted back.

"We're running out of time, hurry up. Let me know the minute you're strapped down."

Leif said to Stacy, "You need to strap down fully. When you pass out from the G's your arms and head will flail around and you could break a wrist, or hit your head."

"I don't need to worry about blackouts. In training missions I held more G's than anyone in my unit."

"My dad didn't tell you then?"

"Didn't tell me what?"

"What he did in the war, who he was with?"

"No, he didn't talk about it. I assume he flew something."

Leif yelled up to the front, "Dad, how come you brag to me incessantly about being a Hammerhead, but no one else?"

"He was a HAMMERHEAD?" Stacy reached down and strapped her ankles down. "I thought all of the Hammerheads were dead."

Jeffrey yelled from the cockpit, "Get those restraints on, now!"

Stacy pulled the strap over her forehead, slid her hands under the wrist straps, and thumbed the button. The straps pulled tight.

"We're in," she shouted out.

The ship pulled up hard. Stacy felt her body crush into the seat, and she growled and flexed her leg and stomach muscles to keep blood in her head. The ship pulled even harder, more than she had experienced in training. The pressure let off a bit, and then the ship fell to the right. Stacy thought back to her training in the centrifuge. She had given it everything that day, pushing herself to stay conscious. With her body smashing down into the centrifuge's padded chair, she got a giddy feeling that she would never pass out, and then the color bled out of her vision, leaving everything shades of dull brown. A quiet tunnel collapsed on her and closed, and she fell into a far-off blackness. She could still hear the sounds of the centrifuge but from a distance, as if she were suspended in a lightless mass of cotton. The blackness had given way to an electric blue that swirled around her with sparks of bright-white light. Then the electricity went out of the blue, it dimmed to black, and she faded back into the decelerating centrifuge. She had pulled more G's before blacking out than the other trainees, and she had a splitting headache for her efforts.

As Jeffrey flipped and spun the gunship in the air, she lost track of which direction was up. G's crushed her into the seat in three quick successions, and then her entire body cavity tickled as they went weightless. The seat straps hauled down on her shoulders, her head pressurized as blood rushed up, and her vision tinted red. The pulling sensation flicked in an instant to a brutal crush down into the seat. The tunnel came immediately to her vision and she thought she was going out, but the crushing went to floating weightlessness again and her vision returned. A less intense but still harsh press into the seat followed. She looked at Leif. He grinned at her.

"What are you—," she stopped, gritted her teeth, and let out a guttural sound as the G-s pushed her down. The pressure let off, and she said, "What are you grinning at?"

"Are you kidding me? My entire childhood I've, oh man…" The crushing weight turned to weightlessness for a split second. "I've had to listen to stories about this guy's flying and always thought it was built up."

"So now you get to experience it firsthand."

"This is amazing," Leif said, and let out a whoop.

"Yeah, great, but," the G-s became severe and the tunnel returned. Stacy tensed every muscle in her body, trying to keep blood in her head and hold onto consciousness. The tunnel widened for a moment and then folded shut, rolling her into darkness. As before, she felt as though she were suspended in cotton. Calm. This time the electric blue came on slowly, but with brilliance, as if a xenon bulb had been rolled open across the sky. She found herself sitting on a field of dark-green grass, which squeaked like oily plastic under her hands. The grass ran off into rolling hills. That was all, just the electric sky and plastic grass.

She touched her face and found smooth, healthy skin where the bandage had been. "I'm dreaming," she said.

"You all right?" a voice to her right asked, and she turned to find Leif sitting next to her. He had turned to stone, sitting like a Buddha under the sky. He said nothing more.

Now the sky sparkled and swirled in deep burgundy spirals. She lay back on the vinyl grass and looked up at the sky and watched the burgundy turn into fractals.

...

Jeffrey ground his teeth trying to stay conscious. He locked his leg and torso muscles tight, and he wondered if the pilots bearing down on him had G-suits on. When he had been given the go by Stacy, he flipped the gunship over and turned east. The other Kiowas had come to weapons range as he hammered the throttle and pulled the ship above Mach 2.5, blasting the desert with a sonic boom. He flew out over the ranches to the Cuyamaca Mountains. He would have preferred steeper mountains, but these had enough to dip down into and make life hard for the pilots behind him.

The three gunships turned, and he lost some ground as they tacked in on him, but he needed them close. Alarms went off as the gunships behind him painted him with their fire-control systems. The Kiowa's countermeasures jammed the targeting and the missiles became useless.

"Guns only, my friends," Jeffrey said, and smiled. He welcomed the other pilots to his turf: close in dogfighting. No lobbing shots from the bleachers. He came low to the deck and dropped his speed subsonic as he lanced into the mountain valleys.

The three gunships stayed above the peaks at first, trying to get a shot off at him from a safe distance. Tracers flicked past him, but the pilots could not gain the accuracy from that distance.

"You're going to have to come in after me and bloody your knuckles," Jeffrey said, and slammed on his air brakes. This had the effect he had hoped for. Two of the pilots overshot him and began turning to re-engage. The one who had slowed in time to stay behind him had the fastest reaction time.

So, you're the best in the group.

Jeffrey would put that pilot down first. He snapped the gunship left and right, threading through the shallow mountain

73

valleys. He flew low now, pulling seven or more G-s at sixty years old with no G-suit. Through a few of the turns his vision lost color, but not a hint of tunnel yet. He still had the edge after all these years, but pushing this hard in mountain valleys put the Devil's price on his head. If he bet wrong, pulled too many G's and lost consciousness, they would all die.

He felt his back spasming, and he thought perhaps his old body could not do enough to get them out. There was a time, decades before, when he could have briefly pulled over seventeen G-s with a suit. Now, nearly forty years later, his natural resistance to black out and the modifications the military had made to his vascular system and genes could only take him so far against twenty-five-year-old pilots in G-suits.

The best pilot had dropped in behind him and tested his guns for range. Jeffrey kept his gunship moving like a pro boxer's chin, weaving left and right and up and down. He would turn on his left wing and nose down to turn right; then he would spin 270 degrees and pull up. There was no firing solution for the other pilot. He was close enough now to do damage, so Jeffrey had to play it right. Years of dog fighting had left him with an immediate toolbox of creativity in flight maneuvers, and he blended movements together; smooth then jagged, steep then shallow, and the other pilot had no pattern to use for prediction.

Jeffrey saw a mountain ridge ahead of him and headed straight at it, weaving and jigging the whole time. Every so often a tracer would flash by close. He imagined the other pilot laying down a coat of foul words as he tried to land even one round in the gunship. Jeffrey knew how the other pilot felt right now. Chasing a faster, stronger pilot was infuriating. When a pilot realized that, even with a dominant 6-o'clock position, the other pilot could not be taken, he or she had to try and read patterns to predict what was going to happen. When no patterns emerged, and if the pilot didn't have enough experience at this level of dog fighting, he or she would become desperate. When a pattern finally did emerge, even if it was blatant bait, the pilot might jump at it. That's what Jeffrey hoped for, and he had seldom been disappointed in a dog fight.

As Jeffrey approached the wall of rock, he gave the pilot a beautiful pattern: left, then right, and then left again. The wall of rock loomed in his windscreen, and there appeared to be no room to turn right again. Seeing this, the other pilot committed fully to the left turn in an attempt to come high and close the distance. Then Jeffrey pulled right, feeling his body crush into the seat. He growled as he clamped his body down to keep as much blood in his head as he could. The side of the mountain came closer. The other pilot, now wider in the turn, should have let him go, but youth and aggression have heavy costs. The pilot turned right to follow. Jeffrey shifted his gunship farther right, down the mountain, taking more escape angle away.

The wall of rock loomed, and Jeffrey's vision began to tunnel. He yelled out as the tunnel gradually collapsed around his vision. He was just about through the turn, but the mountain still came closer. He dared not pull on the stick any harder. For a moment he was not quite sure if he was still conscious, and then he cleared the mountain and righted the ship down into a ravine. He gasped for breath, pushing oxygen deep into his lungs. His vision cleared. He looked at the proximity screen and found no ship behind him. He turned on a wingtip and the mountainside came into view, blanketed with fire, scraps of gunship still rolling into the valley.

He hated to kill such a skilled pilot, but they were not letting off, so Jeffrey had to walk them right out the door. He turned the ship again. When he looked down the valley, he could not believe his luck. One of the gunships flew directly at him about mid-valley, probably looking for him. While Jeffrey had both the ship's IFF transponders on his screen, they had nothing but visual contact. He flew deep into the valley, approximately 500 feet below the other Kiowa. That ship made no move to engage or evade. It just kept coming up the valley. Stupid to go that slow in a fight, Jeffrey thought. Fly fast and crazy and keep looking around. Don't roll along, especially not high like that. But then again, that pilot was probably flying lower in a mountain valley than he ever had before and did not expect a ship to come up off the rocks from below.

Jeffrey did just that.

As he approached the other gunship, he slammed on the airbrakes and fired the nose thrusters. His gunship came up about 60 degrees, and he balanced it on its rear thrusters. The computer vectored the thrust perfectly, and the gunship flew along nose up and belly out. Jeffrey opened up his guns, and– as the other ship flew over him–tracers lanced through it from nose to tail. At a distance of less than 400 feet, the armor piercing sabot rounds ripped all the way through the ship.

Jeffrey slammed the throttle to its stops, and the gunship accelerated up ballistically. He pulled back on the throttle and inverted through the partial loop of a Half Cuban Eight, rolling the ship upright and leveling off behind the other gunship. A thick swath of black smoke rolled out of the gunship. It listed toward the left side of the valley. The canopy blew off, and the pilot's and navigator's seats shot up and away. Their chutes opened. The tail ramp opened, and soldiers jumped out. They fell toward the rocks, their chutes trailing like streamers behind them. Jeffrey willed the chutes to snap open, but the soldiers did not have enough altitude. One at a time, they hit the rocks.

The rocks caught the ship's wing, and the ship spun like a Frisbee back out into the valley, parts scattering. One last soldier flicked out of the back of the gunship. The soldier's sideways angle allowed enough time for the chute to open. Just the kind of blind luck Jeffrey had seen so many times. The ship struck the valley floor, and a fireball swallowed it as Jeffrey pushed his throttle forward. He scanned his proximity screen, found the third gunship, and turned to intercept it, hopping over a ridge and into another valley.

"Call them off," he said through his teeth. "I just walked through two good pilots and killed maybe eight to sixteen more soldiers. You don't need losses like this. Just call them home and figure out your next play."

But the other gunship continued its patrol of the mountains. Jeffrey came to a valley beside the other gunship, flying low and waiting, still hoping.

"Call them off, you bastards," he said. "See this for what it is."

The gunship turned into the next valley and kept a solid patrol pattern.

"Goddammit," Jeffrey said. He couldn't wait forever. More ships were most likely on their way, and he had been lucky to survive three. Then he thought about the IFF transponder.

Of course. I'm invisible to the other ship. Why the hell is that so hard to keep in my head?

He waited for the ship to turn east, and then he turned west and broke the sound barrier deep down in the valley. On a ridge, he saw some hikers staring as the gunship ripped by.

"Sorry," Jeffrey said for the shockwave he knew he had slammed them with. He shot out the west end of the Cuyamaca Mountains and, in a few minutes, flashed over Del Mar and out over the Pacific Ocean.

The flat of the ocean turned to a sheet of glinting light as it caught the high sun. Jeffrey came low over the water and pushed the gunship over Mach 2. He considered the fuel supply and the consumption and did a quick calculation in his head. They had more than enough to get to where he wanted to go, and beyond.

From the troop area he heard Stacy ask in a quiet, pitiful voice, "What's going on?"

"Stacy," Jeffrey said over his shoulder, "You have had one hell of a day, and you're safe for now. Just rest and get some sleep. Leif, how are you doing?"

"Oh, I'm good," Leif responded from the back, his voice thin, "Stacy seems better off than I feel, but I'll make it."

Jeffrey heard the shuffle of a bag and then retching.

Stacy said, "I definitely feel better than that."

"Okay, you both just rest then," Jeffrey said. "We're free from worry for now."

He heard the bag crumple, and Leif asked, "You going to tell me what's going on?"

"Just rest," Jeffrey said. "We'll have all evening to talk, and honestly, I think we may even take another day before we move on. We need to be sharp for what's coming."

"You have a plan?" Stacy asked.

"I'd love to lie and tell you I did."

He turned the gunship north to Alaska's Aleutian Islands. Then, after 300 miles he dropped the ship to 100 feet off the waves and turned south. It never hurt to be cautious. He ran for an hour at this altitude, as long as he could stand the concentration. When he felt exhaustion dulling his mind, he lifted the ship up to a safer 500 feet and flew on.

CHAPTER 9

After almost four hours at Mach 2, the gunship had covered over five thousand miles and burned most of its fuel. Jeffrey ground the heel of his palm into his left eye, yawning wide and slow as he scanned the ocean's surface and the sensor screens for shipping and air traffic. He wanted to pilot well clear of anything to limit errant rumors of a Kiowa in the South Pacific Ocean.

He heard someone settle into the seat behind him and, looking into the mirror, saw Leif.

Leif looked around at the navigation instrumentation. "I'm rested, and you're tired as hell. I wish I could help you fly this thing." He scrubbed his fingers through his hair. "Is there anything I can help you with?"

"I'm okay. We're almost there," Jeffrey said.

He heard Leif's finger tapping on glass.

"We better be," Leif said. "You're getting low on fuel."

"We'll be fine, but not for long."

Out on the ocean, the pale, white rim and dark-green center of an island drew toward them. Jeffrey slowed as they came up on the island, tipped the gunship to the left, and circled the island looking out the window at what was not much more than a sand spit with an elongated palm and sandalwood forest in the center.

"Too small," he said, and aimed the ship at the next island on the horizon.

"Where the hell are we?"

"We're over the Tonga islands east of Fiji," Jeffrey said. "There are well over 100 islands right here, and less than one-quarter are inhabited. It's a great place to disappear." The ship flew by the next island, but it was smaller than the first. Jeffrey did not slow.

"What are you looking for?" Leif asked.

"I need an island that's big enough to hide the shape of this ship. Ideally, it would have a clearing among palm trees we could land in. I assume that this thing doesn't have any form of active camouflage."

"None. No one has figured out how to generate a field large enough to camouflage anything bigger than a person. The power on the field is exponential, so the power requirements go far too high. To make something this big disappear you would need to park it next to a nuclear reactor and suck up all its electricity."

"That would surely be noticed," Jeffrey said. He pointed to the left. "There we go. That's nice." They approached a much larger island with a worn volcanic outcropping. Jade-green vegetation draped the old slopes of the volcano. Dense palm trees grew at the foot of the volcano, and white beaches surrounded the forest. A crease on one side of the volcano formed a short valley. Underbrush broke up the sandy floor of the valley.

Jeffrey circled the island once, looking for boats.

"There's no sign of any heart activity larger than a rat on the surface," Leif said.

"You've got to be kidding me," Jeffrey said. "You can scan for that?"

"Yes. If you can get close enough, these ships can read the electrical activity in the heart."

"Did I fly close enough for an accurate scan?"

"Sure, no problem."

When Jeffrey circled back on the crease in the mountain, he nosed the ship right up to the cliff face and began descending. Ferns and rocks rose up around them, and the light in the cockpit shaded to greens as the ship set down beneath the surrounding palms. Jeffrey shut down the engines, unstrapped, and stood up out of the seat for the first time in some eight hours.

Leif began to rise from his seat. Jeffrey shoved him back down, laughed, and said, "Out of the way, gotta go."

Jeffrey squeezed out of the tight cockpit space and walked into the troop area where he found Stacy fast asleep. Her restraints held her sleeping in a position of perfect posture. Jeffrey reached down and pressed the button to release the pressure on her wrist straps. Then he walked to the back of the troop area and opened the ramp. The ramp hissed down, and bright light and the sound of ocean surf filled the cabin. He walked down the ramp and onto the white sand. He stepped between plants with waxy leaves and patches of white flowers. When he had walked some distance from the ship, he relieved himself. Then, instead of returning to the ship, he cut out under the palms toward the beach.

The sun floated high in the western sky behind palm fronds, dappling Jeffrey with dancing patches of light. They had chased the sun across the Pacific Ocean. Despite eight hours since stealing the gunship in Nevada, it was still early afternoon here. The curve of the island formed a bay of translucent blue water. Far out toward the open ocean, a reef caught the surf. The sound of the waves crashing there slowed Jeffrey's heartbeat.

Jeffrey had no illusions as to why this had been the first place he thought to hide. The scent of saltwater mixed with palms and tropical underbrush returned Jeffrey to nearly forty years earlier when he had crash landed in the South Pacific. Flying at the edge of space, surrounded by the stars and the curving earth, enemy fire had punched holes in his main engine and right wing. His ship fell into the atmosphere. The wing, to his amazement, did not fall apart on re-entry, and he had just enough control surface left to glide. As he came down over the sparkling flatness of the Pacific Ocean, a small dot of an island materialized and curved up to meet him. He ejected and parachuted into the surf.

He had lived on that island, in the shadow of a three pronged volcano, for over a month before they came for him. When they arrived to take him back to the war, he stood hip deep in the water, having just speared a small blue fin trevally on a sharpened, sandalwood branch. The sun caught the blue and red-gold scales of the fish as it flopped on the spear. It had taken him an hour to spear, and its weight shook the branch as it slapped its bladed tail back and forth. Then the thunder of turbines rose up over the crash of the surf. He turned to see the military transport come over the breakers, throw its shadow over him, and land on the beach. He tossed the fish into the water, dying and wasted. As he walked through the shallows up to the beach, tears welled in his eyes. They came not because he was afraid to die, but because the moment he saw the ship, the deep sense of peace he had found over the previous month vanished. He had not been prepared for that.

He had not returned to the South Pacific until now, even though somewhere in his heart he had always intended to do so. While this was not the island he had survived on, it was close enough. That sense of peace returned to him as he stood in the forest shadows on the edge of the white blanket of sand. He stepped out from under the shadows of the palms onto the bright beach. He pulled his boots and socks off, tossed each aside, and dug his toes into the sand. He unzipped his gorilla-operator's jumpsuit, stepped out of it, and then pulled off his t-shirt.

For most of his life he had ignored his scars, but as the island brought him back closer to the war, he looked them over. A long thin scar ran from his ribs under his armpit, across his chest, and over his right shoulder. There on his shoulder the scar cut across a tattooed hammerhead shark, its tail curved underneath it. It's row of exposed teeth and baleful eyes gave the shark a dispassionate and death-focused expression. The scar bisected the tattoo leaving the top and bottom misaligned. Jeffrey looked down at his legs. Mottled scars and sporadic circular burns covered his shins and the tops of his feet, some deeply pitted, others more superficial.

Wearing only his boxer briefs, Jeffrey walked out across the beach and into the water. Its pale-blue clarity made the water merely a suggestion over the immaculate sand, just showing itself in bending flashes of sunlight. He walked out until the water, just on the edge of warm, lapped over his knees. He lifted his arms to his sides and fell backward. The water slapped his back and then its warmth washed over him. He sat up, chest deep, sputtering and blowing saltwater out of his nose, laughing. He leaned forward and lay belly down in the water, head up, and sank his hands in the sand. He pulled himself along until his hands could not touch, and then he swam out into the bay.

...

When Jeffrey returned to the gunship he wore only his underwear and held his jumpsuit and boots pinned under his right arm. He walked on the balls of his feet through the underbrush, keeping to the sand between the bushes. Stacy and Leif sat on the ramp, looking out through the palm trees to the ocean. Water bottles from the gunship's emergency supplies sat beside them on the ramp.

Stacy saw him first and rolled her eyes. "Nice undies, Jeffrey."

"Thanks," Jeffrey said. He walked up the ramp, tossed his jumpsuit inside, and unzipped one of the three large bags of emergency gear. In it he found water bottles and MRE's. He unzipped the second bag and pulled out several pairs of ripstop BDU's in various shades of tan. He found a pair large enough and pulled the pants on. Leif laughed.

"What?" Jeffrey said, looking down at his pant legs. The pants, which fit his waist, floated four inches over his ankles.

"The military never did supply clothes that fit me right," Jeffrey said. He dug into another survival bag, took out a folding knife, and cut each pant leg off just above the knee. He folded the knife, clipped it to the edge of his pocket, and sat down on the ramp. Fishing through the bag again, he found a brown t-shirt. He pulled it over his head. Leaning back on one of the survival bags, he put his hands behind his head and wiggled his toes.

"Are you done?" Leif asked.

"What did I do?" Jeffrey said, holding his arms out and looking over at Stacy who was staring at the burns on his shins and feet. "Pretty ugly, eh?" he said. "That's what happens when you get an electrical fire in your cockpit instrumentation. You see there," he said, pointing to a vertical row of symmetrical circles on his right ankle. "That's where the eyelets on my boot burned me. It was so hot spatters of molten metal burned right through my boot leather." He pointed to the middle of his shin where the scarring turned from spots to more of an overall sheet of mottled skin. "You see how the line is more severe here? That's where my flight boots ended and I only had a layer of fabric. I kept having to reach down while I was flying and slap my shins to put out the fire."

"Dad," Leif said, "I appreciate that Stacy has not heard these stories before, and surely you'll have to share with her the heroic action that led to the loss of your right pinkie tip, but if you wouldn't mind telling me, now that we are finally stopped, what the hell just happened to my day off?"

Jeffrey scowled at Leif and then noticed Stacy leaning over to get a look at his closed right hand. Jeffrey smiled at her, held up his hand, and wiggled his pinkie, which was one joint short.

"Dad?"

"Sorry Leif. I suppose I don't really want to think about the last several hours." He leaned back on the survival bag and looked up at the tops of the palm trees. "Honestly, I'm not exactly sure what happened." He looked at Stacy. "Have you been able to remember anything more?"

Stacy looked at the ground and shook her head. "I remember running down the corridor of a ship. I am fairly sure

I was on the USS Lacedaemon. That's where our CO set up our training exercise. I can recall the day before clearly. I remember the briefing on the exercise that morning and then me sprinting down a ship's corridor. There were people running behind me. I want to say that it was David and Matt, but I can't say for sure."

"Those the guys in the crash with you?"

Stacy nodded, looking out now through the trees to the beach. The wind flipped at her hair and sunlight played across the tip of her nose. Jeffrey looked at Leif who sat on the ramp, staring at Stacy.

"I told you she was pretty," Jeffrey said to Leif.

"What?" Leif's eyes snapped to his father, angry, telling him to shut up. Jeffrey laughed at Leif.

"What's that?" Stacy said, coming out of her thoughts.

"Nothing." Jeffrey tried to suppress his smile and failed. "Please go on. Can you say if you were running to or away from something?"

Stacy stared at him for a moment, probably suspicious of his smile. "Definitely away. I remember being afraid."

"Okay, hold on," Leif said, holding up his hands, the breeze catching his loose Army t-shirt. "I would like to be filled in. What crash, who's dead, and what the hell are you both doing with a new-generation Kiowa gunship? And please, since I could go to prison for what I just did, make it good."

Jeffrey said to Leif, "I really appreciate you're taking the chance on us."

Leif looked down at his hands. "Well dad, you've always been there for me."

"I would like some more detail too," Stacy said. "As far as I know, someone tried to kill you, and you helped me out of a really bad situation. That's it."

"I'd argue we helped each other out," Jeffrey said.

The breeze from the ocean stirred the palms around the ship, and Jeffrey put his hands behind his head. "Well, I guess there's nothing for it but to start from the beginning." He told Leif and Stacy everything he had gone through that day, starting with meeting "Arlo" and moving on to his transport's engines shutting down. He told them about the spider and finding the bodies and Stacy. Then he told Leif about their escape from the soldiers.

They all sat in silence for a moment, and then Leif–now staring at the backs of his hands–said, "This is bad."

"Yeah, I know," Jeffrey said.

"And you don't remember a thing before the crash?" Leif asked Stacy.

"No, I have no idea why someone wants me dead."

"Enough of this for now," Jeffrey said. "As long as we're here, we need to enjoy it. Let's build a fire and see if we can spear some fish."

Stacy smiled at the suggestion and stood.

"What?" Leif said, jumping up. "We need to figure out what we're going to do."

"There's plenty of time for that," Jeffrey said, walking over to Leif and taking hold of his shoulders. "Right now we need to breathe."

Leif shook his head and smiled. "I don't know how you can do that knowing that someone tried to kill you just a few hours ago."

"Oh, they're not the first to try. It's no big deal. Either you die or you live. If you live, you fight back. If you die, well then, who gives a shit?" Jeffrey slapped Leif on the shoulder hard, laughed, and walked out to the beach with Stacy.

Leif jogged to catch up with them.

"First, let's get the material together for a nice fire," Jeffrey said. "While we're doing that, we can look for some good branches for spears. We'll try and catch some fish. I for one do not want to eat an MRE out of that survival kit if I can help it."

"Is a fire a good idea?" Stacy asked. "Will someone see it?"

"No. We're surrounded by thousands of islands in millions of square miles of ocean. We're alone out here and safe for now."

...

Farther up the beach, a stand of sandalwood trees had provided fallen limbs in abundance for a fire. The flames of the fire, now bright against the evening sky, brought out their footprints in long shadows across the sand. The sky had shifted to a heavy red, and Jeffrey thought the clouds, now lit from underneath by the setting sun, looked very much like sand dunes. As darkness folded around them, sparks rode the twisting heat up out of the fire.

Stacy squeezed peanut butter from a brown, plastic pouch. Leif threw the empty packaging of his MRE into the fire, lay back on the sand, put hands behind his head, and looked up at the sky. The first stars glinted near the volcano's peak. Jeffrey held a lemon cake sticking out of a tan pouch and bit at the chemical frosting.

"Come on," Stacy said around the peanut butter in her mouth, "they aren't that bad."

"You'd think in 40 years someone would have figured out how to make this stuff taste better." He ate the rest of the cake and threw the pouch in the fire. He lay back on a survival bag. "So Stacy, tell me how it was that you ended up getting into Navy Special Warfare."

"If I tell you, will you tell me about the Hammerheads?"

"Sure, some of it anyway."

Stacy squeezed out the last of the peanut butter, took a drink of water, and opened a pouch labeled with black letters: fudge brownie.

"I was raised on the Colorado plains. Everybody thinks that Colorado is all amazing mountains, but there's a big chunk that's basically just like Kansas. My dad was a minister. He's retired now. My mom's still a checker at the Safeway. Our house is very conservative, cinnamon scented with cross stitches on the walls. There's a white piano in the living room where we used to sing hymns. I suppose I was a typical Midwestern girl. I had long hair, wore jeans, and loved horses. My life growing up was really good. I can't complain. But, in high school, everything went sideways when I started dating a guy who hit me. I dated him for two years, and only broke it off when I moved to Denver for college."

"I'm sorry you had to go through that," Jeffrey said.

"It's okay. It took me a long time to understand that it was one of the best things that happened to me because of the direction it sent me. In the end it brought me out of my shell and showed me who I really am. Turns out, while I enjoy the quieter things in life, I really enjoy the harder edges as well. I didn't see that at first though. I spent my first year in Denver paranoid."

"The University of Colorado was okay, but—after being in an abusive relationship and being fairly small—I didn't feel safe around men. No one did anything to me, but every time a guy looked at me I felt afraid. There were a few times I was pretty nasty to guys who didn't deserve it. I thought I was being tough, but—now that I look back—I realize I was just afraid."

Stacy bit into the brownie and continued talking with her mouth full. "I finally decided that I was sick of worrying so I looked up self-defense classes. I signed up for one at a martial arts school near the campus. One of the instructors at the class was a woman my size. She changed my understanding of the world. She made me realize how much more I was capable of than I had believed."

"So you enjoyed the class?" Leif asked.

"I went a bit crazy for it," Stacy said with a smile. "At one point they put on full face helmets and had us practice headbutts. They wanted us to put the top of our head into the face of their helmets. Hard and strong," she said, tapping the top of her head, "striking soft and fragile," and she tapped her nose then her chin. "I did the headbutt wrong... with my forehead. One of the instructors brought me a towel. I had no idea why until I looked down and saw blood on my chest and on the floor. I had stripped a ribbon of skin off the bridge of my nose. I was so amped up, I hadn't felt a thing. I liked the self-defense class so much, the next week I joined the school and attended it through the next three years of college."

"How'd your parents like that?"

"The first time I came home with short hair and bruises on my shins and forearms, my mom cried. She's had me in long hair since I was a toddler. My dad said the time there would distract me from my classes."

"On one visit home my younger sister told me some guys were hassling her at school so we went out on the back deck and I showed her a few things. My dad came out and I stopped, but he sat down and said he wanted to watch and to keep going."

"When I came home with this tattoo," Stacy lifted up her jumpsuit leg to expose three Asian characters on the outside of her calf, "my mom freaked out. She screamed at me for an hour, and then—when my dad got home—she made me show him. He told my mom he would take me for a drive and talk to me. We got in the car and he didn't say a word. When my dad got silent, I knew he was really mad."

"Yeah," Leif said, "I can relate. My mom was like that."

"That's definitely true," Jeffrey said.

Stacy said, "Sitting in the restaurant, waiting for our food, my dad finally asked me if I was a lesbian. I laughed so hard I choked on the water I was drinking. I told him that I wasn't, but probably would be better off given the quality of men I had met. At that my dad surprised the hell out of me. He had always been so straight laced and, I assumed, closed minded. But he laughed out loud and told me that, no matter what I chose in life, he always had and always would love me. The rest of the dinner we just talked adult to adult. It was the first conversation like that I'd ever had with him."

"So what does the tattoo stand for?" Leif asked, "Karate?"

"No it's Jeet – Kune – Do," she said, pointing at each character. She looked back at Jeffrey. "After college I went down to the Navy recruiting station and gave them my story. They stuck a bit on the assault charges, but..."

"Assault charges?" Leif said. "You didn't say anything about assault."

"Oh yeah," Stacy said. "Sorry, I skipped that part. My last year of college I went home for Thanksgiving, and some girlfriends took me out to a tavern called MacFinn's. It's one of the two taverns in town. I ran into my ex-boyfriend there. First time I'd seen him in a few years. He was a bigger jerk than ever. He walked up behind me and smacked my butt hard. I didn't give him a chance to speak. I just laid him out. The judge..."

"Wait a minute," Jeffrey said, "him smacking your butt is assault in itself. How did that not go down as self defense or at least a mutually inclusive fight?"

"It would have been, but I went a bit crazy. I really hurt him, and I do feel a bit bad about that."

"What'd you do to the guy?" Leif asked, sitting up.

"He ended up with two broken bones in his foot, three in his right hand, a broken jaw, a shattered molar, a perforated ear drum, and a ruptured testicle."

Jeffrey and Leif stared at Stacy.

"What?"

"I'm just waiting to make sure you were done," Jeffrey said.

"Yes," Stacy said, "that was the extent of it. I felt really bad about it afterwards. In the end, the judge was good to me and gave me a conditional discharge instead of a felony. I had five days in jail, which I served over Christmas break, and then I was on probation for a year."

"I'll make sure to be very nice to you," Leif said.

Stacy made a fist, held it up, and gave Leif a broad, beautiful smile. Leif looked away and Stacy's smile faded. She seemed, to Jeffrey, to be unsure why Leif had not responded well to her joke.

He's shy, and you're not fully aware of how pretty you are.

Jeffrey stretched, yawned, and then said, "Honestly, I don't care what you did to that guy. Life's hard, and he had a lesson coming. If I had a daughter getting treated like that guy was treating you, it would have been me sitting on the other side of the parole officer's desk."

"The Navy recruiter had similar sentiments when I talked with him," Stacy said. "When I told him I had just come from my last appointment with my probation officer, he said the Navy probably wouldn't be able to use me. But, when I told him the details, he just shook his head, called my ex-boyfriend a stupid bastard, and took out the forms to sign me up."

"I made it through basic training, served six months as a yeoman and then asked my CO if I could put in for Special Warfare. I caught a lot of crap because of my size, but they had no reason to block me so off I went. The last thing my CO said was, 'See you back here in a few days.' That one comment gave me all the motivation I needed. Hell Week was terrible. I got hypothermia three times and a hairline fracture on my right elbow, but I made it through. They have this bell that's over 200 years old. You go up and ring it three times if you want to quit. I refused to even walk near it. We had over one hundred candidates when we started. I graduated with 28 other men and women."

"I haven't heard of a bell for Special Forces," Leif said.

"Not Special Forces," Stacy said, "that's Army. We're Navy Special Warfare. They were once called SEALS, but–when the Navy started doing most of its operations in space–the name SEALS was changed to Navy Special Warfare Group, supposedly in respect to an old SEAL team. However, the unique Hell Week the SEALS developed is still the same. The insignia is a holdover from the old days," Stacy said, pointing to her shoulder patch. On the gray background, a black eagle gripped a rocket with its left talon and held an ancient musket in its right. An anchor sat centered in front of the rocket.

"As I continued on with training, I became fascinated with explosives and asked to follow that career path. The officers agreed and set me on a blended training path. That was a year ago, and now here I am sitting on an island... where are we again?"

"Tonga," Jeffrey said with a slow yawn. He stretched out his arms and folded them across his belly and closed his eyes.

Then he asked, his eyes still closed and sleep in his words, "So your training was in explosives?"

"Yes, but it's not complete," Stacy said. "I've got a year in and have the general explosives concepts down, but now I have to learn to apply them."

"Making it through all that is pretty impressive," Leif said.

"Not nearly as impressive as the Hammerheads," Stacy said. "It's not every day that you get to meet a mythic figure. What about it Jeffrey? What about your story?"

Leif, who had been prodding the fire with a stick, dropped his hand to his lap, and his eyes snapped to her. "What the hell do you mean 'mythic'?"

Stacy held up her hands. "It's not like that. Not like those conspiracy nuts who say the war never happened. Let's say 'heroic' then, okay?"

Silence followed, and Stacy and Leif looked over to Jeffrey leaning back on the survival bag, legs stuck out across the sand, his forearms crossed over his belly, asleep.

"Oh that is so unfair," Stacy said. "He owes me. You're my witness." She kicked a bit of sand into the fire, and then asked Leif, "What about you?"

"Me?"

"Yeah, you."

"I don't really have a story. I grew up in Ramona, California playing video games and floated through school. I could have done better, but I just didn't care. I give my dad a lot of credit for not tearing my head off. I'm not his ideal son. I tried sports, but I wasn't any good."

"I gravitated toward the Army because I knew he'd like the idea of me signing up. Honestly, I didn't have a clue what to do with my life. They moved me into electronic countermeasures. Pretty boring really, but I like the life and will probably make a career of it. Hopefully I can stay in San Diego the whole time. The beaches are nice. I'd love to go to Hawaii, but only the Marines get stationed out there anymore."

"Do you surf or something?"

"No."

"That's it? Nothing more?"

"Sorry, I lead a pretty simple life: Work, eat, and sleep."

"Well there is definitely something to be said for simplicity."

Leif and Stacy sat for a time. When the sun had set and darkness folded around the fire, Stacy stood and walked out toward the breakers. As her eyes adjusted to the dark, she found herself under a heavy curtain of stars. In deep space more stars fill the darkness, but they burn as sharp points of light. Here the stars shifted and twinkled, and it felt natural. Out where the breakers rumbled, a wisp of foam curled now and again. Beyond the surf, out across the ocean, a violet line stretched along the horizon.

As she looked out on the vastness of it, with her bare feet in the cool sand and her face and arms catching the night breeze, she felt the reality of having lived through the day. She knew how close she had come to never seeing the world again, and she believed this moment on the beach and every moment beyond was a gift that Jeffrey had given her. Jeffrey kept saying how she had played an important part in their escape, but she didn't feel it. It was his actions, plans, and flying that had saved them in the end. She felt as though he had handed her a box of diamonds, and she had no words to thank him. The diamonds were the stars, and this moment looking at them was hers alone.

CHAPTER 10

The sun lay behind the volcano preserving the cool morning as Jeffrey showed Leif the tarantula. Leif picked through its abdomen with a pair of tweezers. They had left Stacy asleep by the burned-out firepit. The skin on Jeffrey's shoulders and neck crawled as he watched Leif hold the spider with his bare hands. Jeffrey heard Stacy's voice and looked up to see her just entering the palm forest from the beach. She shouted out and then hopped, holding one bare foot. She continued through the bushes with more careful steps. When she reached them, she sat down on the ramp and smiled.

"I had a dream last night," she said, "and I remembered something new."

"What is it?" Jeffrey asked.

"In my dream, I was running down a corridor jumping through hatches. People were running behind me. I could hear their footsteps. It was vivid, as if I was really there. I was scared as hell and running for my life. I turned around to look behind me and David and Matt were right on my heels. I saw Matt's eyes go wide, and I turned around and saw a guy dressed in black BDU's."

Leif and Jeffrey continued to look at her. She just looked back at them, saying nothing.

"Is that it?" Jeffrey asked.

"Well, it's something isn't it?" Stacy said, "I'm just glad to have remembered something. I hope that means I will get the rest of it back."

Leif had gone back to inspecting the spider.

"I hope you're right," Jeffrey said. "I have a feeling whatever is locked up in your head is the only thing that's going to give us any hope of getting out of this situation."

"Oh, man," Leif said, scraping out some gray material from the spider's rear abdomen and rolling it into a ball between his fingers, "that was lucky."

"What's that?" Jeffrey asked.

Leif motioned for Jeffrey to hold out his hand. He pressed a pea sized chunk of a pliable gray material into Jeffrey's palm.

"You know what that is?" Leif asked.

"C4," Stacy said, looking over Jeffrey's shoulder.

"I know what it is," Jeffrey said. "It was in the spider?"

"Yeah, it looks to be some kind of self-destruct mechanism. Probably designed to go off when the spider was done with its injection. It looks like when you stepped on it the collapse of the chassis yanked the blasting cap out. Somewhat of a design flaw, don't you think?" Leif reached over and pointed at the ball, "You see that burn on the side? The cap, not being imbedded, only set it on fire and it must have extinguished under your boot."

"Is this enough to kill someone?" Jeffrey asked, as he touched the ball of C4 in his palm.

Leif looked to Stacy.

Stacy shook her head. "No, it probably would have knocked you off your feet and might have been able to break one of the bones in your foot, but that would be the worst. It would have completely destroyed that little guy though. With that amount of C4, I'd agree with Leif that it's probably just a self-destruct mechanism. You could put a lot of different, modern explosives in to make it more lethal. C4 is old. It has a slow rate of burn compared to what we have now. But it's cheap and destructive enough to obliterate that spider."

Jeffrey said, "So it probably finds its target, jabs it, and blows, covering up any specific detail. Or, if it's caught and tampered with, it blows. When I stomped on it, there was a puff of smoke, but I thought it was electronics shorting out."

"Nope, that was the blasting cap going off," Leif said. He had pulled away the skin of the spider and cut away the broken body panels, exposing the electronics inside. He took up a magnifying glass he had found in the survival gear and looked over the circuit board with it.

"Stupid," he said.

"What?" Jeffrey and Stacy both asked at the same time. Stacy moved to the other side of Leif.

"They left the manufacturer's data matrix right there."

"Why would they do that?" Stacy asked.

"Either they were too confident in their self-destruct system, or they were lazy. Judging by the quality of this spider, I'd guess they were overconfident. It would have taken a lot of extra work to go through and scrub all manufacturing data off the boards and chips, so the self-destruct was a faster, cheaper way. The odds of the blasting cap getting pulled out are pretty small. Maybe the wires for the cap were laid in wrong, you know, caught on the chassis somehow."

"So what do we have here?" Jeffrey asked.

Leif took his sat-phone out of his pocket and zoomed in on the data matrix. Then he scanned the matrix and the text. He handed the phone to Jeffrey. Systemic Alliance Development Board number AX1593C93-000017 showed on the screen. Jeffrey handed the phone off to Stacy.

Stacy said, "Sure, Systemic Alliance does a lot of work for military robotics. That makes perfect sense."

"This is an amazing piece," Leif said, exploring the mechanism with his screwdriver. "The motors that drive the legs are tiny, but really well made. Look at the articulation." He held up the spider and pulled one of the legs out, released it, and it curled back. Jeffrey shuddered and held up his hand.

"That's terrible. Don't do it again."

They all sat looking at the spider, and then Leif said, "So what do we do now?"

"We need to start formulating a plan," Jeffrey said. "We should go over what has happened, what we know is fact, what we think we know, and what we don't know. Then we decide on a way forward. Right now we can't simply walk up to the military and ask for help. We've killed several soldiers and destroyed a lot of equipment. We have to assume those soldiers were innocent, or at least will be perceived as innocent. We need to find out what's going on, gain proof of it, and then go as high as we can for exposure. We don't know who or which branches of the military are compromised. We don't know how far spread it is or how high it goes. So, once we have some more information, we'll have to choose that exposure point very carefully."

"Let's start with this spider," Stacy said. "Where can we find out more about it?"

Leif said, "We can learn more about it from the Systemic Alliance Development's manufacturing records. We can try and hack into their system, but I wouldn't know where to begin, and the minute we fire up a link from this ship, it'll light us up on their boards."

"Can they identify our location in that situation?" Jeffrey asked.

"I honestly don't know."

"Do you think we dropped our pants when you looked up that data matrix on your phone just now?"

Leif looked at the phone for a moment and shrugged. "I don't know. I hope not. If they hack into my phone records and search my data, it will be one tiny piece of data in a long stream of information. Also, I looked it up on a large general table, so knowing the site I went to will not give them specific information. Even if they do figure it out, they only know the one board, which looks like it's used in a lot of different applications. They might come to the right conclusion, but it's a long shot."

"Is your sat-phone reporting location?"

Leif shook his head, "That's old tech, Dad. Sat-phones have better location security by default now."

Jeffrey nodded. "Let's take the risk of making the assumption that whoever has been after us doesn't know we have the spider. I don't want to let them know we have it by having your phone or the computers on this ship start pinging away at the company's servers. If we don't find what we're looking for remotely, they'll know right where we're headed, and they'll likely know what we're looking for. We have to proceed quietly. The less they know about us the better."

"So what do you propose?" Stacy asked.

"We kidnap someone," Jeffrey said.

"Oh, God," Stacy said, dropping her head into her hands.

"But first," Jeffrey said in an upbeat tone as he stood, "we have to get fuel and get to wherever this Systemic Alliance Development is." He looked to Leif for the answer.

"I don't know where it's headquartered," Leif said.

Jeffrey began putting items back into the survival bag. "Okay, well, the first order of business is to get fuel, and then find some way to access the data we need without using this ship's computers or your personal sat-phone." He pointed to the magnifying glass in Leif's hand. "You want that in here, or what?"

"That's as good a place as any," Leif said, and then looked at Stacy. "I guess we're going." He tossed the magnifying glass into the bag.

Jeffrey zipped the bag shut and threw it into the gunship. He held out the ammo can, let Leif set the spider back in it, clamped it shut, and set it in the gunship. Then he looked down at Stacy's bare feet and his own and then out to the half bay where the light-blue water glittered in the morning sun. He breathed in the fresh sea air. "First, I think we should all take one last swim."

"Really?" Leif asked.

"Sure, you don't know how long it's going to be until any of us gets a proper shower again. Can't die smelly." He stepped into the gunship and found the first aid kit. He dug around, took a sheet of self-adhesive plastic out, trimmed it with scissors and then came back out. He walked over to Stacy and lifted her chin with his hand. He saw that the skin just around the edge of the bandage had bloomed with a black and purple bruise, and a deeper green bruise ran off toward her ear.

"Close your eyes," he said.

When she did he blew a bit of sand off the bandage. Then he took the sheet of water proofing adhesive and laid it over the bandage. He pushed down the edges, careful to avoid the injured area of the cheekbone. Stacy winced a bit at the pressure.

"There you go," he said, "ready for a swim."

The three made their way out to the beach. Out on the broad sand, they stripped down to their underwear and waded into the bay. Stacy dunked her head in the warm water and scrubbed the dirt and scraps of blood out of her hair. Jeffrey floated as best he could in the water and then dove down into the deeper center of the bay. He swam along the sandy bottom, feeling his ears pressurize as he went deeper. Then he swam up to the surface, drew a breath, and went down again. When he surfaced, he looked back to where Leif and Stacy lounged in the water. Stacy stood thigh-deep in the water, the sun glowing on her skin, and Jeffrey chuckled to himself when he noticed how often Leif glanced over at her. She was incredibly pretty and a strong woman.

When the sun burned down from high overhead, they made their way out of the water. Jeffrey noticed red on Leif's neck. He touched his own neck feeling the light burn. He looked over his forearms and saw that they had turned pink as well. Stacy, with her black hair and perhaps Greek or Italian skin, had only turned a slight shade browner. She pulled the waterproofing sheet from her face. Then she picked up her jumpsuit and looked it over. It was torn and spattered with blood and she folded it up as she walked away. Leif stared at her as she went.

"You look like a man dying of thirst," Jeffrey said.

Leif lowered his eyes as he blushed.

"I only–" he said, but Jeffrey interrupted him.

"Don't justify it, just play your cards right."

"Yes sir," Leif said, "and I suppose the great Hammerhead will give me some advice on how to play those cards?"

"Are you kidding me?" Jeffrey said, as he buttoned up his shirt. "I was a charity case to your mother," and he laughed. Leif stood on one leg to put on his pants. Jeffrey walked past him and slapped him on the shoulder. Leif hopped several times to regain his balance.

"Come on," Jeffrey shouted over his shoulder. "Let's go hijack some fuel."

...

The gunship fired up with a smooth rumble. Leif settled into the navigator's seat behind Jeffrey, and Stacy strapped into the troop area. Jeffrey waited the few moments for the engines to come up to operating temperature. When the gauges flicked to green, he lifted the gunship straight up out of the palm trees, turned, and flew over the shallow bay. He tilted the ship nose-down and flew sideways so he could look into the water. Regret for having to leave rose in him as he spun the ship around and flew out over the ocean, staying 500 feet above the waves. When there was no land in sight, he pulled back on the stick and put the ship into a hover.

"Is 500 feet enough to get the antenna working?"

"Yes, that will work, no problem," Leif said. "Are you ready?"

"Go for it," Jeffrey said. He heard Leif clicking on the keys of the navigator's console.

"See if you can find what we need in Australia," Jeffrey said.

"I'm going to assume," Leif said, "that everything I search for is going to get logged and targeted, so I'm going to start off searching for trucks transporting aviation fuel all over the Pacific rim, Korea, Japan, Taiwan, New Zealand, even the US Marshal Islands. Then I'll move over to the Chinese mainland. That will create a big mess that hopefully will give them too many targets to focus on."

He clicked on the keyboard for several minutes. In the distance, white clouds were rising up in the heat of the blue sky.

"Oh, and there you are," Leif said.

"Did you find a truck?" Stacy asked from the back.

"Not yet, but a message just popped up on my screen that says, 'Out of fuel?'"

"Really?" Jeffrey asked, looking in his rearview mirror. He saw Leif hunched over the console and could make out Stacy's knees beyond the bulkhead.

"Yeah," Leif said, his fingers still clicking on the keyboard. "You want me to respond?"

"Tell them to go—" Stacy began, but Jeffrey interrupted.

"Not a peep, Leif. Let them wonder if the message was received. The less information they have the better off we are."

"Yes, sir," Leif said, and continued tapping on the keyboard. "Got another message. It says, 'We will allow you to turn yourself in without shots fired. Please acknowledge.'"

Stacy said, "They'll save the shots for when we are in a nice quiet room, hands tied."

"I have what I think is a perfect fuel out in Australia," Leif said. "It's a triple tanker of Jet A-1 bio on the road just out of Coober Pedy heading toward Alice Springs. I assume that's the middle of nowhere, just as we'd like it."

"It sounds good to me," Jeffrey said. "It would be better if we found some JP-5B, but the A-1 has a high enough algae-alcohol percentage, so we'll be able to burn it."

"I'm moving my search north again, through Japan."

The keys clicked.

Jeffrey began to feel uncomfortable, as though a huge spotlight were painted on him as he hovered high out over the open ocean.

Continuing to type, Leif said, "Got another message, 'We have you in the vicinity of Tonga. You are locked via satellite. Interceptors en route. Please acknowledge intention to surrender.' You still want me to ignore them?"

"Give 'em nothing," Jeffrey said over his shoulder. "They have squat."

"I'm almost done with the searches," Leif said. "I'm pulling up more detailed shipments in the Chinese low-population areas. Do you want to start heading there and then I'll shut down?"

"No," Jeffrey said. "It's too obvious. If I saw that many searches I would immediately discount the ones in the direction a ship headed right before it disappeared. Let's just leave them with 20 or so targets that are all equal."

"Okay," Leif said, "I'm shutting down the link. I'll let you know when to move out."

"Good," Jeffrey said. "How many targets did you give them?"

"I gave them 456 trucks to think about," Leif said. "The signal is black, you can move on."

"Excellent." Jeffrey dropped the ship into a freefall and pushed the throttle full on. The gunship lashed out across the ocean 100 feet over the waves, splitting the air with a sonic boom.

CHAPTER 11

Out on the horizon, the surf and low green hills of Australia's Frasier Island came into view and then rolled up on the Kiowa. As the gunship came over the island, the green trees and bright sand seemed strange after so much blue water. The gunship crossed the shallows between the island and the mainland. Jeffrey pushed left a bit to keep the gunship over the less populated forests and farms between the cities of Torquay and Maryborough. As he flew inland, the trees grew thin in the valleys until only dry grass ranches remained. The old worn-down mountain ranges shifted steadily to red dirt. As the rock and sand of the Outback took over, the entire glass bezel of the ship's fuel indicator began to pulse red. Beneath the gauge, the display reported 867 miles of fuel remaining at the current speed. The display decreased one mile every few seconds.

Jeffrey slid his finger along the map display, scanning over the Stuart Highway. From the southern coast, it ran up through the center of the continent, all the way to Darwin. The truck they needed rolled northbound somewhere along that strip of asphalt between Coober Pedy and Alice Springs. Jeffrey could not establish the exact distance to the Stuart Highway, but he was fairly sure it was more than 867 miles. He pulled the throttle back dropping the gunship to .98 Mach and the miles-remaining display rolled up to 1246. Would that be enough? Jeffrey could not set a waypoint in the GPS navigation without risking sending off a signal.

The gunship shot out over the iron-oxide red of Queensland's Central Lowlands, and Jeffrey thought how, aside from the scrubs and sporadic gidgee and gum trees, it looked very much like the dead surface of Mars. The calm air held a few high clouds out over the crystalline line of the horizon.

Leif had moved into the back some time ago, leaving Jeffrey alone in the cockpit.

"How you doing up there?" Stacy called out.

"We're over the continent now," Jeffrey said over his shoulder. He heard shuffling and looked in the mirror to see Stacy coming up and strapping into the navigator's seat.

"How far will our range be when we gas up?"

"From what I can see here for fuel consumption and capacity, I would say that–with full main and secondary tanks and flying sub-Mach–we could potentially get to Russia the long way. We won't have to worry about fuel again after this, I hope. The only trick is not running out before we get to the truck."

"Oh, I see," Stacy said, and Jeffrey heard her finger tick the glass on one of the navigator's instruments. "Do you think we have enough to get to the tanker?"

"I honestly don't know. It either will be, or we are going to be living off the bounty of the Outback. Even if we get there, we might have problems. I don't know what priming the system needs if it runs too low. How's Leif doing?"

"He's sound asleep."

...

For the next two hours, he and Stacy watched the mottled red, light orange, and white hills and bluffs pass by beneath the gunship. They sighted the Stewart Highway just as a buzzing alarm joined the pulsing red light of the fuel gauge. 'Fuel Low' began scrolling across the lower portion of the front cockpit glass. The gauge showed a range of 198 miles. The fuel had lasted to the highway, but they saw no trucks yet. Jeffrey slowed the ship as he came up on the highway and turned north toward Alice Springs. Red gravel flanked the black asphalt, creating a wide ribbon cutting across the desert. The miles remaining on the fuel gauge ticked down to 197.

The truck they wanted had left Coober Pedy this morning. In the time since then, Jeffrey assumed that it must have crossed at least half of the over 400 mile distance to Alice Springs. He flew with the highway to his left, about one thousand feet away. No vehicles moved on the asphalt. On either side of the road, sand and rock stretched to the horizon, broken only by scrubs and a few spidery trees.

After another 15 minutes and sixty miles, Jeffrey saw a tail of dust rising off the asphalt ahead. The dust lifted into the air away from them. Southbound. Not the truck they wanted. Jeffrey pulled wide, out over the desert. Throttling on, he dropped the gunship low, out of the sightline of the truck. The fuel gauge fell from 146 to 98 when Jeffrey accelerated. He cursed under his breath and dropped his speed.

With the highway clear, Jeffrey pulled back toward it. He saw no other dust-trails but decided to keep heading north along the road. In another ten minutes they were only 100 miles from Alice Springs.

Did we miss it?

The fuel gauge rolled below 50 miles. Jeffrey scanned the road. Then, out ahead, he saw another dust-trail. He strained his eyes at it. The dust rose toward them. Northbound.

"Please let that be the one we need," Jeffrey said, drumming his fingers on his leg while the slow flight speed crawled toward the truck.

As they closed in on the truck, Jeffrey leaned forward, squinting his eyes. He saw a glint of chrome.

Is it a tanker?

"Yes," Stacy shouted out, making Jeffrey jump. "That's it, it has to be. Three... no four tanks." In a few seconds they were close enough that Jeffrey could also see the chrome cylinders of a quad-tanker semi.

"I thought it was supposed to be a triple tanker," Jeffrey said.

"Does it matter?" Stacy asked.

"Not as long as it has the right fuel."

"If not?"

"We walk to Alice Springs or die out here." Jeffrey looked over his shoulder. "Leif, wake up, we have ourselves a truck."

Leif said, his voice groggy, "I'm up."

"Everyone clear on the plan?" Jeffrey asked.

"Yes," Stacy said.

"I'm good," Leif said from the back.

"Okay," Jeffrey said, "we've got a good list of crimes going. Let's add piracy to it."

CHAPTER 12

Doug Norton rode in the passenger seat of the fuel tanker, his head aching from last night's whiskey. To his right, Alex McKinney drove with a stupid little grin on his face. Doug shifted in his seat and groaned. He had found a good tussle last night, and his right eye throbbed with his heartbeat. At one moment, the drone of the big fusion engine soothed him, in the next, the rocking of the truck cab made him feel sick.

"You still feeling the effects?" Alex asked in his heavy northern accent.

Doug hated Alex and his stupid mountaineering sunglasses. Alex could drink all night and not seem to feel it the next day. But then again, Alex was an alcoholic.

Despite it all, today was a good day. Yesterday, dust storms plagued them, and Doug still had dust crusted in his nostrils from working outside, fixing three blowouts. The truck had rocked and twitched up the highway all the way from Adelaide to Coober Pedy. Nothing but a stiff whiskey had smoothed

Doug's nerves when they reached town. Now, with the sky blue and clear over the Stuart Highway, Doug felt the need to enjoy the moment. He reached into a cooler, pulled out a bottle of beer, pried off the top on the door of the truck, and flicked the bottle cap at Alex's woolly, blonde head.

"Hey," Alex said, lifting up his arm.

The truck swerved onto the shoulder, and Doug saw a cloud of dust billow up in the rear view mirror. He laughed, drank off a third of the bottle, and then folded his arms across his barreled chest, saying, "Keep your eyes on the road."

"I honestly don't know why I keep drivin' with you," Alex said.

"This fuel run is my route is why," Doug said. "You're a parasite."

Alex shook his head.

They passed a south-bound road-train pulling five trailers of sheep. Doug got on the radio and talked for a moment with the other driving crew and then returned to the bright sun and red dirt, feeling boredom creeping in on him.

Thirty minutes passed.

Alex yawned and said, "I suppose it's just about time to check the tyres and let you drive."

Doug didn't respond. He stared across Alex, out the side window of the truck, at what first appeared to be a large, black bird. But it didn't flap its wings and took an unnaturally straight and fast line through the sky.

"You with me?" Alex said, looking at him.

"I don't believe it," Doug said.

"What?" Alex asked as he turned and looked out his side window.

"There's an American warship out there."

"What the hell do you mean?" Alex said, leaning forward over the steering wheel to get a better look out the side window.

The aircraft flew north, out ahead of them. Its dead-black lines caught and swallowed the harsh sunlight; even the glass of the cockpit, somehow matted, absorbed the light. The ship slowed and turned toward them, flying sideways. It approached the highway and came to a hover over the asphalt. As the truck approached, the ship began flying backwards, maintaining its distance. The ship was close enough that Doug could see the pilot in the cockpit. He wore no helmet and appeared to be an old man with close-cropped, gray hair and a trim beard.

"That's no military pilot," Doug said.

"What should I do? Stop?"

"Not on your life."

The gunship flew in that fashion, backwards with its rotary cannon on them, for about half a kilometer. When it became clear that Alex had no intention of stopping, it turned and arced away. It came back around toward the highway about a kilometer ahead. The nose came down and missiles lanced away, drawing four, fast trails of smoke out from under the down sloped wings. The first missile converged on the highway. A ball of fire erupted and expanded exponentially as each new missile merged into it. From out of the fireball, small bits of pavement and roadbed shot straight away, trailing smoke, while larger chunks of rock and slabs of tarmac flipped end over end through the air. A moment later, the heavy thumps of the explosions shook the truck's windshield.

Alex let off of the gas and pressed on the brakes, slowing the two-hundred-plus tons of fuel and steel. The truck rolled up and, as the smoke blew away, Alex and Doug saw that the pilot had run the missiles in a line, one after the other, creating a series of linked craters about ten meters wide and thirty meters long. The craters extended out into the scrubs on each side of the highway. The truck would not be able to go around, and there was no way to get the road-train through a U-turn on the thin strip of pavement. The gunship turned, its landing gear came out, and it settled just on the other side of the craters.

"They just blew Stuart Highway in half," Alex said.

Doug grabbed the CB radio and turned up the volume. A piercing wail filled the cab. He turned it down and switched channels. Each turn of the knob brought forth the same terrible noise.

"They've filled the airwaves with crap, so we can't radio out." Doug switched the radio off. He took out his sat-phone and scowled at it.

"There's no signal," he said.

"No signal from the sat?"

"They must be jammin' that as well."

Alex pulled off his sunglasses, exposing his dog-blue eyes. "So what do we do?"

"Well, we can't back up or turn around, so I suppose we find out what it is they want." Doug reached into the glove compartment and pulled out a Ruger .357 revolver with a bright nickel finish. He stuffed it in his worn pants pocket, grabbed the warm door handle, and popped open the door. The desert air, hot even in the autumn, hit him in the face. The heat felt good after the air conditioned cab. The metal-grate steps clanged under his boots as he descended to the ground. He walked around the bull-bar to the front of the truck.

Alex still sat in the truck cab. Doug turned and, with an angry jerk of his right hand, motioned for Alex to get out. Alex squinted into the sunlight toward the gunship and pointed.

Doug turned and saw a man... no... a man and a woman come from round the rear of the ship and stand to the right side of the cockpit. The man was young and thin as far as Doug could see. He had blond hair and wore cargo pants and a dark-green t-shirt. The brunette was small, but nice enough on the eyes. She wore fatigues.

The man waved to Doug in a friendly way, and then cupped his hands around his mouth and shouted with an American accent, "We need your fuel. We have no intention of causing you any harm. However, you will need to let us take the fuel for that to work out."

"You and that little waif of a girl are gonna take my fuel?" Doug shouted back across the crater.

Alex stepped around to the front of the truck. "Why not just give them the fuel? It's not our damn fuel."

"You just gonna take a gobful off some Seppo pricks?" Doug said.

"Seppo pricks with guns in a ship with missiles? Yes."

"I sure as hell am not," Doug said. "This is just the type I hate. They need the fuel, so if we stay beside the truck, they can't use their big gun. They don't even look like they have handguns. We just have to wait them out until someone else comes."

"I'm not in for this," Alex said, putting his sunglasses back on. "You want to die, you do it on your own."

Doug turned and thumped Alex in the chest with his fist. "McKinney, if you don't back me up on this, I'll not hesitate. You get me? Did you pocket your pistol?"

"No, it's in the cab," Alex said.

"What the devil's wrong with you?" Doug said, grabbing Alex by the shoulder, spinning him around, and shoving him toward the truck. "Get up there and get it in your pocket."

"All right, all right," Alex said, knocking Doug's arm away and walking back around the side of the truck. He climbed up into the truck. After a few moments, he climbed out of the truck and walked around to the front carrying an old, snub-nosed .380 Smith and Wesson pistol.

"Alex," Doug said, staring at him.

"What?"

"I had hoped for a bit of surprise, but there you are with your pistol out in the sun. Do you suppose they know our intention now?"

They both looked back towards the gunship. The man wagged his finger in the air and then pointed down to the rotary cannon on the nose of the gunship. An electric whine spooled up and the multiple barrels of the gun blurred.

Doug shouted out in his deep voice, "You won't shoot. You need the fuel." The man shrugged and tapped his ear, unable to hear over the spinning cannon. He turned and gave the pilot a thumbs-up, then he and the girl both put their fingers in their ears. The cannon shifted just to Alex and Doug's right, and the barrel erupted in a blast of flame. The roar of hundreds of shots in a few seconds ripped across the desert, and large-caliber bullets whipped past them. The truck's driver-side mirror blew away in a sparkling mist of shattered glass and bits of chrome.

"Holy Christ!" Alex shouted out, and threw his pistol as if it were a baseball. The man standing next to the gunship laughed.

The alarm on Alex's face faded, and anger took its place. "That little whacka."

Doug held up his hand. "These Yanks are either crazy or stupid if they'll shoot at a fuel truck they need. Let's just walk over there. They still don't know about my pistol."

Doug walked off, and Alex followed him through the scrub skirting the craters. The rotary cannon had spooled down, but it still tracked them.

Doug and Alex came around the craters and continued walking toward the man and woman. Doug saw that the woman had a white bandage across one side of her face. Both she and the gangly man looked like easy enough pushovers. When Doug and Alex were a few meters away from the pair, Doug took his revolver from his pocket and leveled it at them. The rotary cannon spun up and Doug side-stepped to put the man and the woman between him and the cannon. Alex took two, quick steps to stand behind Doug.

The man began to move out of the line of fire and Doug pulled back the hammer on his pistol, saying, "Now just stay where you are. This could get messy fast, so let's just take it easy."

The man held up his hands, "Okay, I can do that. All we want is some fuel and then we'll be on our way. You can probably still deliver the rest of what we don't take."

"We can't deliver a drop with the highway blown apart," Doug said. "What do you figure gives you Yanks the right to come down here and start blowing holes in the Outback? And what makes you think we'd just roll over and give up our fuel like a cup a' sugar?"

With her eyes wide and her body rigid, Doug knew the woman wouldn't give him trouble.

The poor girl's probably just got dragged along for the ride. Probably never even seen a gun before, let alone had one pointed at her.

"I think we'll start with you, darlin'," Doug said, motioning with his free hand for her to come over to him. Her eyes went even wider, and she didn't move.

"Now, dearie, this is what happens when you spend time with the wrong blokes. Now come over here nice, or I'll put a bullet in you and your friend. Then we'll deal with the old man."

She didn't move.

"I'm going to count ta three and you're gonna be standing in front of me or laying dead on the road, yes?"

She made no response.

"One!"

She stepped back a bit.

"Two!"

He leveled the pistol at her face. A tremor ran through her and she shouted out, "Okay, okay," and then walked forward. She stopped a pace away from him and he saw she was not just pretty. With her light-hazel eyes flecked with gold and brunette hair cut in a frisky way, she was stunning.

"Come right up here now, darlin'. I won't hurt you if you do what I say."

She took another step. He lowered the pistol, tracing the tip of it around her breast. She looked like she was about to cry. That made Doug smile.

"You're a real pretty one to be out here with these–" and just then the fear in her pretty eyes shifted to a predatorial glare. She shifted sideways, and her hands blurred to the inside of his arm. Her right fist struck him in the soft inside of his bicep. Her open, left hand gripped the top of the gun and levered down on it. As the gun popped out of his grip, he pulled the trigger. The gun clicked, but did not fire. Pain overtook the inside of Doug's arm and burned down to his fingertips. His arm dropped to his side, nothing more than weight hanging off his shoulder. The woman stepped a few feet away, and pulled the pistol's hammer back, drawing the web of her hand out. A bit of blood bloomed there. She pulled the trigger, set the hammer down, and pointed the gun at Doug.

"Not that I want to insult you," she said to him, "but that was stupid."

Doug's entire arm burned with pins and needles. No matter what his brain commanded it to do, it hung limp at his side.

The man walked up to Alex and pulled some large cable ties out of his back pocket.

"Put your hands up on your head like this," he said. Alex did just as he was told. Then the man walked around behind Alex, pulled each arm off of his head, and zip-tied them behind him. Then the man pulled Doug's arm behind his back and a flash of pain burned down to his fingers. As the man let go of Doug's wrists, he tried to straighten his arms and realized the man had zip-tied his belt in along with his wrists.

"Why don't you gentlemen come have a seat in the back of the gunship," the man said. "It's air-conditioned."

"I don't mind if I do," Alex said as he glared at Doug and then walked out ahead of them.

Doug watched Alex go.

He's stupid to just go along with them. We'll both probably be dead in an hour.

The man looked at Doug and motioned for him to follow Alex.

"What reason do I have to trust that you won't just kill us?" Doug asked.

"None," the man said, and he pulled a tazer out of his pocket and pressed it against Doug's chest. "You can either walk to the ship, or be dragged."

Doug waited, feeling the pressure of the tazer on his chest. He wondered what it felt like to be shot with it. Looking back at the woman, he said, "I'll walk," and followed Alex.

In the cockpit, the man told them to sit back to back and used more zip-ties to bind their arms together. The man and woman sat down, the engines screamed, and the ship lifted off with the ramp wide open. They flew over the craters and landed behind the tanker. The man got out, walked along the tanks to the cab, and returned with the shipping manifest.

"We're in luck," he said, looking the manifest over. "Jet A-1 bio in all four tanks." He tossed the clipboard out onto the road and stepped off the ramp, opened a panel, and pulled a thick, rubberized hose out, dragging it over to the truck. He climbed up the side ladder, pulled open the top access port, and worked the hose down into the tank. He held his thumb up, and the woman flipped a switch. A pump spun up.

"What are you doing in the Outback stealing fuel?" Alex asked the woman as she made her way past him. Doug swiveled his head around to see the woman shrug her shoulders and keep walking. Doug tried to listen for a hint as to what they were doing or where they might be going, but they only spoke about taking the fuel.

The pump shut off and the pilot shouted, "That's it. Mains and secondaries are full. We're ready to roll."

The man pulled the hose from the tank. With the hose in one hand, he came down the semi-tank's ladder, and hopped down to the asphalt. The woman pressed another button on the rear control panel and the hose retracted. The man walked back carrying the end of the hose. As it came up into the gunship's body, he stepped aside and let the hose fall. A final splatter of jet fuel poured from it. The spilled fuel filled Doug's nose and lungs with a chemical heat.

The man walked up the ramp, and he and the woman sat in the seats. The gunship lifted off, the ramp still open. Doug looked out at the empty square of blue sky. As the wind from the open ramp rushed around him, he understood their plan.

"You're gonna drop us out the back aren't you?" he shouted at the man, but the man just pointed to his ear and then shook his head. The ship accelerated and Doug had to brace his feet to keep from tipping over toward the open ramp.

"Why not just get it over with then?" Doug tried to shout over the jet blast. The man looked away from him toward the open ramp. Alex shouted something to Doug, but the jet blast and wind overrode it. The ship slowed, and Doug and Alex tilted and fell onto their sides on the decking. Doug shoved himself back to sitting, pulling Alex with him. He felt sure that now they would throw them out the back. But the man and woman remained seated, and the desert floor came up under the ramp and the ship thumped on the ground. Doug stared at the dirt touching the end of the ramp. The engines spooled down to an idle.

"Get up," the man said. Doug and Alex pressed back-to-back, shoving their heels along the decking to stand. The man gestured toward the desert and said, "Walk." They both tried to move at the same time. Then Doug yanked on Alex and walked down the ramp, Alex back-stepping behind him. After walking a distance from the ship, the man patted Doug's pockets and pulled out his sat-phone, and then patted Alex's pockets.

"No phone on you?" he said.

"I have one in the cab of the truck," Alex said.

For the love of Christ you're a damn fool. They mean to leave us out here and you just told 'em...

"That's fine," the man said. "Your truck is six miles to the west. We just need a bit of a head start before you're able to contact anyone." The man took two bottles of water out of his cargo pocket and tossed them to the dirt. Then he took out a knife and cut the zip-ties holding Alex and Doug together. Their arms remained zip-tied behind their backs. The man walked around behind Alex and cut his hands free. Doug stared at Alex's free hands.

Now here's my chance. When the Yank cuts me loose, I'll make a run at him. If I can get the knife, they'll be down a man. Then I'll see about the bitch and the old man.

The man smiled at Doug and pitched the knife into the scrubs, beyond a shallow dirt berm.

"Aren't ya gonna cut me loose?" Doug asked.

"I'm not as dumb as you think I am," he said to Doug. "You should see the look on your face. You'd kill me if you had the chance." The man looked at Alex. "Don't move from that spot until we're gone, or–" and the man took Doug's Ruger out of his pocket and tapped the end of the barrel to Doug's forehead. The man smiled, turned, and walked back to the gunship.

Doug looked to Alex, "Now's your chance. Go find that knife and…"

"Shut it Doug, ya goddamn figjam," Alex said. "He could have left us tied up on the tarmac burnin' ta death, but instead he's made it so we can call for help in the air-conditioned cab of our truck. As far as I'm concerned, he left us with three full tanks of fuel and our lives. He even gave us water. What the bloody hell else matters?"

Doug wasn't sure of the answer to that, but in the weeks to come, each time he saw the heavy bruise in the inside of his right bicep, he would feel a bitter anger at the woman.

The man stepped up onto the gunship's ramp. He turned and looked back at Doug and Alex. Waving, he gave them one last smile, and the ramp lifted and sealed. The turbines of the gunship spooled up to a roaring shriek. As the gunship lifted off, dust blew out in all directions. A bit of grit clipped into Doug's eye. He tried to lift his still-tied arm to his face and shouted out from the pain in his bicep.

CHAPTER 13

Jeffrey flew the gunship north, beyond Alice Springs, to the King's Canyon area. There he found an isolated canyon with a flat, sandy floor and landed the gunship. The three stepped out into the afternoon shadows. The canyon walls continued to reflect the heat of the day. Stacy turned around and looked back at the ship.

"Are you kidding me?" she said.

"What?" Jeffrey said, looking the ship over for some kind of problem.

Stacy pointed at each wingtip hanging out over the scrub brush. "There's barely two feet of clearance from the canyon walls for either wingtip. Why would you land here?" She turned and pointed down the canyon, "The canyon's twice as wide right over there."

"I suppose I just knew I could, so I did."

Stacy laughed with an undertone of derision, shook her head, and turned and walked away from them.

"Stacy–" Leif started, but Jeffrey held up his hand.

"It's okay, Leif," Jeffrey said, and called after Stacy, "I didn't mean anything by it. It wasn't a risk. We're fine."

"Look," Stacy said, as she turned and walked up to Jeffrey. For a moment he thought she might hit him. "I, for one, don't need you flying like a high schooler in his sports car when I have nearly died twice in as many days."

"Stacy, we've made it through so far, and we're safe now—"

"I don't feel safe. You may have this whole insane, warrior's attitude, but I'm scared. I just about got shot in the face back there, and it was my own stupid fault. I can't believe I let a guy with a gun just walk up to me like that. We totally misread them." She kicked a rock, which flipped away in the dust.

Leif started to speak, but Stacy pointed at him and yelled, "You keep your mouth shut. I'm sick of you too, you know." She turned on Jeffrey. "You may be eight feet tall, and," she turned back to Leif, "you may think hangin' with dad is fun, but I don't want to hear any warrior-poet bullshit from either of you."

"Stacy," Jeffrey said, and waited. Stacy turned and glared at him.

"What?" she spit the word through her teeth.

"I'm sorry."

Stacy scowled at him, waiting for more, and—when no more came—her eyes went softer. She turned and looked down the canyon and ran a hand through her hair.

Jeffrey said, "I have to remember to step out of my own skin once in awhile. After years of stuff much worse than this, it's very easy to just jump in and run with it." He sat down on the side of the ramp and looked up at her. "I have to admit that, as an old man closer than I care to be to the end of my life, this has been–in a strange way–fun. I forgot what it felt like to be on the edge. How it shouldn't be exhilarating, but damn if it isn't. I've had death on my tail so many times in my past that I feel like I really know when it's close. I honestly haven't felt we've been in an end-of-the-line situation yet. So, here I am feeling we're running fine, and I've forgotten that you and Leif will respond to the situation differently. I need to consider that more carefully."

Stacy looked back at him and then to Leif.

"What about you?" she asked. "Isn't this freaking you out at all?"

Leif gave a nervous laugh. "Yeah, I'm trying not to think about it, but I have to admit that you looking down the barrel of that gun scared the hell out of me. I had no idea what to do."

"You did pretty well. I thought it didn't even faze you."

"Are you kidding me? I'm lost here. You both have a lot more experience with this sort of thing."

"I don't have any experience with this," Stacy said.

"Well, I suppose we're doing okay," Leif said. "Sure, people are trying to kill us, but no one has a clue where we are, and now we have full fuel tanks. We've had a few close scrapes, but we're averaging out on the positive side."

"All we have to do," Stacy said, "is slip a little below average, and we're dead."

Jeffrey said, "I think we'll make it through."

"No you don't," Stacy said. "You have your doubts at least."

Jeffrey nodded and then said, "I'll do everything I can to get us there though. I'd rather die than let anything happen to you."

"Yeah, right," Stacy said.

"It's true."

"You just met me." She crossed her arms. "I don't see how you could feel that way about someone you just met. I can understand why you want revenge on the people who tried to kill you, but—"

"This isn't about revenge, Stacy. It's about avoiding grief. I've lost too many people in my life." Jeffrey hesitated and then held up a finger. "I think I know how to get this across. You said you want to know about the Hammerheads, so I'll tell you something about them, about one pilot I flew with."

"What does that have to do with–"

"Trust me."

Looking at Leif, he said, "I don't think I've told you this one either." He jammed his boot heel into the sand, trying to figure out where to begin. After a moment, he said, "While there are some other surviving members of the Hammerheads, I have the unpleasant distinction of being the only surviving member of the first group. From the start of the war we fought every day. As exhaustion set in, we made more and more mistakes, and more and more of us died. Within six months, over half were gone. The Marines had more men and women on their way to us, but it was a long process. The pilots had to be selected, modified, and trained."

"When the second group of trainees arrived, we all thought they flew for crap. We felt doomed. These were the best pilots in the world and had been exposed to extensive gene therapy to improve hand-eye coordination, reaction time, and vascular stability for G-forces. They were physically ready for the challenge and had all the flight theory ever written jammed into their heads, but their instincts and attitude were terrible. On the first mission, two hot shots flew right into each other. The attack formation fell apart as debris scattered."

"They were all arrogant, but it didn't last. They walked onto the flight deck the first day like roosters, and came home with hollow eyes. I think we lost one in ten of the new pilots in the first week. I don't remember if I was that arrogant when I started. Probably was. I definitely was bloodthirsty after what happened on Jupiter Station."

"Well, after awhile, I started to realize they weren't all crap; it was just the fools that stood out. The stupid and unlucky ones died off, and we were left with a hard-core group of amazing pilots. Evan Welch stood out in that group. He came from Canada somewhere: Moose Jaw, or Yellowknife, or some such place. You'd never have expected excellence from him. He was short, thin, and lanky. He had a big nose, and his eyes were always red, like he was sick. A lot of the pilots, including myself, thought he was slow in the head. Even the CO did. He set his call sign as Dopey. At first we couldn't figure out how he got into the Hammerheads."

"During flight briefings he would sit off to the side and look at the floor as if he wasn't paying attention. If you made eye contact with him, he'd look away quick. He was so passive I personally expected him to die in the first dogfight."

"But he didn't die on the first day. On the second day he came home as well. During the briefing for the third day, the CO told us that Dopey had taken two enemy ships, one each on the first and second engagement. I didn't believe it though. I thought maybe it was a mistake, or he had taken out a ship already damaged by another pilot."

"That day the CO assigned him as my wingman. We were working the asteroid belt looking for enemy fighters. I was young, tired, and hot-headed. I told my CO that we should let the newbies kill each other, and that I didn't want one covering me. I suppose it was pretty ugly of me to say right in front of

Evan, but he didn't react. He just walked past me to the hangar. My CO stared at me and pointed out to the hangar."

"We left the carrier in a close, fingertip formation, and having him three feet off my wing made me nervous as hell. I felt as though, at any moment, he would run into me, shoot me, or something else just as stupid. As soon as I could, I ordered the group to slide out to route formation, and got my first hint that Evan was more than he let on. The other lead pilot gave me a verbal confirmation, and his rookie wingman had to say something cute. Typical idiot. From Evan all I got was two clicks on his radio. Nothing to say, just doing as he was told."

"As I flew lead, thinking of all the different ways I could be killed by my wingman, I got my second hint about Evan. My proximity marker showed him at exactly 90 meters. We trained to stay 85 to 95 meters off our lead in route formation. That's a pretty tight margin as it is, but he was focused right on the center of that. When I realized it, I sped up, slowed down, and turned. The other two pilots faded and caught up and faded again, but Evan stayed at 90 meters. He would slip up to about 92 or down to around 88 and then, in a split second, he was back at 90. We're talking about six-G turns and changes in velocity of hundreds of miles an hour, and he kept his variation under twelve feet. It was staggering. I had the unsettling realization that if Evan were to go to guns on me, he would kill me in seconds. He was a much better pilot."

"Later in the flight, we engaged the enemy, and I soon realized that Evan was the most precise pilot I had ever flown with. He slid out to combat position and stayed within my trailing cone through every maneuver. You expect your wingman to fall off a bit here and there, but here was a rookie who had no problem following me through my best patterns. I was pushing to my own G-limit and throwing every tactic I knew at the enemy. He followed me through it all. He clipped two enemy ships off me that day, and never once left me, even when he had a ship lock on him. Some rookies would peel off and try to save themselves when that happens, which is exactly what the enemy wants. Divide and eliminate, just like taking a weak animal out of a herd. The wingman needs to trust the lead to pull him or her out of the tail, and he did. The guy didn't know me at all, and I had been an ass to him. But he handed me his life and trusted me with it, covering me through the entire fight."

"After a few weeks, and several more kills, the CO changed Evan's call sign from Dopey to Mako."

Stacy sat down next to Jeffrey on the gunship's ramp. "Why Mako?"

"It was a special call sign, which goes back to the beginning. We were Hammerheads originally not after the sharks, but because we could take so many G's. The joke was that we had steel in our skulls." Jeffrey tapped his knuckles to his forehead. "Hard as a hammer. The centrifuge operators started the nickname. Then, when the experiment was moving into an actual combat unit, Gunnery Sergeant Richter drew the insignia of the hammerhead shark on a training-room board. It stuck. Later, the CO's decided that pilots who distinguished themselves would have the name of a shark as a call sign."

"It was interesting how much power we put into a name. As Dopey, Evan appeared passive and sickly, but as Mako his hooked nose, hunched shoulders, and quiet off-to-the-side demeanor seemed much more predatorial. He was good at flying lead, but as a wingman he shined. I pretty much knew that, if I had Mako behind me, I was coming home. Knowing that, I could push myself to my own limit. I felt immortal."

"Evan had a lot of close calls because of his dedication to the slot. He would never leave his wingman no matter how much heat came down on him. He often came home with holes in his ship, but his luck held on for just over a year. Now remember, a tour of one year was a long time for a Hammerhead. The average Hammerhead died in six months, but killed on average over 50 enemy ships. The kill ratio was staggering, and there wasn't a single member of our unit, man or woman, who wasn't okay with the price. At first the enemy had us with sheer numbers. But they were a long way from home, and we were chewing through them like chainsaws on fallen trees."

"A little after a year into his tour, Evan and I were deep in a fight as I chased a particularly quick ship. The enemy had recently destroyed Deimos and a belt of crap was floating around Mars. They were holing up in the debris. I came around one rock, about the size of a four-story building, and the ship I was chasing turned right and went square into another rock behind it. I pulled harder right and went between the two."

"I knew Evan would have no problem with the maneuver, but it was so tight I looked back anyway to watch him come through. As he passed through the gap, his ship obliterated in a big, yellow ball of fire that started at the engines and blew forward. The explosion snuffed out when it had burned off the ship's escaping oxygen and hydrogen, leaving only dark scrap scattering in all directions. I couldn't tell what happened. He might have hit some smaller rock, or gotten shot from an angle I didn't see, but honestly I think his ship just gave out. We pushed those things to the limit day after day and there were failures, although most not quite that spectacular."

Jeffrey drew a slow breath, exhaled, and then looked at Stacy. "That's only one story I have of a good friend's death. There are a lot more. I've had to work through each one throughout the years, which has been a terrible process." He kicked at the sand. "During the fight, when each one died, I had to ignore that something horrible had just happened, or I would have died as well. I shoved each aside and they dissolved into my bones. I didn't even realize they were still with me. Years later, something would trigger a memory, a song or a smell, and I would find myself thinking about a good friend I had forced myself to forget ever lived."

"It was that way with Evan. It's not that I couldn't remember him. I had chosen not to remember. However, no matter how much I didn't want them to, the dead always found their way back to me. My memories of Evan were triggered several years after the end of the war. I was with Leif and his mother watching fireworks. One of the fireworks exploded with the same bright yellow flame as Evan's ship. At first I tried to block it out, but he pushed right through. I left my son and wife in the field and sat in the car alone, working through events I hadn't faced since I had survived them."

"It's a very confusing experience for someone like me. I always believed I had to be strong at all times. I attack and I win. Once I'd won, the situation was over, end of story. But until you've reconciled each loss, the dead won't let you rest. When the memories first started coming back, I tried to stop them, but I learned that, if I blocked them out, they would only come back again another time. Others turned to drinking or drugs to hold back the ghosts, but I couldn't let myself go that way with a wife and new son." Jeffrey turned to Leif. "You don't realize it, but you being born may have saved me from the self-destruction I'd seen others go through."

Leif shifted his weight and twisted his hands together.

Jeffrey said, "I don't worry too much about my own death. I've had a long life, much longer than I expected when I was young. What troubles me is outliving others. It's you two who I have to see through this, and I want you to believe, Stacy, that I will not carelessly put you in harm's way. I couldn't stand to do it. I'll lay down my own life without hesitation before I let anything happen to you."

Stacy stood up and motioned for Jeffrey to stand as well. He did, and she hugged him, saying, "Thank you." She held onto him a moment longer and then let him go. She looked up at him. "What was your call sign? Great White?"

"No, at first it was 'Grinch' because I was a real grouch in training. But then, because of my flying, they changed my name to Orca. The CO said I was deadly, but too big to be a shark."

"That's a good name," Stacy said.

"Not so much," Jeffrey said, chuckling. "You try catching hell for six years being named after a whale in a tank of sharks."

Stacy laughed at this and then looked out to the canyon walls. "What do we do now?"

Jeffrey followed her sightline up to where the rust-red edge of the canyon cut a ragged line under the sky. The sky held nothing, no wisps of cloud, no birds, no aircraft, and it's smooth, blue perfection gave it a depth that drew Jeffrey in. He drew another deep breath, exhaled, and let Evan Welch go one more time.

He looked at Stacy. "I need information on System Alliance Development. That spider's the only lead we have. We need the name and address—home address I mean—of somebody important in their robotics division, someone who can get us access to their manufacturing data."

"What are you planning?"

Jeffrey smiled. "You ever kidnap anyone before?"

Stacy shrugged her shoulders. "Why the hell not? I mean if we're going to prison, let's go whole hog, right?"

"That's the spirit," Jeffrey said, and looked over to Leif who sat hunched over a sat-phone, tapping on the screen with his thumbs.

"What are you doing?" Jeffrey asked.

"Relax dad, I took this from the truckdriver."

"Stop," Jeffrey said. "What have you looked up on that thing?"

"I was about to look up some information on management in System Alliance's robotic division."

"Have you searched anything yet?" Jeffrey asked.

"No. I was just about to hit 'enter'. Do you want me to?"

"No. They might search that phone's records when our friends are able to get connected with civilization. It's a long shot, but if they think of it, then we just dropped our pants."

"What do we do then?" Leif asked.

"I don't know," Jeffrey said, sitting back down on the ramp and putting his head in his hands. Stacy sat down as well. The three stared at the sandy ground. A cooler breeze blew down from the narrower reaches of the canyon now, flushing out the heat of the day. The shadows had reached halfway up the side of the canyon wall.

"I've got an idea," Leif said. "How many vehicles did you pass when we were coming across the Outback?"

"Oh, I suppose I saw dust trails from two or three trucks," Jeffrey said. "Why?"

CHAPTER 14

Just beyond the orbit of the thin, crescent Moon, a long blade of darkness blocked out the stars. The faint moonlight illuminated dozens of large cannons. The dark shape, the USS Lycurgus, was the command center for the Navy fleet. While not as large as standard battle cruisers, it was much more heavily armed and armored. Docked against the black metal of the Lycurgus via the fixed cylinder of an airlock, a small, civilian yacht caught and reflected more than its share of the dim light.

The sleek lines and oversized hydrogen-oxygen engines illustrated the yacht's opulence, and shining white ceramic tiles gave it away as an atmospheric re-entry vehicle. While unmarked, its uniqueness made it easy to identify as the Corona Mundus, the flagship for United Aerospace, which—for over a century—had been the United States' largest military contractor for spacecraft and aircraft.

Along the starboard side of the yacht, large circular windows faced out toward the Earth. In one of the windows, a woman stood in her private suite and looked out on the Moon and the nightside of the Earth. The terminus of dawn glowed along the rim of the planet, matching the Moon's crescent.

The woman turned and faced Carter Roberts, anger flaring in her eyes. "What do you mean you don't know where they are?" Despite Carter's years of military experience, he winced at her derisive look.

She continued, "You had their location in the South Pacific and knowledge of their search for fuel trucks but have found nothing?" She jammed the silver nail of her index finger into the "United Aerospace" patch on his chest. Carter's heart accelerated at her touch.

She said, "Mr. Roberts, this is totally unacceptable. Those two people could undo all we have worked for. If it weren't for that nosy bitch we would have no opposition," She turned back to the window.

"Yes, Mrs. King…"

"Oh dear God, please don't use that name," she said, reaching up and pressing her palm to her forehead. "I suffered far too much being married to that old bastard. Now that he's gone, I don't want to be reminded of it." She placed her hands back on the window sill. Carter Roberts looked out, over her shoulder, at the dark sphere of the Earth and the electrified edges of North and South America, their major cities illuminated webs.

He looked back to Maxine King and thought she looked rather Grecian in her long, white gown with one pale shoulder bared and the other covered by a draped length of fabric, which shifted in subtle colors as she moved. For tonight's meeting with military commanders, her hairdresser had pinned her hair back into a formal twist with pearled clips. She normally wore it down between her shoulder blades. Carter did not like the severe style. It, blended with her uncharacteristic anger, made him unsure how to proceed.

"Maxine," Carter said after a pause, "they identified several hundred fuel trucks, and there is nothing to suggest which one they selected as their actual target. We have no idea of their fuel range, their ultimate destination, or their intent."

"And they made no response to your messages," she said.

"Exactly. They're cautious and resourceful."

"What do we know then?" her voice went softer, closer to where Carter felt it should be for the mother of the New World: tender and caring. She touched the sides of her neck with her fingertips. Carter stared at her neck where the silver nails caressed the skin.

"Mr. Roberts?"

Carter pulled his gaze away from her neck. "I have some more information on the shipbreaker from the landing strip. It turns out that he was a Hammerhead."

"WHAT?!" Maxine turned on Carter, glaring. "How is it that we are only finding this out now?" She held up a hand and, as she inhaled, pulled her shoulders back and her chin up. "It doesn't matter," she said. "The Hammerheads were a myth, and any member of their group is useless. It will not be a problem."

"I agree that the Hammerheads were just one more element in the military's ruse to justify itself. However, we can only assume that this Holt is the reason Stacy Zack was able to escape. That, and the luck of the devil. We still can't understand why the freighter's bridge did not burn out on re-entry. It was an error on our part."

"A significant error, on your part."

Carter acknowledged the comment with a pause and then continued. "Regardless, this Holt has proved to be a skilled pilot. According to the records, he was decorated many times during the war—"

Maxine cut him off. "Why are you speaking as if the war happened? It was a lie. You know that. The Hammerheads were a lie. It means nothing. Anyone saying they are a member of any combat unit during that war should be easy pickings for our troops. They did nothing for years, aside from having false memories implanted, while society quavered in fear thinking a mythical, alien race was about to destroy life on earth. Meanwhile, my husband's father made his fortune." She stopped and pursed her burgundy lips, closing her eyes.

"Yes," Carter said, "but it still doesn't change the fact that this Holt has been able to out-fly our best pilots."

"What do we know of this Holt's weaknesses?"

"The only living member of his family is his son, Leif Holt."

"No one else?"

"No one else."

"I think it is time we took custody of this son, don't you?"

"Yes, well." Carter took a deep breath and exhaled. "We went to his quarters in San Diego and—"

Maxine's eyes went flat. "San Diego?"

"Yes."

"So that's whom he picked up in Ramona then."

"We can only assume so, as we haven't been able to locate the son. However, he is not scheduled for duty for another 12 hours, so we will not be able to verify an AWOL status until then."

Carter saw Maxine's jaw muscles working, and he hesitated.

"What do you have to add?"

"It appears preventing us from using him as leverage is not the only reason Holt took his son," Carter said, looking back over his notepad. "Leif Holt is an electronic warfare technician, countermeasures specifically. We lost the Kiowa's IFF transponder a few moments after they picked him up."

"I am displeased with this situation, Mr. Roberts," Maxine said, stepping closer to him. "It was your decision to dispose of the Special Warfare unit via the freighter, so it is your problem. The fact that this Holt was not eliminated before the cleaning crew arrived is also your fault. I expect a resolution within 24 hours or you will answer for the failure, is that clear?"

"Yes, ma'am," Carter said, looking slightly up at her. He remained quiet, letting himself be drawn into her eyes. He stared at the long, blonde lashes, moved across the pure white, and then followed the delicate fan of sea-green around her pupil. Transfixed by her eyes, he felt electricity in his legs.

"Is there something else, Mr. Roberts?"

Carter felt the sudden urge to reach out and pull her hair free. He saw himself taking hold of her by the waist and wrist, and then pressing his palm to the small of her back, feeling the silvered fabric and the line of the zipper. He would pull her close and, as her ear brushed his cheek, inhale the luminous scent of her blonde waves. His chest swelled with heat and his pulse tapped in his neck.

"Well, Mr. Roberts?"

The vision shattered. He was left with her scowling at him.

"No, ma'am."

"Then get to work, Mr. Roberts."

"Yes, ma'am," Carter said, and turned and walked out of the room, his face red, and his heart pounding.

CHAPTER 15

Leif fashioned a backpack with handles from the survival bag's straps and thought it looked convincing enough. He finished the costume by rubbing dirt on his legs, chest, and arms and then brushed it away. They took off and flew out over the Outback. As the sky darkened, Jeffrey spotted, along a lonely dirt road, a tail of dust rising from a 4x4. Jeffrey flew well ahead of the 4x4 and landed beside the road, which was really nothing more than two ruts. Leif walked down the ramp to the dirt.

The ramp of the gunship lifted up, Leif turned away, covered his ears, and jet blast hammered his back. He felt dirt scattering across his neck, and then the roar diminished. He turned and saw the gunship fly away and land on a ridge a short distance off. Its black paint against the dark sky made it invisible, unless one knew exactly where to look.

Leif waited by the side of the road and considered the last few days. He had surprised himself because he hadn't screwed up yet, even when that thug had pointed a gun at Stacy. He had always wondered how he would do if presented with life-or-death scenarios like in his dad's war stories. Did he have some of that do-or-die in his blood? He had thought his dad had never been scared, because how could you be scared and still do the right thing? Now he realized that fear and ability were not mutually exclusive. He had been scared as hell but had done well. He smiled at himself.

The dirt track cut over a low hill, the edge of which now glowed with the headlights of the approaching 4x4.

Leif considered that the chase had brought something new into his heart, something he'd not felt before. He had grown up small and witty, but afraid of pain and failure. Nothing like his father. But now he felt a surge of unfamiliar confidence in himself. He felt as though he couldn't fail. He understood that they might fail, that they could be killed or captured; he wasn't kidding himself. But the primal aspects of his personality did not seem to respond to that knowledge. He felt at ease and secure.

The 4x4's headlights broke over the hill and bore down on him followed by a whine of gears and crunch of tires on rocks and dirt. Leif stuck out his hand and waved. The 4x4's brakes screeched and it idled to a stop beside him. The smell of burned oil drifted from the hot engine. The old 4x4 had no doors. Its worn canvas top caught the evening breeze.

Despite himself, Leif asked, "Does this thing run on gas?"

The man in the 4x4 took off his dirty hat and set it on the patched knee of his dungarees. He said in a heavy Australian accent, "It's converted. But what kind of question is that to greet a man with on the side of the road?"

"Sorry," Leif said, "it was the first thing that came to mind."

The man stared at him for a moment and then turned and spit into the desert.

"Um," Leif stammered a bit, "I... my friends and I, that is, are camping... out that way," and he pointed directly at the gunship out in the darkness and then cursed himself. The man looked over Leif's shoulder to the ridge, squinting.

"It's really more that way," Leif said, pointing farther north.

The man put his hat back on his head. "You all right? Feeling okay?"

"Oh, I'm fine. I have a pregnant wife back home, and I wanted to check in on her, but our sat-phone's dead, so I..."

"You shouldn't be in the Outback on foot at all, lest alone without a sat-phone."

"You're right, but I thought I'd wait here to see if I could flag someone down and use their sat-phone to check in with my wife. The pregnant one."

Dammit Leif get your shit together.

He drew a deep breath. "I'm pretty nervous about the whole thing."

The man shifted his weight in his seat, took out his sat-phone, and looked at it. "Not nervous enough to stay home where you shoulda. Right?"

"Sure, but I really would appreciate the help."

"You must be daft or lucky, probably both," the man said, looking out along the dirt tracks. "No one drives down this road. Why, I bet I'm the first one to drive down this way in a month or more."

"That's lucky for me then," Leif said, feeling irritation rising.

Just give me the damn phone, and I'll let you get on your way.

The man looked at the phone and then leaned over the passenger seat and handed it to Leif. He said, "Get in the truck and sit down, no reason to be uncomfortable while you talk.

I'll give you a few moments to yourself." He took the key out of the ignition and stepped down out of the 4x4, walking out into the scrub a good distance. Without ceremony the man, now facing the sunset, unzipped his fly and relieved himself.

Leif tapped on the phone's screen, calling up a search on System Alliance Development. He found the headquarters and then looked through the corporate information. No officers listed. He found a submission area with a security flaw, hacked into the corporate site, and browsed the listings. He noted a few names of scientists, but then came to Roger Freisman, VP of Robotics, based in Bremerton, Washington.

"Good stuff," Leif said to himself.

He looked up to see the man watching the horizon, giving him privacy with his wife. Despite the fact that the man had given him a hard time at first, Leif felt a pang of guilt for lying to someone who was now being so good to him.

Leif looked back down to the phone and found Freisman's HR records, medical benefits, etc. He took out a scrap of paper and a pen and jotted down Freisman's home address and a few facts. Married. 16 year old daughter. Out in the scrub, the man turned and starting walking back to the 4x4. Leif tapped quickly into the phone and then lifted it to his ear. "I love you too," he said, and pretended to end the call.

The man, now standing beside the 4x4, said, "Your wife okay?"

"Sure is," Leif said, handing back the phone and stepping out of the 4X4. "Thank you."

The man climbed into the 4x4 and looked at Leif. "You need a ride back to your camp? This thing'll make it there."

"No, I'm fine, but thanks very much."

The man shrugged. "Suit yourself." He pushed the 4x4 into gear and drove away.

...

Jeffrey and Stacy sat in the gunship's cockpit watching the headlights of the 4x4 off in the distance. It held its position for some time, and then the headlights began sweeping and bouncing down the road again. Jeffrey let the lights move out a mile or so before he flew back. Leif came on board and shouted over the engines, "Roger Freisman is our man. He's the VP for Robotics. We get him, we'll have the keys to the castle."

After the ramp had sealed shut, Stacy said, "Great work."

"Thanks."

Jeffrey asked, "Where do we go?" He looked over his shoulder at Leif and saw a solid confidence in his son's expression.

"System Alliance Development's robotics division is headquartered in Bremerton, Washington, up near Seattle. There's a Navy base nearby. I've been there. I had to fly in to do some repairs on a Dakota gunship's main boards last year, so I'm somewhat familiar with the area."

"What if the guy looks up what you did on his phone?"

"He'll find nothing. He could call the provider for logs, but his phone is clean."

"Excellent," Jeffrey said. "Where's Bremerton in relation to Seattle?"

"You know the Olympic Peninsula?"

"Yes, the mountains to the west, right?"

"That's them. Bremerton is on the inside of that, across Puget Sound from Seattle."

With their target in hand and several hours to fly, Stacy and Leif settled into the rear seats, and Jeffrey pushed the gunship across the Pacific one more time. He knew he should have flown to some desolate area and gotten a good night's sleep before moving on, but he was too eager to get closer to a potential solution. He washed a caffeine tablet down with a swig of water and flew out across the Great Barrier reef, into the black sky.

Out over the open ocean, the bright half-moon hung in a field of stars. Ahead, a storm front rose up off the water's surface. Jeffrey pulled back on the stick and brought the gunship up to 35 thousand feet. The storm clouds, glowing in the moonlight, rolled beneath the gunship's belly. The night and storm brought Jeffrey relief as the gunship melted into the darkness. A few red and blue markers strobed in the distance, but far enough off that no one would make out the black gunship in the night sky.

Jeffrey considered saving fuel by flying below the speed of sound, but over seven thousand miles of ocean separated Australia from the northern U.S. coastline. He wasn't sure he had it left in him for over ten more hours of flying. He pushed the gunship past Mach-3 and it drank deeply of its fuel. Yet, this speed would cut the trip time down to just under three-and-a-half hours. Even so, they would be jumping seven time zones and when they arrived again on U.S. soil it would be nearly 8AM.

Halfway across the Pacific, the horizon glowed a deep red over the blanket of clouds. Then, with the gunship speeding toward it, the sun cut into the sky in a blinding red disk. Jeffrey scanned the controls again and found a dial with the graphic of a sun half blazing and half covered in a dark square. He turned it and the cockpit glass went black.

"Oh, wow," he said, and backed off the dial, reducing the tint so he could see out the shaded glass. The sun now hung above the horizon as a solid plate of copper. As he flew, the sheet of clouds broke up, allowing him to see down to the gray chop whipped up from the dark-green sea. The high clouds thinned out more, and fog built up over the ocean, pressing itself up against the landmass of the Washington coastline.

"Hey Leif," Jeffrey shouted into the back.

"I'm up, I'm up," Leif said. A thumping and a curse came from the back, and then Leif appeared in Jeffrey's rearview mirror. He sat down, and Jeffrey saw him grinding the heels of his hands into his eye sockets.

"You'll grind out your eyeballs if you keep that up," he said.

"It feels good to grind out your eyeballs," Leif said through his hands. He stopped and looked over the navigation controls. "What can I help you with?"

"I need you to help me locate this town. I'm riding the IFR signal into Seattle, but I don't know Bremerton's frequency, or even if they have an airport. I haven't looked for it on the GPS. Locate it, and then show me where a good area for a landing site might be. We need a nice, secluded landing site as close to Bremerton as we can manage. Also, I need you to scan for people like you did before." Jeffrey slowed the gunship, and began to let it lose altitude.

"Should be easy enough," Leif said. "When I was up here, I did a bit of hiking in the evenings. The entire Olympic Peninsula has gone back to wilderness. You go fifty miles west of Bremerton and you won't find a soul."

"Maybe we should try to risk a bit closer," Jeffrey said. "I, for one, do not want to hike fifty miles there and back."

"Got it."

The blanket of fog caught in ripped sheets on the glaciated peaks of the Olympic mountains. Farther inland, the fog ran thin, and only eddies of it remained in the valleys and over the lower forested peaks. The majority of the peaks passed to their left. Then the gunship flew over a thin inlet, its tree rimmed water still dark in the morning light.

The gunship crossed the inlet and was back over forested land, when Leif said, "Hold up."

Jeffrey pulled back on the stick and hovered, "What?"

"You see that larger body of water just past the last hills there?" A glitter of blue-green ran north to south, separating the forest.

"Yes."

"That's Puget Sound, so Bremerton is just on this side of it in the trees there. You see the city over there?"

Jeffrey squinted and saw the forest broken by a gray swath along the water.

"Okay," he said.

"That's Seattle, so it's probably a good time to start looking for a place to land."

"I think we can get closer," Jeffrey said. "What do you see on the ground?"

"There are heartbeats everywhere, many big enough to be people. The forest is littered with signals. It's most likely deer and other animals."

"We'll just have to risk it then."

Jeffrey scanned the ground, coming closer and closer to the city. Now he saw buildings over the trees and he dropped the gunship just a few feet above the tree tops. To the right, a road ran along, cutting a path through the forest. Jeffrey veered away from it. The forest consisted of immense pine trees with branches so heavy they could have been trees themselves in other areas of the country. Here and there, gaps in the trees revealed a forest floor clogged with briars and ferns. As Jeffrey turned the gunship away from the road, he flew out over a clearing and thought he had just appeared over some kind of facility in the woods. However, when he looked for buildings, he saw nothing. The area had simply been recently logged. Young saplings grew in the clearing and he considered that this probably meant that the area, currently growing back, would be vacant. He lowered the gunship into the clearing and set it down behind a low rise on the southern side of the clearcut. The gunship settled at a slight angle, and he shut off the engines. As he pulled off his straps, he heard the ramp hiss open.

Stacy said, her voice distant in the back of the gunship, "This is definitely a change." Then her voice became even fainter as she stepped out of the ship. "Oh my God. Look at this place, it's... mossy." As Jeffrey unstrapped himself, the outside air rolled through the cockpit, carrying with it the scents of spring flowers, pine resin, and morning mist.

Jeffrey and Leif moved out of the cockpit, through the back, and down the ramp to join Stacy standing among old broken stumps on a bed of ferns and grasses. Young pine saplings surrounded them, reaching up shoulder high. Delicate purple foxgloves, blue lupine, and yellow daises grew up among the grasses. On several of the mossy stumps large, yellow banana slugs shifted through the morning dew. Jeffrey inhaled the cool air through his nose, let it fill his chest, and let it out again.

"What's the next step?" Stacy asked.

"I sleep," Jeffrey said, rubbing his head and yawning. "We'll stand our ground for awhile to see if this place is abandoned or if we get guests. Then we'll have to risk leaving the ship and pray to God no one finds it."

"We could leave someone with the ship and let the other two go," Stacy said.

"You mean, leave me with the ship," Jeffrey said. "I'm the only pilot right?"

"Yes."

"You ever kidnap someone before?" Jeffrey asked.

Indignation slid into Stacy's voice. "No. Have you?"

"No, but I'm fairly confident I can. What about you?"

"I'm pretty sure I could do it," Stacy said, and turned to Leif. "What about you?"

"I'm not gonna make any claims at all," Leif said. "I'm gonna vote for all three of us, and risk the Kiowa. We don't know what we're up against here, and in that situation we need all the experience and help we can muster."

Stacy looked at the gunship. "What about the ramp? If we close it, will it lock us out?"

Leif said, "I disabled the fingerprint scanner when we were on the island. It only operates on the secondary switch now. It won't lock us out, but we can't lock anyone else out either."

Stacy nodded, and then said to Jeffrey, "So go get some sleep and we'll get you up... when?"

"Let's leave at dusk," Jeffrey said. "You two scout out a path to the highway and then try and get some sleep this afternoon."

Jeffrey stepped back into the gunship, took some BDU's from the survival bags, and set them out for a pillow. He lay down. In a few moments, the sound of his breathing rolled out of the gunship.

CHAPTER 16

Stacy followed Leif to the edge of the clearcut and found that the briars there grew higher than their heads, a solid wall of thorns. Farther east, the briars thinned to ferns and broad-leafed plants. They hiked through the underbrush to the south and found a deer trail. Branches grew over the trail, and Stacy had to stoop and push bushes aside to enter the forest. As they walked, the air remained cool in the deep shade of the old trees.

"So do you have a boyfriend or…?" Leif asked.

The question made Stacy uneasy, and she considered lying, but then said, "No."

"Oh," Leif said.

Stacy felt that he wanted to say more and wished he wouldn't. She said nothing more. As she walked, listening to the cracks of twigs under their feet and the buzzing of insects, the moment passed.

Within the hour, after a few dead ends, they stepped down a steep bank to the gravel shoulder of the road. The new pavement lay under a hallway of trees. Moss tinted the edges of the blacktop green. In a moment, an electric whine rose up from around the corner and a car flashed by. The driver looked at them as he passed.

"I think we should set out before nightfall so we can get someone to pick us up and take us to town before dark," Leif said. "We'll have a hard time catching a ride on this road at night."

A semi rolled by as Stacy spoke.

"What?" Leif asked.

"I said, sounds good to me."

They stood on the road for a moment more. Stacy felt as if there was something more she should do, some more planning or surveillance, but nothing came to mind. Another car passed and, when it had gone, Stacy turned and walked back into the forest. Leif followed her up the bank.

...

When they returned to the gunship, they found Jeffrey snoring in tremendous draws of breath. His boots stuck out onto the ramp in a slightly shifted position. A fat, round winter wren landed on one boot toe, hopped to the next, picked at the sole, and then, when Jeffrey drew in another snoring breath, flitted away.

Despite the bright afternoon sun, the air remained pleasantly cool as it filtered in through the forest. Leif and Stacy walked up the low hill to see the rest of the clear-cut. The area extended out about 500 meters square. A red-tailed hawk glided out from over the surrounding trees and circled, its wings outstretched, pinion feathers splayed wide. Stacy and Leif watched as it completed another circle and then glided back over the trees and out of sight. They turned and walked back to the ship.

Stacy listened to Jeffrey's snoring for a moment and then looked out across the clear-cut. "I think I'll try to get a bit of rest away from the ship." She walked up into the ship, took out a few BDU's from the survival gear, rolled them up to serve as a pillow, and walked along the tree line. Most of the moss still held the dampness of the morning fog, but she found a spot of dry grass, lay back on it, and looked up at the trees. The pines shifted as the breeze hushed through them. Small, fat clouds moved across the blue sky. Every so often, one crossed the sun, dropping her into shadow and the air chilled. As the cloud moved on, the sun beamed back out warm and bright. In this shifting of light, Stacy fell asleep.

...

When Stacy woke, a deep afternoon shadow lay across the clear-cut and she felt cold. She sat up and saw a banana slug making its way across the toe of her boot. She heard the crack of a twig and looked over to see Leif walking toward her.

"I was just coming over to wake you up," Leif said. "Did you sleep well?"

She touched the bandage on her face. The deep-bone soreness lanced into her skull as she pressed on it. She stretched her neck and shoulders and realized that, aside from her face, she felt wonderful. "Actually, yes. I slept very well."

"That's good."

Leif had the bleary look of someone who had been awake too long.

"Did you get some sleep?" she asked him.

"No, I just rested."

"Will you be okay tonight?"

"Sure, a caffeine pill and I'll be alert enough."

"Okay," Stacy said, "but just let me know if you're feeling tired, okay? We have to support each other."

She lifted the slug off her boot, tossed it into the bushes, wiped her hand on her thigh, and stood up. She felt where wetness from the ground had soaked into the seat of her pants. She stretched her arms out and then walked back toward the gunship. Leif followed. As they approached the gunship, she noticed Jeffrey still fast asleep.

"Do you think we should wake him?"

"Yeah, I suppose." Leif walked up the ramp and kicked the sole of Jeffrey's boot.

"Rise and shine, Pop."

"Nice," Stacy said.

Jeffrey rolled to one side, sat up, and pressed on the small of his back groaning.

"You should have slept in the ferns," Stacy said, "The deck can't be good on your back."

"Doesn't matter," Jeffrey said. "Did you find a path to the road?"

CHAPTER 17

Jeffrey pushed the last bite of his MRE into his mouth, swallowed, and then washed the chalky texture down with water. He stood, shoved the bags back into the gunship with his foot, and stepped off the ramp. He nodded to Leif, who pressed the switch. The ramp hissed up and sealed. Stacy and Leif led Jeffrey to the deer trail, and Jeffrey peered into the darkening forest.

"You couldn't find a wider trail?"

"We found a trail that went to the road," Stacy said. "We're lucky it didn't wander into the wilderness."

"How can you fit down that?" Jeffrey asked.

Leif pushed aside a branch and walked down the trail. Stacy followed. Jeffrey cursed under his breath and then leaned under a bramble. It caught the back of his shirt. He pulled at it and the bramble bent toward him and pricked his back. He grabbed the bramble with his hand, pricked a finger, and pulled it off, only to catch it on his shirt sleeve.

"Son of a," Jeffrey said and grasped the bramble between his thumb and middle finger and plucked it off. He turned and walked down the deer trail, catching on more brambles and branches every few feet.

When Jeffrey emerged from the forest, out onto the empty space of the highway, he found Stacy and Leif at the side of the road, sitting on a fallen log. Stacy ran her fingers over a fern, which grew out of the log. When they saw Jeffrey, they stood.

"We thought you were lost," Leif said, and smiled.

"Funny." Jeffrey walked past them, down the road. A car came around the bend. He turned, walked backwards, and stuck out his thumb. The car flashed by and curved around the next corner.

"No one's going to stop if you scowl at them like that," Stacy said, catching up with him.

As each car came around the corner, Jeffrey held out his thumb and did his best to look friendly, but none slowed. Among the broad bases of the trees, darkness came on early. Above them, the strip of sky between the trees still shone dim blue, but the cars now ran with their headlights on.

As they walked, they approached a green, reflective sign with a white '17' on it.

"This must be 17 miles from Bremerton," Jeffrey said. "There's our mark on the way back."

More cars passed, and Jeffrey stuck his thumb out to each, but still none stopped. The sky through the trees shifted from blue, to dark blue, to black. No moon shone and, as stars materialized in the dark strip of sky, the road and forest around them vanished into blackness. The next car had blazing high beams, and Jeffrey squinted as he looked at them. Only Stacy held out her thumb, and the car blurred past and down the road, disappearing around the corner.

Leif shook his head in the darkness. "This could be a long night."

Just as he finished speaking, the corner up ahead began to glow. Then high beams blasted out. The car slowed down as it went by, the same low sedan which had just passed them. It turned a half-turn across the highway, and its reverse lights came on. It backed up, finished the turn, and pulled in behind them. The high beams flicked down, and the door swung open. A man stepped out. Jeffrey held his hand over the glare of the headlights trying to clarify him, but he remained only a dark shape.

"You folks break down or something?"

"No," Stacy said, smiling, "we went for a walk today, which got longer than we thought."

The man motioned to his car. "Jump in if you want a ride," and he got back in the car. The passenger-side door clicked and swung open.

Stacy and Leif climbed into the back seat of the car, and Jeffrey settled into the front. The man, elderly, with glasses and a thin black tie, turned to Jeffrey. "You their dad?"

"His," Jeffrey said, pointing to Leif.

"You folks from the area?"

"No," Jeffrey said, "just visiting."

The man looked at Jeffrey, searching his face for a moment.

"Thank you for the ride," Stacy said, and the man nodded and smiled at her. Then Stacy proceeded to ask the man more questions. At first Jeffrey felt an irritation at her unending questions, but then he realized what she was doing. She kept him talking about himself to the degree that, during the entire ride to Bremerton, she had prevented him from asking any questions of them.

He drove them to downtown Bremerton. When he dropped them off, he motioned Stacy over to his window. He took her hand in both of his and smiled.

"You're a wonderful young lady."

"It was a real pleasure meeting you," she said. He let her hand go, and she waved as he drove away.

Jeffrey said, "Let's get going." He looked around at the downtown area. Many people milled along the shopfronts. The warmth of the day had been compressed out by a damp cold, and the beginnings of fog hung around the sodium streetlamps. Jeffrey stopped a middle-aged woman and asked her for directions to Marine Drive.

She gave his camouflage, cut-off shorts a look and then pointed toward the next intersection. "That street is Sixth. You take that to Adele. Turn right on Adele, and it will turn into Marine."

"Thanks." Jeffrey gave her his best smile.

She grimaced back at him and walked away.

They made their way out of downtown and into a residential area. Jeffrey felt they were taking far too long to reach their target, and he found himself regretting not just dropping the gunship on Freisman's lawn and pulling him out. However, he needed any advantage he could gain, and it was not time to be so bold. If it went well, Freisman would simply disappear and not be immediately connected to them. Hopefully their pursuers were still sweeping the South Pacific.

In an hour-and-a-half of walking, they found themselves on Marine Drive passing large multistory homes with gated driveways. The black asphalt of the drives, lined with elaborate landscaping, wound up to each home. Despite the cold, a few crickets chirped at a slow tempo from the bushes. Long stretches of lawn and trees separated each of the estates, and it took some time until Jeffrey saw number 16547. Walking up to the gate's call button, Jeffrey saw the name 'Freisman' on an iron plaque. Jeffrey pointed to a hedge, and Stacy and Leif followed him into the shadows.

Jeffrey said, "Now we just have to figure out how to get in there without setting off the alarms I'm sure he has. If we can cut power, perhaps we can disable the system."

"That won't work," Leif said, "if the system is sat-phone enabled with a battery backup. The only way to get around that type of system is to not set it off."

"What if we get up on the roof and rip out an attic vent and drop in that way?" Stacy asked.

"And wake up the entire neighborhood?" Jeffrey said. "No, what we want is a dark entry-point. From there we'll need to disable a door or window system and–" he stopped talking as an expensive sedan rolled up the street and slowed.

"What are the odds?" Jeffrey said, as he turned and walked, still in the shadow of the hedge, toward the car.

"What are you doing?" Leif whispered out to him, but Jeffrey motioned for him to be quiet and reached into his pocket, gripping his pistol. The car turned, and the gate jerked to life, rolling open. Jeffrey crouched over and ran up to the car as it crossed the sidewalk. He kicked the passenger door, cried out, and fell onto the trunk as the car jerked to a halt. A middle-aged man wearing a black suit jumped out, anger on his face. He brushed his hand over his thin hair as he came around the back of the car. A slight belly protruded from his unbuttoned suit coat.

"What the hell is going on?"

"You ran over my foot you son of a bitch," Jeffrey said.

"What the hell?" A touch of doubt entered his voice as he asked, "Are you hurt?"

Jeffrey stood, grabbed the man by the forearm, and pulled him close. He pressed the muzzle of the Colt 1911 into the man's stomach.

"Give me your wallet," Jeffrey said.

The anger in the man's eyes widened to fear. "You're mugging me?"

Jeffrey yanked on his arm. "If you want to live, you'll do what I say when I say it."

The man reached into his back pocket and took out his wallet.

"Take out your driver's license," Jeffrey said.

"I don't understand. Just take the money, please."

Jeffrey pressed the gun into the man's ribs. "The license."

The man whimpered a bit and his fingers scattered through his wallet spilling cards on the ground.

"Damn it," Jeffrey said.

"Oh, God," the man said, dropping more cards. He did not find what he was looking for and then saw it on the ground. He bent down and picked up his driver's license and handed it to Jeffrey. Jeffrey took it and looked at the name.

"Good," Jeffrey said. "Now pick up the rest of that crap and get in the back seat of the car." Roger Freisman scrambled on the ground picking up cards while Jeffrey motioned for Stacy and Leif to join him. He scanned the street for the glow of headlights, his heart pounding in his chest.

He pointed at Leif. "You get in the back seat with him." He opened the back door and pushed Freisman in and then reached down and flicked the child restraint lock on and slammed the door. Leif and Stacy ran to the far side of the car. They pulled open the car doors and each sat down, Leif in the back and Stacy in front. Jeffrey looked down and saw a credit card on the ground and picked it up. Then he squeezed into the driver's seat. He pressed a switch, moving the seat to gain leg room. Throwing the car into reverse, he backed out into the street and stopped the car with a jolt, letting momentum slam his door shut. Then he threw the car into drive. "Roger, how do I close the gate?"

"Oh, God," Freisman said. "Oh, God, this can't be happening."

"The gate, Roger, NOW!"

"I… uh… the center button there." He pointed to the rear view mirror. Jeffrey pressed the center button, and the gate rolled closed. Jeffrey then drove the car down the street at the speed limit.

"Oh, that worked great!" Stacy said, her bright tone strange in contrast to Freisman's panting. "But what if it hadn't been him?"

Jeffrey winked at Stacy and then held up his hand for quiet. "Do you have the phone?"

Leif took the Australian trucker's sat-phone from his pocket and pressed it into Jeffrey's hand.

Freisman asked, "What are you going to do with me?"

Jeffrey looked into the rearview mirror at him. "Worry about your wife and daughter. The more you cooperate, the less pain they'll feel." Jeffrey tapped on the phone and then pressed the end-call button. He lifted the phone to his ear and waited.

"Yes, it's me," he said into the dead phone. He paused. After a moment, he said, "Yes, we have him. Do you have the wife and daughter secured?"

He paused again and looked at Freisman in the mirror. The flash of fear in Freisman's eyes told Jeffrey that his gamble had paid off. Freisman's wife and daughter were home tonight.

"Good, that was perfectly timed," Jeffrey said into the phone. "Remember that nothing happens to the daughter until I say so." He paused again and then shook his head, saying, "No, no, no, not unless I say, dammit. You leave that girl alone, you got me?"

One more pause.

"Keep it that way." Jeffrey pressed the end-call button again and handed the phone to Leif, saying, "Those guys are sick in the head."

Freisman asked, his voice catching, "What do you want from me?"

"Right now," Jeffrey said, "I want silence."

CHAPTER 18

Jeffrey turned the car down the forest highway and looked into the rearview mirror at Freisman. Dark shadows lay across Freisman's face, but Jeffrey could see enough to know that something was wrong. The fear in Freisman's eyes had diminished and been replaced by a searching look of curiosity.

Freisman leaned forward. "I can't place it, but I know you don't I?"

"No."

"No. I never forget a face." He leaned back into the seat, and more confidence blended into his voice. "We've met some time before. Is that what this is about? I've done you some wrong?" Freisman looked over to Leif. "I don't think that's possible. I'm a very fair man. At least I'd like to think so."

"Shut him up," Jeffrey said to Leif.

"Be quiet," Leif said.

Freisman's voice now had the tone of a negotiation. "If I don't?" He paused. When Leif did nothing, he said, "Not a thing. Am I right?"

Stacy looked at Jeffrey with a flick of her eyes and then looked away. In the mirror Jeffrey could see Freisman looking at Leif. Then Freisman turned and looked at Jeffrey.

"If I can just figure out how I know you," Freisman said. He took a handkerchief from his breast pocket and wiped it across his forehead. "You don't want to say?"

"You've never met me before this moment," Jeffrey said. "Now stop talking."

Freisman looked at Jeffrey in the mirror for a moment longer and then said, "I'm a good judge of what people say. What you just told me may be the truth, but there's no other group with my wife and daughter. Am I right? It's just you three isn't it?"

Stacy turned to look at Freisman, and Jeffrey saw the expression on her face shift, for just a moment, to 'how did he know that?'

Freisman smiled at Stacy. "I thought so. You almost had me." The smile faded from his face, and his expression became flat, businesslike. "I suppose my butt's still in a sling here, but I'm guessing that you aren't planning on hurting me." He looked to Jeffrey for a reaction. Jeffrey gave him nothing.

Freisman continued, "What is it that you want? Money?"

Leif said, "You need to be quiet now."

"I think we need to start negotiating right now," Freisman said. "Let's end this as quickly as possible."

Jeffrey yanked the car to the right. Stacy, Leif, and Freisman—all caught by surprise at the sudden movement—snatched at the car's interior to brace themselves through the turn. The car shot up a gravel road a few hundred yards.

Jeffrey slammed on the brakes, and the car slid sideways in the gravel. A cloud of dust, glowing red with the brake lights, drifted past the windows. Jeffrey put the car in park, shoved his door open, and got out. He yanked open Freisman's door, grabbed his arm, and pulled him out of the car. Freisman looked up at Jeffrey, confident.

"Look," Freisman said, "we don't need to do this intimidation act. We're rational men, and I'm sure we–"

Jeffrey slammed his fist into Freisman's ribcage. Freisman's face twisted in pain. Jeffrey hit him again and felt Freisman's side give in as a rib broke. He drove a left hook into the opposite side of Freisman's chest and then grabbed him by the back of his skull and slammed him face-first into the rear window, cracking the glass. Jeffrey pushed down on Freisman's head, and the crack spidered up the widow. Freisman made a trilling sound of pain and fear as he fought to push himself away from the car.

"You thought I wouldn't hurt you. If you were wrong there, the next question is, is your daughter safe?" He gripped Freisman by his hair and pulled him up, bending his head back. Jeffrey stared down at him, "When I say 'shut up', you shut the fuck up. Do I make myself clear?"

He released his grip on Freisman's hair. Freisman fell to his hands and knees on the gravel, wheezing.

Jeffrey brushed bits of Freisman's hair off the palm of his hand and then kicked Freisman's side where the rib had broken. Freisman yelped like a dog and fell to his side. He lay for a moment wheezing.

"It hurts..." Freisman said, his voice quiet and pleading. "Oh God, it hurts so bad."

With one hand, Jeffrey grabbed Freisman under the armpit and pulled him to his feet. He shoved Freisman's head down and pushed him into the car. Freisman gave a sharp scream as he folded into the car. Jeffrey kicked Freisman's feet in and slammed the door. He got in the front seat, the car sinking under his weight, and pulled the door closed. He looked at Stacy and tried to mask the regret he felt at hurting the man. Had he gone too far? She dipped her chin in a nod.

She's still with me.

Jeffrey felt something let go in his chest. He drew a breath and exhaled.

Freisman wheezed in the back seat, his head on Leif's shoulder. Jeffrey pushed the mirror so he could no longer see him. Every so often Freisman let out a quiet, "Oh God," and went back to his shallow breathing. Jeffrey put the car in gear, spun the steering wheel, and crushed the accelerator under his boot. The car's rear end whipped around, and he flipped the steering wheel. The car straightened and accelerated back down the road, fishtailing. Jeffrey pulled back out on the highway and drove away at the speed limit.

They sat in silence for a few minutes, the highway empty and the headlights glowing on the bases of the trees. The tree trunks went up into darkness in a ghostly way. Ahead, a car came around the corner and approached. As it passed, Jeffrey saw the light bar and side markings of a police cruiser. Jeffrey watched the cruiser growing distant in his rearview mirror.

"Was that a cop?" Leif said, as he turned and looked through the cracked rear window.

"Nothing to worry about," Jeffrey said. "There's no reason for him to notice us."

The police cruiser's brake lights came on. It pulled onto the shoulder and swung through a U-turn. Its bright headlights flashed across Jeffrey's eyes and then came at them, fast.

What the hell did I do to attract this guy's attention?

At that moment, the blue and red strobing LED's came blasting on, filling the interior of the sedan. For a moment, Jeffrey considered smashing down the accelerator and running, but he knew they couldn't run from a police cruiser in the sedan. Even if he could pull away, the deer trail to the gunship was too long and difficult to make a getaway on, especially with a wounded hostage. They would be caught. It left him only one choice. Jeffrey pulled the car over on the pine-needled shoulder. The police cruiser pulled up behind him, the spotlights glittering along the crack in the rear window. The blue and red lights flared off the surrounding trees.

Jeffrey's heart rate doubled as adrenaline flashed through his limbs. He reached into his right thigh pocket, touching the handle of the pistol. Stacy took hold of his wrist and, with gentle pressure, pulled his hand out of his pocket.

"One step at a time," she said.

"I have no idea why this guy just pulled me over," Jeffrey said, "but we don't have time to find out. The minute he sees Freisman and runs the plates, we're cooked. Then, it's either this cop dies, or we take him too. If he gets suspicious, and is well trained, it will be very dangerous to both him and us to try and take him. We either kill him or we play 'broken wing' and trap him."

"I vote for trapping," Stacy said.

"I agree," Leif said. "If we can get to the end of this, we're going to have to try and clear our names. Killing an innocent cop won't help."

Jeffrey nodded. He looked at Freisman in the rearview mirror. Blood from a cut on Freisman's forehead darkened the bridge of his nose and his mouth.

Jeffrey said, "Freisman, you hear me?"

Freisman answered in a whisper, "Yes."

"You fell hiking, got it? We're taking you for medical help."

There was no answer, just his soft wheezing.

"You make this cop suspicious, he dies. You gain nothing. Got it?"

Freisman dropped his head. For a moment, Jeffrey thought he was not going to answer, but then he said, in a quiet rasp, 'Yes.'

The police cruiser's door opened, and the cop got out. He adjusted his belt and walked up to the side of the sedan, shining his flashlight into the backseat and then the front. The sides of his shaved scalp showed under the wide brim of his hat. Jeffrey felt his stomach tighten when he saw the size of the cop. His biceps stretched his shirtsleeves, and his barrelled chest pressed the edges of his bullet-proof vest outward. The cop shined his flashlight on Freisman and then back to Jeffrey. He tapped the glass with the knuckle of his index finger. Jeffrey lowered the window.

"Sir," Jeffrey said.

"Everything all right?" the cop asked, his jaw squared and his expression humorless. The coals of his eyes glittered in the strobing lights.

"Well, not really sir. We were doing some hiking, and my friend took a fall. We need to get him to a hospital," Jeffrey said.

"You were heading out of town with your high-beams on, and your friend took a fall," the cop said, playing the light across Jeffrey's cut-off BDU's, and then into the back on Freisman.

Jeffrey looked down to the dashboard and saw the blue high-beam indicator light.

Forgot to dim my lights...

He thought about his first kill from yesterday, the soldier's silhouette glittering in the intense sunlight.

It's always the stupid little mistakes that take you down.

"I'm not good with blood," Jeffrey said. "That must be why I forgot to dim my lights. We were trying to decide what to do."

The cop stepped away from the door. "Step out of the car, sir."

Jeffrey opened the door and shifted his weight off the seat. He stood and saw that he had the cop by a few inches.

This isn't good. This guy's not used to looking up at people. If he's startled by my size, he's going to be even more cautious.

The cop placed his hand on his holstered tazer and pointed behind the sedan. "Now step around the back of the car and talk with me."

Jeffrey walked around to the back of the car, squinting into the intense spotlights.

No one else in the cruiser. He's alone at least.

The cop clicked off his flashlight and hung it on his belt. He kept his distance from Jeffrey, standing where he could see both Jeffrey and the sedan. With the cop's hand on his tazer, Jeffrey was not ready to risk lunging at him.

"Place your hands on the trunk and spread your feet."

Jeffrey turned and the cop stepped forward, pushing Jeffrey toward the trunk. Jeffrey placed his hands on the trunk lid. The cop patted him down his left side, then started down his right toward the pistol.

I'm done when he reaches the gun. Now or never.

The cop's hand moved past Jeffrey's waist. Jeffrey tensed, preparing to whip around and strike. The passenger door shoved open, and Stacy got out of the sedan.

"What the hell do you think you're doing?" Stacy yelled at the cop. "My uncle is badly hurt and you're frisking my dad?"

The cop stopped his search. "Ma'am you need to get back in the car, now. Sit down."

Jeffrey spun away from the cop, but the cop, having planted his weight well, did not fall forward as Jeffrey had hoped. Jeffrey grabbed the cop's forearm, lifted it, and hooked a punch into the cop's ribcage. His fist hit a wall of muscle. He swung again, this time at the cop's jaw, but the cop raised his shoulder and ducked under the punch. The cop threw a hook, landing it in Jeffrey's midsection. The punch compressed through Jeffrey's torso, causing him to hesitate. In that half second, the cop pulled his tazer, planted it in Jeffrey's chest, and fired. The electricity burned through Jeffrey, and he bit his tongue. His neck muscles pulled his face back, and the arches of his feet tightened, lifting him onto his toes. With his legs and feet locked up, he tipped forward and fell face first to the gravel. A pistol shot fractured the air, and a muzzle flash lit the trees.

"That's enough of that," he heard Stacy say.

The officer took a step back and Stacy fired another shot. A head-sized spider web cracked into the windshield of the police cruiser.

"Now, if you keep backing away from me," Stacy said, "I'm going to have to stop you, so if you stop yourself, we'll be a lot better off."

Jeffrey felt his muscles going slack. He forced his arm down into his pocket, and drew his pistol. Reaching out, he tapped its muzzle on the cop's shin. The cop looked down at Jeffrey. Jeffrey, half-blind from the cruiser's spotlights, said, "If you take it easy, you won't be hurt."

The cop put his hands up and said, "Bullshit."

Jeffrey pushed himself up to his knees. Then, using the bumper of the sedan for support, got to his feet. He leaned on the trunk as his back spasmed.

"Put your hands on the trunk," he said to the cop. The cop stepped forward and placed his hands palms-down on the car. Stacy side-stepped around to the sedan, her gun trained on him. Jeffrey took the handcuffs off the cop's belt and pulled one arm back, slapping the cuff on it. His back spasmed again, and he shifted forward, nearly falling into the cop.

"You all right?" Stacy asked.

"Fine."

Jeffrey pulled the cop's other arm and the cop did not let him draw it back. Jeffrey grabbed the cop's pinkie and ring fingers and pulled them backwards, and the cop's arm followed. Jeffrey connected the cuff and then hauled the cop off the trunk. He took the cop's pistol, tazer, and flashlight, handing each to Stacy.

"Leif, open the cruiser's trunk."

Leif got out of the car and jogged to the police cruiser, the headlights flicking across his legs.

"A car's coming," he said, looking past the cruiser.

Jeffrey looked to where the road bent out of sight and saw the trees glowing with headlights.

"Get it open," he said to Leif. Leif leaned into the cruiser and pressed the trunk release. Jeffrey shoved the cop to the rear of the cruiser. He lifted the trunk lid and called to Stacy.

"Can you get this stuff into the back seat for me?"

She grabbed road flares, rain gear, and emergency supplies and tossed them into the rear seat of the police cruiser. Jeffrey took out a flashlight and then pushed the cop into the trunk.

The cop looked up at him. "You realize how much trouble you're in, don't you?"

"Brother," Jeffrey said, "I'm in a lot more trouble than you can possibly imagine. You'll be lucky to see me alive again to testify against me."

He shoved the cop's legs in, and–for the first time–the cop's coal-dark eyes showed fear.

Jeffrey put his palm on the cop's chest. "You'll be fine."

He shut the trunk. The cop began kicking dents outward on the quarter panel of the cruiser. Headlights emerged from around the corner. Jeffrey motioned for them to get back in the sedan. Even in the sedan they heard the cop kicking the hell out of the trunk of his cruiser. A taillight broke.

"Aren't we going to get out of here?" Stacy asked.

"Not yet. I want that guy's shotgun from his car. We're just a car pulled over by a cop. Someone driving by won't notice the cop's missing."

The headlights bore down on them, and the semi roared by pulling a silver trailer. It continued down the road, red taillights diminishing. Jeffrey got out of the sedan and went back to the cruiser, found the shotgun release, and pulled the gun from its holder.

From the radio came: "Unit 364, please report in."

Jeffrey opened the glove box and found a box of shells. Beside the passenger seat he found another heavy, black flashlight. All the while, the cop kicked at the inside of the trunk.

As he closed the cruiser's door, he heard: "Unit 361 please check on unit 364."

The cop continued to kick at the inside of the trunk. Jeffrey walked to the sedan's driver side door. He reached in, handing Stacy the shotgun and shells. Sitting down in the sedan, he pulled the door closed. He threw the sedan into gear and spun his tires, pelting the police cruiser with gravel.

Jeffrey drove at twice the speed limit and, in a few moments, came up on the semi rolling down the highway. The trailer's tall doors glittered in the sedan's headlights. Jeffrey felt exposed behind the semi, but he didn't know where the trail ran off the road and might miss it if he passed the semi. The back of Jeffrey's neck cooled with sweat, and he kept looking into his rearview mirror, expecting blue and red lights to come strobing around the last bend at any moment. He saw highway marker 17 and pulled over to the right. The semi rolled off into the distance again. Jeffrey drove a few hundred more yards and spotted the embankment up to the deer trail.

He pulled the car to a stop and gripped the steering wheel. Then he let out a breath.

"That was good work back there," he said, looking over at Stacy and then at Leif in the rearview mirror. "A bit rough on the delivery, but we got done what we needed to. You both good?"

"Great," Leif said.

Stacy nodded and said, "We need to get out of here."

"Always the practical one," Jeffrey said, and threw his door open. He opened the rear door, gripped Freisman by the upper-arm, and pulled him out of the car. Freisman gave a sharp bark in pain.

Stacy took the lead with one of the flashlights. Leif followed her up the trail, carrying the shotgun. Behind them, Jeffrey pushed the flashlight into Freisman's back, forcing him to move ahead. Freisman walked along holding his side. He groaned each time he had to step over a root or lean under a branch. They heard a siren in the distance.

"They'll have patrols all over this area in no time," Freisman said. "You can't hide in the woods."

"We aren't going to hide in the woods," Leif said.

"Just let him think what he wants to think," Stacy said. "He'll get the idea soon enough."

Freisman walked along, seemingly resigned to his fate. Out in the forest, every so often, they heard the shuffle of small animals and the crack of sticks. At one point, a large pounding burst from the darkness beside them and ran off. They heard at least two aircraft now and distant shouts. Far behind them, search lights illuminated the tops of the trees.

They broke out into the clear-cut, and Freisman–seeing the Kiowa–said, "I don't understand. Who are you people?"

Stacy jogged up to the rear of the gunship and pressed the ramp switch. The ramp cracked open and hissed down to the grass. She pointed for Freisman to walk up into the ship. He did as she directed, and Leif shoved him down into a seat, strapping down his legs and head. Taking out a roll of tape from one of the survival bags, Leif taped Freisman's arms down. The ramp clamped closed.

Jeffrey sat down next to Freisman and pulled out Freisman's sat-phone. He dialed and then hit the end-call key. He held the phone to his ear.

"Yes, we're out." He sat quietly for a moment and then said, "He's a bit worse for wear, but he'll live if he chooses to. You need to get the woman and the girl out of the house fast. We were pulled over and had to tie up a cop... What?... Yeah, we put him in his own trunk. They've probably already identified Freisman's car and may be on the way to the house right now." Jeffrey fell silent for a moment. Freisman wheezed next to him.

"Good, I'll contact you when he's told us what we need to know. Then you can let the woman and the girl go. If he won't talk you can start with the wife. We'll give him a second chance on the girl."

He fell silent for a moment, then asked into the phone, "What's that?" Quiet again. "No we don't work that way. You may be used to that, but if he talks he gets his wife and daughter back, untouched. I'm a man of my word, you got that? If you prove me wrong, I deal with you, understand?" A short silence, and then, "Good, now take the woman and the girl and get out of there." He put the phone back in his pocket, saying, "Goddamn punks."

Freisman looked at him, his eyes wincing with each breath.

"Any more speeches on your ability to read people?" Jeffrey asked.

Freisman lowered his eyes. "No."

Leif and Stacy settled into their seats. Standing, Jeffrey walked into the cockpit. He settled down into the seat, pulled on the harnesses, and fired the engines. The small trees and grasses around the cockpit blew around in the jet wash. Jeffrey looked up at the tree tops, along the edge of the clear-cut, wondering if a police pursuit would come into view. The Kiowa's engines had cooled fully and the temperature gauges rose in a slow arc.

Jeffrey saw a searchlight begin playing at the tops of the trees. The temperature gauges went green, and he lifted the gunship off the ground. He flew across the clear-cut staying below the surrounding trees, and then, as he lifted up at the north side, he turned the ship sideways. Toward the highway, two police-patrol aircraft shined their search lights into the forest canopy.

A fast response. Not quite fast enough though.

Jeffrey turned the gunship away from the patrolling aircraft and, coming up over the trees, flew north. Acceleration pushed him back into the seat, and he relaxed with the speed and power of the gunship.

CHAPTER 19

The Kiowa nosed up, and the engines thrummed with the effort of hovering. The floor gave a kick as the landing gear thumped into position. The wavering of being airborne disappeared as the gunship touched down on solid ground.

Stacy and Leif unstrapped themselves. Jeffrey came into the back from the cockpit.

"No one saw us leave the area and their aircraft were right over their own search party. That would cover our engine noise. They most likely don't even know we had an aircraft and will be searching that forest until morning."

"Where are we now?" Stacy asked.

"Deep in the Olympic Peninsula," Jeffrey said, and pressed the ramp release. It opened, and the sound of rushing water on stone filled the cab. Reaching up, Jeffrey turned off the lights. The gunship sat on a broad, gravel shoal–a dark, rushing river on either side. The moonlight caught the water, sparkling its black surface with arcs and crests of light. Beyond the river, black silhouettes of treetops underlined the deep stars.

"You definitely know how to pick your spots," Stacy said, as she stepped out onto the gravel. Leif followed her. Jeffrey unstrapped Freisman and walked him out onto the shoal. Downed trees lay here and there across the gravel, gray in the moonlight. Jeffrey walked Freisman over to a log, their footfalls noisy and shifting in the loose stones.

"Sit down," he said.

Freisman sat.

"I need some information from you." He took the ammo can from the bag and unclamped it. He lifted the spider out of the ammo can. Moonlight glinted off the broken edges of carbon fiber.

Holding up the spider, he willed himself to not shudder. "What can you tell me about this?"

Freisman's eyes searched Jeffrey's face, and Jeffrey saw realization and understanding materialize in them.

Freisman looked away. "I have no idea what that is."

"Now, I may not have your deft skills at reading people, but I know a lie when I hear one."

"I'm not lying."

"Oh, good. Well, what we'll do is just squeeze this here..." The mechanism for the syringe extended the bevel cut needle out of the mouth of the spider. "...and jab it in your arm."

Freisman looked back at the spider. Jeffrey took hold of Freisman's wrist. Freisman tried to keep his arm close to his chest, but could not fight Jeffrey's strength. Jeffrey pulled Freisman's arm level and held the spider on Freisman's forearm. He slid the spider forward, and the needle penetrated Freisman's shirt fabric. Freisman pulled at Jeffrey's grip, his arm and shoulder trembling with effort.

"Stop. Please, stop."

Jeffrey let go of Freisman's wrist.

"You're afraid of this liquid."

Freisman said nothing.

"Let's start there. What's in the needle?"

Freisman looked out at the river. Jeffrey lifted his boot and heel-kicked Freisman in the center of the shin. Freisman cried out, but kept his eyes on the river.

"You realize that someone who knew nothing would be begging right now. Your stubbornness is telling me you know even more than I thought you did. I think you understand that."

Freisman's eyes locked on Jeffrey's, and the confident anger there surprised Jeffrey.

"I won't talk. You can kill me if you want. If I talk, she kills me, so I'm better off here."

"Who is 'she'?" Jeffrey asked. Freisman's eyes went back to the river. On his knee, a rip hung open where he had fallen earlier. Below the rip, blood soaked the fabric. Jeffrey pressed his fist into Freisman's broken rib, hard. Freisman tried to push him away, but Jeffrey grabbed Freisman's arm with his free hand.

"Who is 'she'?" Jeffrey asked again, his anger showing in his voice. Freisman yanked his arm and Jeffrey let it go. Freisman fell backwards off the log, and Jeffrey jumped on him, kneeling over him, his knee in Freisman's chest. He shifted his weight so almost all of his 260 pounds drove straight down on Freisman's ribs and lungs. Freisman's mouth opened and closed, but he could not pull air with the weight on his chest and his broken rib.

Jeffrey shouted at Fresiman, "Who is 'SHE'? Who will kill you?"

Jeffrey lifted his knee. Freisman gasped for air against the pain of his broken rib but said nothing. Jeffrey stood and motioned for Freisman to get back up on the log. Freisman rolled to his side, pushed himself onto his hands and knees, and then climbed back onto the log. As he sat up, he pressed the flat of his hand on his broken rib.

"No answer?" Jeffrey asked, his voice calm again.

Freisman stared at the gravel.

"Don't force my hand, Roger," Jeffrey said. "I don't really want to hurt you. Do you know that?"

"You could have fooled me," Freisman said, his voice quiet.

"No, I'm not talking about a broken rib." Jeffrey stood and grabbed Freisman's hand. He pulled out Freisman's middle finger and put backward tension on it. "I'm talking about cutting the flesh of each finger open, burning the blood vessels so you won't bleed, and then trimming away the muscle and skin."

Freisman tugged at his hand but could not get it free.

"I think you would start talking when you had three fingers with the bones fully exposed. If not, I could keep working up the hand to the wrist, then the other hand." Jeffrey let the hand go, sat down beside Freisman, and looked out at the river. "But I want something more than that. I'm going to be open with you. You know more than I thought you did. We came to you to find the source of this spider. Your company made it, and I thought you could tell me where it was sent or at least something about it. But now I'm sensing that you've got something better for me. You really do know me don't you? You know that I'm supposed to be dead. You just couldn't place me because you didn't expect me to show up on your doorstep."

Freisman stared at the gravel.

"And with each silence I know more and more. It stinks though, doesn't it, when the dirt you like to keep away from your villa comes crawling up the driveway?"

Freisman looked up at Jeffrey. "I won't talk. Kill me, torture me, it won't help."

"No," Jeffrey said, patting Freisman's knee, "you don't have the training to keep quiet. Once I start cutting the muscles off your arms one at a time and cauterizing the wounds, when you see nothing but skeleton and tendon below both elbows, you'll talk. But I think I can get it done without having to listen to you scream, and I can ruin your life at the same time."

Freisman had a question in his eyes now. Jeffrey took the sat-phone from his pocket. He dialed a number.

Leif, who had walked with Stacy upriver along the gravel shoal a good distance, answered, "We're ready."

"It's me," Jeffrey paused, listening to nothing as Leif remained silent on the other end.

"Yeah, it's time," Jeffrey said. "He won't talk. Tell his wife that he could stop it at any time, but won't. Rape the wife first, make it bad. Put it on speakerphone so he can listen."

Jeffrey activated the speakerphone and held it out in front of Freisman. A man laughed as fabric ripped. The crack of a brutal slap came over the phone followed by a woman sobbing and cursing through a gag. Jeffrey shrugged his shoulders at Freisman.

"When he's done with her, you'll get another chance before we do the same with your daughter."

Freisman's eyes went from Jeffrey's calm stare, to the phone in his hand, and back. More tearing of fabric was followed by sobs and muffled pleading.

"You know she'll never forgive you," Jeffrey said. "We'll let you talk with her while the boys work over your daughter. You know you won't let it happen. You know you'll talk to save your girl."

Freisman stared at the phone, his eyes frantic now.

"You can stop it right now." Jeffrey paused as a shriek came from the phone. "You are going to break Freisman. The minute your daughter screams, you're going to break, so you might as well do it now and save your wife too."

Freisman, eyes wild with rage, looked from the phone to Jeffrey. He seemed ready to throw himself at Jeffrey. His eyes measured the larger man. He looked back to the phone, and another scream came from it. Freisman gripped his hands into fists, and then let out a breath through his teeth. He looked at Jeffrey and the wildness bled away, leaving only desperation. "Please make them stop. I'll tell you what I know." He lowered his gaze to the gravel and sobbed. A tear ran down his nose. "Just don't let them hurt her, please."

Jeffrey took the phone off speaker and held it to his ear, saying, "Boys, stop. He says he's going to talk." He paused to listen. "No you will NOT. I am in control of this situation, and when I tell you to stop, you STOP." He listened again. "Good, because if you cross me, I'll have another crew have a go at you. Got it?" He listened. "Good." He hung up the phone.

"Look at me," he said to Freisman.

Freisman did as he was told.

"Your wife is somewhat roughed up, torn clothes and a few slaps, but not violated. You made the right decision fast enough, and I am sure she'll be grateful. The bad news is that those boys are not very reliable, and—as you can imagine—they're pretty worked up right now. We need to get this over with quickly so I can get your wife and daughter away from them."

Freisman nodded, tears running down his face. He said, "Okay, sure, I'll help. Just don't tell her I told you anything, okay? Can you at least give me that?"

"Oh, I think she'll probably guess as much no matter what happens." Jeffrey put an arm around Freisman and squeezed him. Freisman pulled away from Jeffrey's embrace.

"But," Jeffrey said, letting go of Freisman so he fell sideways and yelped in pain, "you have my personal guarantee that I will not put a name to any information you share with me. Hell," Jeffrey said with a laugh, "after what I've been through, whoever is responsible might not live long enough to ask questions anyway."

"You can't stop her," Freisman said, "not now."

"I thrive on low odds. But we need progress here. Begin with who 'she' is."

Freisman looked at his hands. His face glistened with tears. He shook his head as if he could not get himself to talk, but then in a quiet voice said, "Maxine King."

Jeffrey said nothing for a moment, processing what Freisman had just said. He looked at the river, let out a long sigh, and said in measured words, "By that, do you mean Maxine King, President of United Aerospace?"

"The same," Freisman said.

CHAPTER 20

Glass doors hushed open, and Carter Roberts followed Maxine King into an expansive space under a dark, vaulted ceiling. The only light came from the far corner where medical staff had set up a temporary hospital area. The doors shifted closed behind Roberts, and he followed Maxine across the dense carpeting. A large, multi-lensed lamp hung over the bed, illuminating the area in a subdued light. In the bed lay a man in his mid-twenties. His mop of blonde hair stuck out in all directions. A scar on the left side of his face lifted his upper lip into a slight sneer. A stainless steel device encased the left side of his chest. Metal-braided hoses led away from the device to a cabinet-sized machine, the surface of which was smooth and white. At its center, a screen glowed with various images: a tracing heart-rate, respiration, and half-formed ribs latticed with glowing green lines. The cabinet filled the area with a low-frequency resonation, which Carter felt in the center of his chest.

A doctor stood in front of the machine. He touched the screen and the ribs expanded. The green lattice traced the future path of the ribs. The marrow of some had already joined.

Maxine cleared her throat.

The doctor looked over at them and said, "Welcome back. Did you have a good flight?"

Maxine smiled at the doctor. "Yes, thank you."

Sitting down on the edge of the bed, she leaned over the man. She touched the metal enclosure, scowling, and then stroked the man's face with her fingertips.

"He is a handsome young man, isn't he?" she said in an absent tone, her fingernails combing into his blonde hair.

"I wouldn't know," Carter said, taking up the man's chart from the end of the bed. It identified the soldier as 'Lieutenant Commander Brennan Morgan', age 28.

This one doesn't look 28, even with the scar, which should add age to his face.

"Are we sure this is the right information for this man?" he asked the doctor.

"Yes," the doctor said. "I performed the standard DNA verification."

Carter drew his finger across the chart. The screen shifted, showing data on the progress made by the nano-machines now crawling around the empty cavity of Morgan's chest, rebuilding its framework: ribs, tendons, and major blood vessels.

"Barely alive," he said, and put down the chart. He walked over to a long, glass tank, which sat beyond the bed, against the wall. There, half-formed and suspended in a light-green nutrient bath, grew a whitish-pink lung and several strips of red muscle.

"What do we hope to gain for this effort?" Carter asked, looking back at the bed.

Stupid punk gets himself shot, and she moons over him as if he were a hero.

Maxine looked at Carter. "This man was willing to give his life for our cause. Do you not appreciate that?"

"I apologize," Carter said. "I'm sure he's a good man."

"Oh, he is. I can see it," she said, looking back at Morgan. The platinum links of her bracelet clinked as she moved her hand to feel the pulse on his neck.

"Shall we rouse him, Doctor?" Carter asked, and then looked to Maxine to see if he had overstepped his bounds. She continued looking at Morgan.

The doctor walked to a stand and filled a syringe with clear liquid from a vial. He connected the syringe to the Y-adapter on Morgan's IV and pressed the liquid in.

A few moments passed, filled only with the low hum of the equipment. Then Morgan's eyelids split open and his eyes rolled in their sockets. When he looked up at the light, he grimaced and clamped his eyes shut.

"Do you know who I am?" Maxine asked.

Morgan opened his eyes again, squinting at her through the light, and said in a weak voice, "Yes," and then, "Where am I?"

"You are at my estate," Maxine said. "You have served the cause well, and I wanted to make sure you had the best medical care available. You were very near death when we found you."

"How long…" Morgan began, but then faltered, looking up and around him, confused. "He shot me." His eyes searched out into the darkness beyond the lamp's light. "I was dying."

"Please do not worry yourself," Maxine said, petting his forehead, her voice as smooth and soft as the silk of her shirt. The seductive tone of her voice made Carter clench his jaw.

Maxine continued, "You have been in an induced coma for a few days now. You are doing very well, and will suffer no long-term injury. You are by no means dying." She moved her left hand to his thigh just above his knee. "You are young and healthy. You will heal well."

"But," Morgan said, and his hand groped along the metal surface clamped across his chest. He looked down, eyes frantic again.

"Do not worry," Maxine said, took his hand with both of hers, and turned it over, stroking his palm. She smiled at him and Carter remembered years ago when Maxine had treated him that way. It had been years since his time with her, and he grew less tolerant of each man she drew in. As she had sent each one out, addicted to her beauty and her vision, only Carter had remained by her side. She had mentioned many times how important he was to her for his ability to avoid "animalistic jealousy," but with each new lover she took, Carter's sense of infidelity cut more deeply.

"Maxine," Carter said, "we don't know how badly this interview will impact his recovery. We need to ask our questions and return him to his coma so he won't disturb the healing process."

"Yes," Maxine King said, without taking her eyes off Morgan, "of course. You always were one to pull me back to the purpose."

She patted Morgan's chest. "I think it a crime that I have not come to know you before this."

"Yes, ma'am," Morgan said, his face still bewildered.

"Please," she said, "call me Maxine," and she leaned forward and kissed him on the forehead. Carter felt anger flushing his face and neck.

"What do you know of the man who shot you?" Carter said.

Maxine looked over her shoulder at Carter, eyes hard and a slight smile on her lips.

She's pushing me again… always pushing.

"He," Morgan began, and then covered his eyes with his hand and went silent.

The doctor held up a smaller syringe, saying, "I have something that will help him remain focused, but it will counteract his pain medication to a degree." He attached it to the Y-connector and pressed it in.

After a moment, Morgan opened his eyes. "I remember. We flew into the landing strip." He looked at Carter and then back at Maxine, his eyes clearer now. "We came up on the wreckage. A demolition mech sat parked beside it. I sent my men out camouflaged and then made an attempt to attain the situation's status before proceeding with the cleaning of the area." He lowered his hand and looked at Maxine. "I guess if I could do it over again, I would have just shot missiles into the area and leveled it, but those weren't my orders."

Maxine glanced over her shoulder at Carter again and said, "Another failure."

Carter looked at the electrical plugs on the machines and thought of yanking them from the wall.

Morgan winced and gripped at the metal housing on his chest. "I found the shipbreaker up in the bridge of the freighter. I thought the guy was an idiot. He played me right into his trap. I let him make me angry. I walked right up to where he could get his hands on me. The guy was huge. I don't know what I was thinking. I suppose I saw just what he wanted me to see."

"And what was that?" Carter asked.

"I only saw an old-timer who wouldn't shut up, the kind of guy who sees military and wants to be part of the gang."

"When did he shoot you?" Maxine asked, still holding Morgan's hand.

"He didn't shoot me," Morgan said. "One of my own men shot me."

Maxine spoke the next words slowly: "Are you sure?"

"Yes," Morgan said, looking down at the metal casing on his chest. "My chest's really starting to burn."

"Just answer the questions," Carter said, "then we can put you back to sleep."

Maxine looked at Carter with disapproval.

Morgan said, "The 'breaker grabbed me and spun me around and held me so I was in one of my own men's line of fire. My man fired before he assessed what was happening. He intended to shoot the 'breaker, but hit me instead."

Carter scowled. He didn't believe one man could take out five soldiers, one by friendly fire. "Didn't you try to break free?" he asked Morgan.

Morgan shook his head, his face pinching with pain. "You don't understand. It was so damn fast. The 'breaker spun me around, killed a soldier with one shot, then fired into a second, and then I was shot. Someone else shot the man who shot me. I was looking right at my own man; he fired on me, and then his head blew apart."

"Holt shot three soldiers that fast?" Carter said with a slight scoff.

"No. You're not listening." Morgan looked at Maxine. "There was someone to my left."

He put his hand on his forehead, where sweat had begun beading. "It was the body. I couldn't piece it together until now." A smile touched the corners of his mouth at the solution. "It was the girl in the chair. She wasn't dead." He coughed and gritted his teeth. "I knew it. There was something strange about that arm."

"What about an arm?" Maxine asked. She took up his hand and placed it on the silk fabric of her pant leg and held it there. Carter stared at the contact.

Morgan sighed, his hand on the casing trembling now, "There was a body propped in a chair. I thought it was strange that it was clear of the rubble, but I only thought that for a moment. Then he started distracting me by pissing me off."

"Are you trying to tell me—" Carter began, but Maxine cut him off.

"Mr. Roberts," she said, not taking her eyes off Morgan, "our good friend here is not on trial. Why are you speaking to him as if he were?"

Carter could stand it no longer. "He failed utterly in his duty, and you are treating him as if he is a hero. He had five men, and all he had to do was go in and do a quick sweep and assure the area was clean."

Maxine King jumped up from the bed with such speed that Carter did not get the idea through his head to move back. She slapped him across the face hard enough to bring on a stinging numbness. The coppery tang of blood bloomed in Carter's mouth.

"How dare you," she said. "Your incompetence created this situation. That freighter was supposed to burn up on re-entry, kill those three, and turn their bodies to ash. You recommended we kill off the scrap yard worker so we could have time to inspect the crash site, then you failed to finish him off." She jabbed him in the chest with her fingernail, as she said, "This is your fault, Roberts. No one else's."

Carter shoved her hand aside and Maxine's face flashed with rage. He should not have dared touch her.

He said, "We had no other choice. We couldn't kill them on the Lacedaemon. There was no way to safely move the bodies away from the fleet without detection."

She said through her clenched teeth, "You should have shot them in the head before the freighter was sent down."

"A gunshot would have set off alarms and put everyone's lives at risk."

"Then you should have choked the life out of each one."

"I—"

"Get out," she said.

"I only—"

"Get out... now."

Carter turned and walked back across the room, the heavy carpet swallowing his footfalls. The doors hushed open for him, he stepped through, and they slid closed. He turned into the empty, tiled hallway, blinding bright after the dim room.

...

Carter returned to his office. As he sat down, a female officer stepped into the doorway and knocked on the door frame. She smiled, but when Carter looked up, her smile faded.

"What?"

"I..." She hesitated. "I was asked to bring this transfer request to you."

"Why me? That's Abram Soltova's responsibility."

"He wanted you to review it because it regards the wounded soldier."

Carter motioned for her to enter. He tapped two fingers on his desk, and she slid the paperwork over to him. He picked it up and looked it over.

As he reviewed the papers, the officer said, "He's asking permission to leave his duty station in South Florida to come here and be near his brother."

"How does he even know his brother's injured?" Carter asked.

"It's in the report, sir," she said, pointing to the paperwork.

Carter looked over the document.

"God damn it," Carter said and held the paperwork out for her. "I don't need this right now. Find out who forwarded the call to the doctor."

"Yes, sir," she said, not reaching for the paperwork. "All you have to do is sign the back page, sir."

"No. Brennan Morgan's brother can rot in Florida for all I care."

The officer only asked, "Sir?" but her expression said, 'the man's brother? Really?'

"This isn't the goddamn Red Cross." Carter stared at her, willing her to take the papers and get out of his office. She stared at him. He saw her digging deep for boldness, and finding it.

"Fine," Carter said. He grabbed the sheet of paper, scratched his name across the signature line, and tossed it across the desk. It flipped off the desk and landed on the floor. She picked it up off the floor, said, "Thank you, sir," smiled, and walked out.

Carter looked at the pen in his hand and threw it at the wall. He stared at the mark it left and then picked up a document and tried to put gutless Brennan Morgan out of his mind.

CHAPTER 21

Stacy and Leif sat in the rear area of the gunship when Jeffrey came walking up the ramp gripping Freisman by the back of the neck. Jeffrey shoved Freisman forward.

"Get into one of those chairs, and tell them what you just told me."

Freisman lowered himself into the chair, wincing and pressing his hand into his ribs.

"Talk... now," Jeffrey said.

Stacy asked, "What did he say?"

Jeffrey kicked Freisman's shin. Freisman yelped.

"Talk."

"Go on," Leif said.

Freisman looked away from them to the corner. The sound of the river cascading over rocks filled the quiet cabin.

Freisman, still holding his ribs, began to speak in a defeated tone, "Maxine King took over United Aerospace last year when Reginald King died. She actually had control for many years before that. Reginald King was totally in love with her, and completely blinded by it. She is the most beautiful woman." At this Freisman stopped. He let his ribs go, and leaned over, settling his elbows on his knees.

"Come back to us," Jeffrey said, snapping his fingers in front of Freisman's face, "I don't have a lot of time."

"She brought me into her group about five years ago to develop equipment to assist her. I have never met a more sincere or pleasant woman to be around." He looked over at Stacy and smiled. "Please don't tell my wife that part."

"I'll mail your wife your lower jaw if you don't get on with it," Jeffrey said.

Stacy turned to Jeffrey as if to say something to him, but he held up his hand and pointed to Freisman.

"She has so many connections now, you can't stop her. Or 'us' rather. You can't stop us. It doesn't matter what I've told you. It's so close, it can't be stopped."

"What can't be stopped?" Stacy asked.

"The destruction of the entire military fleet."

"What?" Leif asked, as if he had not heard the man correctly.

"Tell them why," Jeffrey said.

"The military is no longer necessary. The human race no longer wars with itself." A confident tone rose in Freisman's voice. "The military realized this some fifty years ago. In order to preserve their way of life, top commanders fabricated a war with an alien race to justify their own existence. The war never came near Earth, which seems strange if you consider how fearsome the alien race was reported to have been."

Jeffrey sat in the seat across from Freisman and asked him, "Do you know how many good men and women died keeping them from Earth?"

"Say what you want," Freisman said. "You're just one of the programmed." Freisman turned to Stacy and Leif. "You see, many soldiers were put into psychotropic states and had detailed memories of war induced." He looked back to Jeffrey. "It's all an illusion. You're just a victim of their plan."

"I lived through six years of war and decades of dealing with those years." Jeffrey said, balling up his fists.

Stacy moved over to sit beside Jeffrey and took hold of one of his hands, lowering it to her lap. "It's all right, Jeffrey. He's an idiot."

"How will you destroy the fleet?" Leif asked, and Stacy looked at Leif and then to Jeffrey. She looked confused, and then the color faded from her face. She shook her head.

"Are you all right?" Leif asked, touching her shoulder.

"I remember it now," she said. "It just came back to me, all at once. Oh, God." She looked at Jeffrey, and he saw terror in her eyes.

Jeffrey put a hand on her back.

"Nukes," She said, and looked at Freisman. "She's using nuclear warheads planted in each fusion reactor on the ships, isn't she?"

Freisman nodded.

Jeffrey took hold of Stacy's hand. "What do you remember?"

Stacy said, "I remember it all now. We found the device by mistake. Our objective was to infiltrate the Lacedaemon cruiser and get to the fusion reactor. We were on a training mission. Only the admiral commanding the ship and other key personnel knew we were coming aboard. We didn't know who was informed of our presence, so we had to be extremely careful. I can only assume that's why we found what we did."

"When we came into the reactor room, we surprised two maintenance crew members installing a piece of equipment. We assumed it was part of the drill, so we restrained them. Then, when we looked over what they had been installing, we realized they weren't maintenance. The device they had installed was small, but powerful enough."

"We tried to report what we found, but our com signal was blocked. At that moment, someone knocked on the reactor room door. We opened the door and found four soldiers standing with weapons holstered. By the surprised look on their faces, I knew they had not expected us to be there. As they drew their weapons, Matt reacted first. He tossed a flash bang in among them. As the soldiers watched it roll between their legs, he ran. Dave followed. Being behind the other two, I didn't have as much time, so I looked away from the flash bang and covered my ears. When I heard it go off, I ran through the group of soldiers. I saw Dave turn right around one of the cores and followed him. We reached the exit to the reactor area only to find another group of soldiers. They already had their weapons drawn. After they had disarmed us and beat the hell out of David and Matt, they moved us all to the freighter. They didn't say a damn thing, just strapped us in and sent us down."

She looked at Freisman, "So it wasn't just the Lacedaemon was it? They have nukes on all the ships."

"Yes," Freisman said, wiping his forehead with the back of his sleeve. "We've been installing them for the last year, concealed in along with a series of upgrades to each reactor. The Lacedaemon was the last cruiser in the fleet."

Leif asked, "So how do we stop this?"

"You don't," Freisman said. "There's no way to shut them down. They're hard-coded and sealed. The coding can't be undone. If the charges that compress the plutonium cores receive any other information than a smooth countdown—any interruption at all—they'll detonate. I was part of the team that designed the detonation control. It's flawless."

"Like your spider?" Jeffrey said.

Freisman met Jeffrey's gaze. Jeffrey saw in Freisman's eyes, not nervous defense, but surety.

"That spider's a toy compared to the quality of the bombs we've built. The military's done. We have contracts with enough nations that very few military ships will remain after the event. Those ships will be easily destroyed in a conventional manner. When they're gone, we can move on to a peaceful world without the hate-mongers like you tearing it down."

"You haven't stopped to think about what the world is like without people like us to defend it," Jeffrey said.

"People like you?" Freisman laughed so hard he winced and held his side. "You defend nothing. You only teach young men and women," he indicated Stacy and Leif, "to hate and be violent."

"I don't know about you," Stacy said to Leif, "but I learned to be violent long before I was in the military."

"No, you don't understand," Freisman said. "Society is poisoned throughout by military actions. Violence is no longer innate in the human race. It's an echo of the past, and only a world without weapons can foster real peace."

Leif asked, "But what about the alien race that attacked us forty years ago? If we don't have a military, we will be exposed—"

"Didn't you hear what I said? It was all a lie. It never happened. There never was and never will be an alien invasion."

"Okay," Jeffrey said, "you claim that my memories are not real, but what about my wounds?"

"They were inflicted upon you to match the memories."

"Convenient," Jeffrey said.

"True."

"I fought in a battle which the public was never made aware of. It happened just off the rim of Earth's atmosphere. I crash landed in the South Pacific. Explain why they would implant me with that memory." Jeffrey felt himself getting angry again.

"Just a flaw in their overall design I'm sure," Freisman said. "Perhaps they had considered bringing the battle closer to Earth and then decided against it."

"This is insane," Jeffrey said. "You—"

Stacy held up her hand. "It doesn't matter one way or the other. You have no right to kill the thousands of innocent men and women who serve on those ships."

"They're not innocent," Freisman said.

"Oh, that is it," she said, stood, and brought the heel of her hand down on the bridge of Freisman's nose. His head snapped back and a shocked look passed over his eyes before they went glassy. He fell forward. Stacy stepped back, allowing him to fall out of his chair, face-first, onto the decking, unconscious.

"That was totally appropriate," Leif said, and looked to Jeffrey, "don't you think?"

"Considering the circumstances, I think it was well timed," Jeffrey said.

Freisman groaned, rolled over, and his eyes searched the ceiling. He sat up and looked at Stacy.

"You bitch," he said, as he touched his nose.

Stacy shrugged her shoulders.

"It doesn't matter," Freisman said, still holding his face. "Do what you want to me. I don't care."

"Don't forget why you're talking," Jeffrey said, and tapped the sat-phone in his shirt pocket. Freisman's eyes darted from the phone to Jeffrey.

"You forget about the leverage?" Jeffrey asked. "How could you do that to your poor wife and daughter?"

"You gave me your word. If I told you what I know, you wouldn't hurt them."

"The deal may have changed," Jeffrey said. "How do we shut off the nukes?"

Freisman sat up on his heels, knees on the deck. He kept his eyes down and tears began dripping off his nose and chin. He opened his mouth to speak, but his voice caught. He closed his eyes. He swallowed and then looked up at Jeffrey, his eyes red. With quiet grief, as if he had been told his wife and daughter were already dead, he said, "I knew there would be sacrifices, but I didn't think it would be them."

"There's no need to sacrifice them," Jeffrey said. "Just tell us how to shut down the nukes."

"There's no way to do it, I told you that. If my wife and daughter rest on shutting them down, then you'll have to do what you want with them. The bombs are infallible."

Jeffrey reached out and picked Freisman up off the deck. He pushed Freisman back into the seat, strapped down his legs, and then taped his arms. Then he motioned for Stacy and Leif to follow him outside. They walked away from the gunship. The moon had set to the west, its light still glowing along the treeline. The river rushed by now, unseen in the darkness.

"So what's the next step?" Stacy asked.

"We need to find out if he's telling the truth about those bombs," Leif said. "We'll have to push him more."

"No," Jeffrey said. "He's at his limit. At this point, I believe we can take him at face value. We need to focus now on somehow getting in touch with the military and getting those ships emptied of as many crew members as possible, but I'm not sure how to get them to believe us." Jeffrey looked back to the gunship and Freisman sitting in his seat, head back against the bulkhead. "We need to be rid of this guy. We'll drop him here."

"What if we need more information from him?" Leif asked.

"He'll be stuck out here. No one will find him for a day or so. We can have someone come back and get him, but I don't want him with us now. He's pissing me off too much."

Jeffrey turned and walked back to the ship. Stacy and Leif followed him across the gravel and back up into the gunship. Jeffrey untied Freisman, walked him toward the ramp, let go of him, and pushed him forward. Freisman limped down the ramp.

Jeffrey said, "You're trash, Freisman. If I live through this, I'll see you in a federal prison."

Freisman turned and smiled. The interior lights of the gunship threw his shadow out along the gravel bar. "When the military goes down, the only force of power will be Maxine King's private army. She'll take control and maintain peace through it, and you'll be on the receiving end of our justice."

"Will I?" Jeffrey said.

"Yes."

Jeffrey pulled the sat-phone from his shirt pocket, dialed, and then held the phone up to his ear.

"Yes," he said, then a pause, and then, "Yes," another pause, "No, he's a weasel and doesn't deserve it. Do what you want with the woman and the girl. Just make sure their bodies aren't found when you're done."

Freisman's face went pale. Then his eyes narrowed, and he said, "You son of a bitch," and he ran at Jeffrey, hands reaching out, his rage apparently overriding the pain of his injuries. Jeffrey braced his feet and, when Freisman reached him, planted the palm of his left hand in Freisman's chest. Freisman's feet came off the ground, and he fell square onto his back on the ramp. He rolled over and fell off the side of the ramp to the gravel. After several seconds he drew a gasping breath.

"I'm taking off now," Jeffrey said. "Get away from my gunship." He pressed the switch to raise the ramp. Freisman reached out for the ramp and caught it, but his fingers slipped off as it lifted. Jeffrey watched the narrowing trapezoid of light close on the gravel. The ramp thumped shut.

Jeffrey turned and walked toward the cockpit saying, "That was almost too much." The adrenaline fire had burned out, and he felt empty. Anger had muddied his mind.

I have to stay focused. I finally have something valuable: a target and a purpose. But not even a guess at how much time...

"What do we do now?" Leif asked.

Jeffrey stopped and looked at Stacy and Leif. They were both so young. He wasn't sure how this was going to end, but he had a feeling it was going to get worse. Suppressing the desire to leave them there, in the relative safety of the wilderness, he stepped into the cockpit.

As he strapped himself in, he said, "We need to put a few miles between us and our friend out there. Then we play our hand." He looked at the rear monitors and saw nothing but blackness. He turned on the floodlights, illuminating Freisman limping away from the gunship. Jeffrey turned the floodlights off and said over his shoulder, "I have to get in touch with Sam Cantwell."

"Admiral Cantwell?" Leif asked.

"Yes." Jeffrey fired the turbines, let the temperature rise to operational levels, and jumped the gunship off the gravel. He wondered for a moment if Freisman had moved far enough away. "It's the only thing I can think of to get those ships evacuated fast."

"How much time do you figure we have?" Stacy asked.

"Just enough, I hope." Jeffrey looked up at the stars overhead. The hair on his arms rose as he imagined yellow blooms of nuclear explosions flowering out of the dark spaces between them.

CHAPTER 22

Carter Roberts walked down the wide hallway past Greco-Roman statuary, some replicas, others original. The hallway led to Maxine King's expansive bedchamber. Carter had not been invited there in years. As he walked, he recalled the room she slept and entertained in. The broad space lay under a domed ceiling. Alcoves along the walls displayed an eclectic collection of sculptures. Arching windows near her bed looked out on a courtyard garden, dense with exotic plants from around the world. Throughout the chamber, fine rugs lay over marble flooring. In the center of the room, a fountain and heated pool glowed with wavering light.

He walked up three steps and stood between the pillars that flanked the chamber's entrance. He listened, but the thick oak of the door allowed no sound through. He lifted his fist to knock. Then, armed with dire news, felt the bold desire to shock her. He gripped the door handle, shoving the door open, and turned on the light. In the tall, banistered bed the covers shifted and then Maxine sat up, naked. She scrambled for the sheet and covered her torso. A soldier rolled off the bed and stood: naked, angry, ready for a fight.

"What is the meaning of this?" She looked at Carter, confusion in her eyes. "Carter? What are you thinking?"

Carter said nothing for a moment. He looked over the young soldier who, now realizing who had just come through the door, covered his crotch with his hands.

Carter said to the soldier, "Get your clothes and get out."

"You don't dare move from that spot," Maxine said to the soldier. She looked at Carter. "You are going to leave, now."

Carter felt fury rise up, stuttering the breath in his chest.

She wants to play it this way? Fine.

"Roger Freisman has been kidnapped," he said.

Maxine had opened her mouth to cut Carter off, but now it hung open, silent.

"I can continue," Carter said, "if you don't mind your pet hearing more."

Maxine pulled the sheet from the bed and wrapped it around her. She said to the soldier, "Go. I will send for you."

The soldier collected his scattered uniform and walked toward Carter. Carter remained centered in the doorway. The soldier stopped in front of Carter and waited to be let by. Carter stared at the soldier.

"Sir?" the soldier asked.

Carter did not move. The soldier looked over his shoulder at Maxine. Maxine pointed at the door. The soldier looked back at Carter, dropped his gaze, and then side-stepped around Carter, pressing his back against the wall to avoid touching Carter's shoulder. He left the room, and Carter felt a cruel smile pull at his lips as pushed the door closed. But, despite his smile, he felt terrible. He had failed her, had put the entire project at risk. Worst of all, he had allowed jealousy to draw him in.

Maxine stared at him with derision in her eyes. "Not your finest moment," she said, and turned and walked across the room. "You will give me a moment to dress."

He watched her as she made her way across the chamber toward her closets, the sheet wrapped around her. He felt his desire for her crest, but it broke on frustration and jealousy. As she left the room his conflicting emotions left him feeling displaced and tired.

He walked to the heated pool. Intricate, white tiles glowed under blue lights. Floating in the pool, a half-submerged champagne bottle turned in an eddy. The torn away foil at the neck glinted silvery as the bottle drifted.

Maxine came back into the room wearing a white robe and walked up to Carter. Carter caught her eyes and then looked back to the champagne bottle.

"Having a good night were you?"

Maxine looked down into the pool at the bottle.

"How dare you." She swung her open palm at his face, but this time Carter was ready for her and snatched her hand out of the air and gripped it. For a moment Carter relished the look of frustration on her face. Then he let her fingers slide away from his, feeling the sweat on her hand for just a moment.

"You know how this works," she said. "You knew it when you signed on. I will not tolerate–"

"I know, I know," Carter said, holding up his hands. "I understand, and I apologize. I normally do very well..." He paused choosing his next word... "coping."

"What do you mean coping? Coping with what?"

"With being in love with you all these years." It was out before he realized he had said it. He looked back down to the pool, wishing he hadn't. He knew she loved nothing but her cause, and while he loved it as well, he wished for more.

"You..." she paused, and then said, "love me?"

A rush of hope filled Carter, and he said, "Yes, ever since we first met. I always have."

She looked down at the champagne bottle. "You know what this means, don't you?"

He shrugged his shoulders not wanting anything to show on his face, not wanting to risk anything more.

Should I have told her years ago?

She looked back at him, and the depth of the anger in her eyes collapsed Carter's hopes. "This means that you are nothing more than a sentimental fool." She turned and walked to the intercom desk. "You will be removed from my presence now."

"No."

Maxine looked back at him, her hand suspended over the desk.

"Please, listen. What about Freisman? Don't you want to be briefed on his disappearance?"

"Abram Soltova is your second, yes? He will replace you immediately. Send him to me with the information."

"I've been loyal to you for ten years, how could you just throw me aside? You still need me."

"No, I need the best counsel at this level, and you are compromised by idolatry."

This made Carter angry. He walked over to her and grabbed her arm. "You will not throw me aside. Not after everything we have been through. I love you, but I won't let it be a problem. I've spent all these years feeling this way, and have still done well, haven't I?"

"Let go of me," she said, pushing at his hand. Carter had never seen her fearful before, but he thought that might be what he saw in her widening eyes. Her voice rose as she pushed harder, "You could have ruined everything for me at any moment."

"But I didn't." Carter said, his anger fading. "Please let me stay and assist you, at least through the destruction of the fleet."

Perhaps I can convince her to let me stay longer... after it's over.

"Please," he said, releasing his grip and smoothing the fabric along her arm.

She glared at him, but then her look faded to sternness. "Fine. But this is why Stacy Zack is still alive. You were distracted and made poor decisions. You have failed, and it is costing me dearly. If she gets to the wrong people before detonation, there will be far too many questions as well as potential failure. You have put years of planning at risk."

"I agree," he said. "I've been foolish, and perhaps distracted. I will avoid it. I can avoid it."

"Enough of this." She poured herself a glass of water and then motioned for him to do the same if he should care to.

"No, thank you."

"If I see any evidence of distraction in your performance—" She took a long drink of water.

"It won't happen."

She lowered the glass, and looked at him as she might a stain on her dress. "If you do, you will be commanding the machine shops." She set the glass down, walked to a large couch, and sat. Carter walked over to the couch, pulled up a straight-back chair, and sat across from her.

"Roger Freisman disappeared from his home this evening. Rather, he never reached his home."

"How do we know it was a kidnapping?"

"The security camera caught it. As he drove up to his house, a man walked up to his vehicle and kicked it. Freisman got out to confront the man and was forced into the backseat at gunpoint. In total, three individuals got in the car with Freisman." He took a handheld screen from his pocket and passed it to Maxine.

Maxine looked at the screen. "This is whom?"

"Jeffrey Holt, the Hammerhead."

"He definitely looks the part." Her eyes traced over the face on the screen. "Dear God, he's a handsome man isn't he?"

Carter exhaled, closing his eyes. "If you say so." He opened his eyes and looked at her again. He felt jealousy rising as she looked at the image. He pushed the feeling aside and reached out, tapping the screen. "Approximately thirty minutes after this was taken, a sheriff's deputy stopped Freisman's car west of Bremerton."

Maxine looked up at Carter, her eyes brightening.

Carter held up his hand to mute her optimism. "The deputy was found trapped in his trunk a short while later."

"How can one man be so hard to stop?"

"It's not just one man. Apparently the three worked very well together to subdue the officer."

"Well, at least the military is more highly trained than the local police force," she said, looking back at Holt's image.

"I would say it was more luck than anything," Carter said, wanting to be unimpressed with the group that was causing him so much trouble. "At some point their luck will run out, and we'll end this."

"Yes, see that you do." She handed the screen back to Carter, who shut it off and put it in his pocket.

"I'm concerned about what Freisman may reveal to them," Carter said.

"He will hold up well. He is totally committed to the cause."

"I'm still concerned. Has he been trained on dealing with interrogation?"

"I would doubt it."

"We should remove you from this area."

"Are you serious?" She raised her hands and slapped them down on the couch. "We should hope they come here. I have 200 highly trained men and women on-site. We have three Kiowas here now, that should be more than a match to their one."

"Remember what Holt has done to our troops and equipment over the last few days."

"Totally different," Maxine said. "He has proven that he can run, but to attack is a different matter."

"We need to get you to a safer location."

She stood and walked to the bar. "There is no safer location than here."

"The safest location is the one that no one can find."

"No." She filled her glass with water and smiled at Carter. "I have a different plan." She walked up to him and stroked his face, causing his heart to race. She leaned in close to him, close enough to kiss. He caught the waxy, talcum scent of her lipstick.

"We have no leverage on Holt," she said. "Find me Stacy Zack's family. She must have a mother, father, brother? A sister?"

"A mother, father, and one sister, all in Colorado."

"Excellent," she said, and turned and walked to her bed. "Now get out of here and send my soldier back to me."

CHAPTER 23

As Jeffrey lifted the gunship up above the trees, he saw the moon resting, half-submerged on the distant ocean horizon. He throttled on and chased the moon for no reason but to give himself something to do. He ran out of land, and the gunship flew out over the empty darkness of the Pacific Ocean. Slowing the gunship, he watched the moon slip down out of sight, leaving him to fly over the vast blackness of the ocean with the swath of the Milky Way above. He turned the Kiowa back toward land. The faint hope of dawn glowed along the hills and mountains. Jeffrey pushed the throttle forward. As he approached the coastline, he saw a broad strip of beach, its sand catching just enough light from the forming dawn to make it stand out against the surrounding blackness.

He descended to the beach in a spiral and set the ship down on the sand, shut off the engines, unstrapped, and stepped into the back of the cabin.

"So, what's next?" Leif said, as he unhooked his harness.

"I need a moment," Jeffrey said. He hit the switch to lower the ramp. Cool ocean air pressed the heat out of the cabin. When the ramp touched down, Jeffrey walked out onto the sand. "I'm going for a walk to think. I need to make sure I have this clear in my head."

Jeffrey walked away from the gunship and considered the man who might be their only hope. He wondered if Admiral Cantwell was part of this mess. Jeffrey had known him for many years, and while Cantwell had also fought in the war, their paths had not crossed in those days. Cantwell held the reputation of a strict but fair man. Still, Cantwell had just been interviewed in the grounding of the Jules Verne freighter a few days ago. Did that hint at involvement? If he wasn't involved, then he was Jeffrey's man. If he was part of Maxine King's group, then Jeffrey had a problem. Jeffrey had isolated himself from the military machine for so long that he had no other personal contacts. Other official channels, and the press, would be unreliable and slow to initiate action.

Jeffrey thought back to what Freisman had said about implanted memories and intentional scarring.

Could it be possible?

He extended his pinkie, one joint short, and remembered having the tip crushed so badly that it had required amputation.

No artificial memory implant could be that detailed, could it? Were those six years of war all a fabrication? The decades coping with the memories just wasted time?

He shook his head.

None of that is important, right now. I've got to stay focused.

Jeffrey turned and walked back toward the gunship as dawn spread in among the stars. His boots pressed into the beach where retreating waves had left the sand smooth and wet. As he walked, something on the edge of his senses bothered him. He closed his eyes.

Is that a jet engine?

He strained his ears at the void and heard the breaking surf. He opened his eyes and looked across the sky and saw the small shapes of gulls wheeling in the cold air. Then he heard it. Off in the distance, the faint sound of thunder rumbled continuously. The sky held no heavy clouds.

He looked along the horizon.

There you are.

Far out over the ocean, up high, maybe five thousand feet, the tiny, bladed shape of a Kiowa gunship skitted through icy wisps of clouds. Jeffrey turned and ran toward his gunship. As he approached, he saw that Stacy and Leif had walked north, up the beach. He shouted to them. They couldn't hear him over the surf. As he ran, his back spasmed and he had to slow to a jog. Stacy stopped and looked out over the ocean, and then back at Jeffrey.

She hears it.

He pointed to his ear and then over the cliffs to the north. There was another source of thunder, he was sure of it.

"We need to get out of here now," he yelled over the surf. He began jogging toward the gunship again, but his back spiked with pain and he slowed to a walk.

He reached the gunship and walked up the ramp as quickly as his back would allow. Stacy and Leif ran up the ramp a few moments later. Jeffrey strapped in and fired the compressors, spooling the engines. The ramp lifted and sealed, shutting out the sound of the engines.

Leif said, "We're in."

"Tell me when you're strapped in."

A moment later, Stacy said, "Okay, we're good."

A fast, black shape flashed out from around the cliff to the north.

"And there you are," Jeffrey said, as he watched the second gunship fly out over the water. He tapped the temperature gauges, willing them up. The gunship turned south. As it passed, Jeffrey saw that the pilot was looking out to sea. Jeffrey's eyes shifted from the pilot to the navigator, whose eyes were locked on his.

"Dammit," Jeffrey said, looking from the second gunship to the temperature gauges and back again. The gunship, now halfway down the beach, hooked left, turning in behind them.

"Dammit, dammit, dammit," Jeffrey said, staring at the temperature gauges. The stick felt dead and heavy to him as he waited for the indicators to turn green. The second gunship had rounded on them, and Jeffrey had to look at his rear camera displays to see it. The small, dark shape came up from behind, fast. At any moment the pilot would open up, tearing them apart with depleted uranium sabot rounds. Or perhaps the pilot would use missiles to scatter them across the sand as Jeffrey had done to the highway in Australia. The needles on his temperature gauges rose quickly now, but were still below the lower limit.

We must be within their firing range now.

The needles swept up and the engine temperature lights ticked from red to green. Jeffrey yanked on the vertical controls. The Kiowa jumped off the sand, its massive thrust bringing a dizzy lightness to his head. He fired the nose thrusters at full power and flipped the ship nose over tail like a pancake off a spatula. Weightlessness tickled at his gut as the ground dropped away and then rolled back into view upside down. He slammed the throttle forward and his gunship leapt head on, the oncoming gunship now lined up in his center windshield.

The oncoming gunship's cannon lit up orange and Jeffrey shifted his ship sideways, spinning it on a belly-out axis, circling around the path of the other pilot's bullets. Tracer rounds flashed by the right side of his cockpit. Jeffrey pulled the yoke's trigger, firing the big nose cannon. The other pilot, realizing at the last moment that the advantage was lost, tried to evade, but too late. Jeffrey landed a burst of armor-piercing rounds through the cockpit glass. The glass caved in, and one engine split outward in a brilliant fireball. Jeffrey flew just under the other ship, which flashed past, leaving a trail of black smoke.

Another pilot and navigator gone, along with God knows how many troops.

Jeffrey tried to level the Kiowa, but it tipped and then dropped sickeningly sideways and fell toward the beach. Warning indicators lit up across the panel. He shoved the stick sideways, attempting to control the ship. It leveled, but continued to fall toward the ground. He pulled back on the throttle, set the airbrakes, and slammed the gunship into a hover. The left side flipped up and the gunship barrel-rolled, the horizon spinning in front of Jeffrey. The ship had gone insane in his hands.

He looked out the right side, and the problem became clear. He thought he had avoided the gunfire, but the other pilot had made his last act count for something. Jeffrey's gunship had no right wing. Only a torn stump extended out beyond the fuselage now. Ragged carbon fiber flipped in the wind, and fuel drooled out of the remnants of the right tank.

The ship dropped toward the beach and, instead of fighting the barrel roll, Jeffrey shoved the stick right, accelerating the roll. He timed the acceleration well, and as the ship came through an upright position it slammed into the sand. The impact broke the front landing gear and the gunship's nose dug into the beach. The windscreen shattered, covering Jeffrey with small bits of glass. Jeffrey flipped up a red and white cover and pulled the emergency lever under it, shutting the ship down.

"What the hell was that?" Stacy called up from the back.

Jeffrey brushed bits of glass aside and unbuckled his harness. He jumped up, slamming his head into the roofline. He groaned, pressing his hand onto his head, and stepped into the back.

"Everyone grab one survival bag," he said. "Make sure to get the ones with food."

"Did we just crash?" Leif asked.

"Yes. I took one down, but this ship is done, and the right side is covered in jet fuel. It could ignite at any moment. We need to get out of here and up into the forest, now."

Stacy and Leif hustled out of their seats. With the power off, Jeffrey cranked a handle, lowering the ramp. Stacy and Leif grabbed emergency bags, pulled out the shoulder straps and flipped them onto their shoulders. With the ramp half way down, they slid out the side and jumped to the sand. Leif helped Jeffrey put his pack on.

"Oh my God," Stacy said, as she saw the shredded nub of the wing.

"I'm sorry," Jeffrey said. "I should have turned faster."

"Are you kidding me?" she said, and pointed down the beach to where the other gunship had crashed, black smoke now reaching up several hundred feet high. "Your flying is the only reason we're not a ball of flame."

Jeffrey looked at the inland forest and realized the magnitude of his more critical mistake: He had landed on a beach, which was separated from the forest by a cliff wall. The sandstone precipice rose high above the beach and, at the top, hung with loose roots and scrubs. Jeffrey looked north, up the beach. There the cliff face ended in a black-basalt wall with waves crashing at its base. South, the beach ran out long and flat, with little cover. However, at the far end, the cliff leaned back and might be climbable.

During the last few days, he had regularly derided those chasing him for their lack of foresight. Now, he had fallen prey to his own arrogance. Never imagining they could be found on the beach, he had dropped his guard. They should have stayed inland, where the forest surrounded the gunship, cutting off visual lines. Due to his mistake, their best hope of getting out of this mess, and saving the entire spaceborne fleet, lay on the sand with one wing ripped off.

Stacy and Leif began to jog away. Jeffrey moved out after them, but his back spiked with pain, slowing him. Leif glanced over his shoulder, stopped, and jogged back to Jeffrey.

"Drop the pack, dad. Your back can't take it."

Jeffrey let Leif help him pull off the bag. They left it on the beach, and Leif helped him walk. Jeffrey looked over his shoulder one last time to see the gunship catch fire. The ship went up quickly, and an explosion thumped the air as a pocket of fuel vapor ignited. Flames ran down the side, tracing the path of jet fuel, and swallowed the fuselage.

The gunship that had carried them halfway around the world leaned sideways and burned, lifting its own stack of black smoke up into the sky.

Stacy had stopped running and stood waiting for Leif and Jeffrey. Jeffrey shooed her away, saying, "You both need to get up that cliff. I'll be right behind you."

"Good luck getting us to leave you alone," Stacy said.

They walked together, and Jeffrey moved as quickly as he could with the pain shooting down his leg. It seemed to increase with each step, and he was unsure how much longer he could keep up the pace. The outside edge of his left foot began to go numb.

Over the rumbling of the waves and his own breath, Jeffrey heard the faint, consistent thunder of a jet engine again. Stacy slowed and looked out over the ocean. Jeffrey looked as well.

The distant gunship had turned toward them, but the thunder Jeffrey heard could not be coming from it. It was too far away, and its jet exhausts were pointing away from them. Jeffrey listened, and his ears led him to the cliff. Above the cliff, the pale, blue sky had washed out the stars, and sunlight glowed behind the treetops. Somewhere beyond that ridge, at least one more gunship patrolled the area.

"I don't think we'll make it down the beach," Stacy said, and pointed to a tangle of gray logs, which lay at the base of the cliff. "Should we hole up there?"

"They'll find us with their heart sensors," Leif said.

"That's better than getting strafed running out on the beach," she said.

"Yes," Jeffrey said, "but in the long run, they'll have us. Our only hope is the end of the beach." He gave Leif a gentle push. "You both need to run there, now."

"I won't," Leif said.

"Please. Go." Jeffrey saw in their faces that they understood what he left unsaid: *I've lost too much in life already.*

They ran.

Jeffrey tried to walk faster, but the intense pain checked him. He looked over his shoulder and saw that the gunship over the ocean had come about half the distance to the beach. Inland, beyond the cliff, the third jet engine continued to rumble.

If it holds off just a bit longer, Stacy and Leif can make it to the trees.

They only had a few hundred more yards to the base of the cliff when the third gunship came up over the trees directly ahead of them. It flew out over the beach, pulled to a hover, and lay down a line of cannon fire in the sand just in front of Stacy and Leif. They stopped running and stood, looking up at the hovering gunship. Jeffrey continued limping toward them.

As Jeffrey approached Stacy and Leif, the gunship coming in from over the ocean arrived and landed behind them. The gunship, which had fired on them, landed on the sand just as another gunship came out over the trees and turned in a patrol pattern around them. It was not going to land.

"I see you do learn from your mistakes," Jeffrey said.

I wonder if I'll live long enough to learn once more from mine.

Leif lifted his arms in surrender. Stacy looked at him and then did the same. It made Jeffrey's heart sink to see them standing in submission. He kept his arms at his sides as he walked up and stood with them. Eight troops carrying rifles came around from behind the gunship. Jeffrey noted that two soldiers' guns were trained on Leif, two on Stacy, two on himself, and two roved.

These guys are ready for the game.

A tall, thin man, wearing slacks and a black military sweater, came around. The soldiers established a line, and the man crossed it, walking toward Jeffrey.

He smiled and said, "An old man and two children have caused us all these troubles? Ridiculous."

"Is it?" Jeffrey asked.

I wonder if he'll drop his guard, get close enough...

He felt the weight of the Colt in his cargo pocket and he wanted to reach for it, but not yet.

The commander stopped a safe distance from Jeffrey and nodded "Yes, perfectly ridiculous."

A soldier flipped a long metallic object end over end through the air. It landed at Jeffrey's feet.

"So much for taking a hostage," Jeffrey said.

"What?" Stacy asked, just as the shock grenade popped open, exposing a web of electrical antennas. Arcs of blue static flashed out. Then darkness and nothing.

CHAPTER 24

Maxine King sat at her breakfast table, a crystal cup filled with tea in her hand. She looked out on the sun-covered gardens. Birds hopped on the lawn, turning their heads sideways, listening for worms. Maxine set the cup down and crossed her hands on the marble tabletop. Her breakfast sat before her, untouched. She heard footsteps coming down the far hallway.

A young soldier came into the room, stopped just inside the door, and squared his shoulders. "Ma'am."

Maxine looked over the young man and sighed. His thin skull and large eyes did not match well, and his ample Adam's apple made his long neck appear jointed.

Why do they trouble me with these ugly ones?

"What is so important that my breakfast must be interrupted?"

"I'm sorry, ma'am," the soldier said, shifting his weight. "Mr. Roberts asked that I come get you."

"What does he want?"

Maxine now understood this poor example of a young man as Carter's doing. She had made it expressly clear that she was to be surrounded by the finest examples of young soldiers her security detail had to offer. She would remind Mr. Roberts of this fact.

"He said to tell you that the three fugitives have been captured."

"What?" She jumped up, tipping her chair backwards onto the slate floor.

"The three fugitives have—"

"I know. I heard you." She walked over to him. "When did this occur?"

The young soldier shifted away from her. "I don't know, ma'am. You'll have to ask Mr. Roberts."

She stared at the sorry excuse for a soldier. "Why didn't Mr. Roberts come here to tell me of this himself?"

"I don't know, ma'am." The soldier looked over his shoulder and then back to her. "You'll have to ask him."

"I will indeed," she said, pushing past the soldier and walking down the hallway.

...

Even before she was through the door to the cell area, Maxine said, "Why was I not awakened to be told Holt and the others had been captured?" She looked around at the gray cinderblock walls and concrete slab floor. No rugs. She hated the basement cell area. Unpleasant odors hung in the chilled air.

Carter Roberts stood with a pair of soldiers, each a far better specimen than the scarecrow she had just had to deal with. Carter turned to look at her.

"Maxine. Hello. What did you say?"

"You did not wake me when Holt was captured. Why?"

"You were not asleep. The call came in five minutes ago. I sent Thompson to get you the moment I received it."

She walked across the room and looked Carter over.

"Why did you send *that* soldier?"

"What are you talking about?"

"The soldier you sent to me." She looked at her nails. "He was not aesthetically pleasing. You know my preferences. Why did you send him? Is this a new game of yours?"

"Are you seriously suggesting–" Carter began, but Maxine's glare stopped him. He drew a deep breath. "I had four soldiers in the room. I told someone to go get you. They chose which among them on their own."

"Please be more specific next time. I do not need to deal with that along with all the stress I am facing."

Carter stared at her for a moment and then said, "Of course."

"Why did you not come yourself?"

"Maxine, I am preparing to receive the prisoners." He held up a clipboard.

She snatched the clipboard from his hand. On it, she found a list of locations: the Aleutian Islands, the Tonga Islands, New Zealand, Papua New Guinea, the Philippines. She scanned down the list to the last item, which was circled in black ink: Washington State coastline.

She tapped the list. "This search took far too long."

She set the clipboard on the desk and walked down the cell hallway. Carter walked with her. Each cell was clean and furnished with a low cot covered with a wool blanket, an aluminum toilet, and a sink. Only the last cell contained a prisoner, two in fact. Maxine approached the cell and saw an older couple sitting on the cot, holding each other's hands. Maxine stopped a few feet from the bars, and the man looked up.

Low, angry tones lay in his voice as he said, "Are you the monster responsible for this?"

Redness mottled the skin around his eyes, but a strength Maxine did not care for still burned in them. She said, "There is a greater good at work here. You will understand and accept that soon enough."

The man stood up and walked to the bars. Maxine gave him her warm matron's smile.

Spit hit her face, warm and wet.

"Oh, Gerald, dear," the woman in the cell said.

"She deserves no better, Ingrid," the man said. "She's trying to kill our daughter. The Good Book says to turn the other cheek, but if I could reach through these bars, I'd gladly take my place in Hell for what I'd do."

Maxine had lifted her hands halfway to her face and then, in disgust, gone still. Carter walked away and came back with a towel. He set it on her hand. Taking hold of it, she pressed it to her face. She held the towel away from her and noticed that a significant amount of makeup had come off on it. Folding it, she handed it back to Carter. She looked at the wall above the sink in the cell, but no mirror had been installed for the inmates.

She pressed her hands together. "Your daughter is getting in the way of the progress of civilization. Her life is meaningless when considering the thousands and millions who will be saved."

"It takes an immature and unholy mind to think that way."

Anger flared in Maxine, but she reminded herself that she was the one in control and let it go. She turned and walked past Carter saying, "Break him, Mr. Roberts. Make it look terrible so when Ms. Zack gets here she knows what she has coming."

"Yes, ma'am."

...

Maxine stood in the hallway just outside the re-education room and listened as they worked on the Reverend Gerald Zack of Midwestern America. While actually watching would have made her physically ill, his screams made her chest flutter.

When they had finished with him, she stepped into the doorway. Her throat closed slightly, and her stomach tightened. Red speckled the white tile floor. He sat in the center of the room, strapped to a stainless-steel chair. She forced herself to walk over to him, wishing she had not come in, but she had to show him that she took pride in his re-education. Snot and blood drooled down his face and onto his chest. A tooth lay on the floor nearby. Maxine's smooth-soled shoes slid a bit on the blood, and she felt bile rising in her esophagus.

"How do you feel about spitting on me now?"

He mumbled something, the blood bubbling in his throat. She noticed that one finger lay twisted up over the back of his hand. She signaled a soldier to give her a towel and used it to push on the finger. He yelled out in pain.

"What did you say?" she asked.

He said, in a whisper, "I'm sorry, so sorry. Please make them stop."

"Do you see why your daughter is in the wrong now? Do you see the beauty in the cause?"

He began to sob, and she could see that the sobbing caused him agony. She felt joy rise at that. His pain confirmed the strength of her group and the justness of her cause.

Those like you and your bitch daughter will be washed aside in the New World.

Maxine walked over to a rack of tools and, setting the towel down, picked up a smooth nylon baton. She walked back to him and pressed the end of the baton into his ribs. He did not respond. She tried a few other areas on his chest until he screamed out in primal terror and pain. She smiled at him.

"Please, I can't remember." He gasped for air. "I don't know."

"Don't know what?"

"I can't..." and he wandered into mumbling.

Maxine smiled. He had broken. Now his soul, exposed and weak, lay before her.

"You remember Stacy though, yes? That she is going to die terribly?"

Tears began dripping from his eyes, mixing with the blood and mucus on his face.

"Do you remember her?"

He turned his head left and right, saying, "No. no. no. no."

"She is your daughter. She is why you are suffering so much. She is a traitor and a terrorist." Maxine smiled at the old man. "Don't you hate her for letting this happen to you?"

He looked up at her and his lips moved, but she heard nothing. In his eyes, she no longer saw the fear she wanted. She grabbed him by his blood soaked hair, too angry to care about the drying, glutinous mess, and pulled his head back. His eyes rolled in their sockets, wild, like a roped goat whose throat had just been slit open, life pumping in thick streams from its neck. His lips continued to form words. She leaned in closely to him so she could hear.

"...the valley of the shadow of death, I will fear no evil: For thou art with me; Thy rod and thy staff, they comfort me. Thou preparest a table before me in the presence of mine enemies..."

She let go of his hair, and his head dropped. She walked toward the door and, remembering the baton in her hand, threw it at him. It hit his shoulder and then clattered to the tile floor. He kept up his mumbling prayer. She took a towel from the tray, wiped her hand off, and left the room feeling unsatisfied.

She walked down the hallway and arrived at the cell area as soldiers wheeled in three bodies on gurneys. She followed them into the cell area. A sheet covered each, leaving the head and one arm exposed. Each gurney had an IV stand with a clear bag of green liquid hanging from it. The liquid fed into a long, curling tube that ended in a needle taped into each figure's exposed arm. One of the figures, the largest, had a strong jawline, almost Viking. The others were smaller, one an irritatingly pretty woman with a dirty bandage on her face. She noted the weak, yet handsome features of the younger man's face and his likeness to the older man. They all seemed to be having a pleasant dream. She touched the young man's face gently. It felt warm and soft.

She looked at Carter. "These are the three who have been causing us so much difficulty?"

CHAPTER 25

Darkness surrounded Jeffrey. Off to his left, he heard the ocean. He felt a mattress beneath him and a blanket draped over him. His breath drew in and out in the rhythm of sleep. He tried to lift his arm, but it would not move. The separation he felt from his body startled him. He felt the urgent desire to draw a deep breath, but his breathing continued in its steady rhythm. Being unable to take in additional air made him feel as though he were suffocating. He wanted to open his eyes, but they remained closed.

Panic rose in him. He tried to wrench his hands up and felt one finger twitch. He wrenched again. Nothing but the breathing. He gave one more tremendous jerk on his body, and his eyes fluttered open. Pushing himself up, back burning with pain, he threw off the green blanket and shifted to a sitting position on the edge of the cot. His boots squeaked on the epoxied floor.

Something spiked at his forearm. In the dim light, he squinted at his forearm and saw a needle planted there, held in place with clear tape. He followed the tubing away from the needle, up to a bag, which hung empty on a chrome hook. He looked back at the needle. Picking at the edge of the tape, he pulled it loose and drew the needle out of his arm. A black bead of blood sprang from the wound, and he sealed the tape over it.

In front of him stood a cinderblock wall, its gray mortar neatly set. Airflow from a ventilation fan, mounted high up behind a steel grate, filled the area with a sound like that of distant ocean surf. He looked to his left and saw a shadowy, stainless-steel sink and toilet. Despite the pain it caused him, he twisted to look behind himself. He found another solid wall. He looked to his right and saw metal bars.

I'm in a cell. Great.

Beyond the bars, electric light came from down the hallway, dim as a winter evening.

"Leif?" he called out.

Even sitting upright, he felt sleep tugging at him. He leaned forward, pushed on his knees, and stood. Pulling the IV bag from its hook, he held it close to his eyes, examining it in the murky light. Asian characters covered the rubbery plastic. He tossed the bag onto the cot.

He looked out into the hallway. "Stacy?"

He heard the scrape of a chair being shoved back, and footfalls came down the hallway. A switch clicked and fluorescent lights stuttered on, blinding Jeffrey for a moment. As his eyes adjusted to the bright light, a soldier came into view dressed in standard, black BDU's. He stood perhaps a foot shorter than Jeffrey, but had a powerful build. The name patch above his right pocket was blank. He stared at Jeffrey, his eyes narrow and malicious.

"You'll be quiet in your cell. If not, I'll muzzle you."

Jeffrey said nothing.

The soldier stared at Jeffrey for a moment longer and then walked farther down the hallway. Soon he returned, walking past Jeffrey's cell with only a passing glance.

He had gone down the hallway to check on someone else? Were Stacy and Leif down there?

Jeffrey wanted to shout out again to them, wanted to know where they were, but he suppressed the urge. Right now, he needed the soldier to stay calm. He sat down on the cot and pain pierced his lower back. He lowered himself onto the mattress and stared at the ceiling. Even with the bright fluorescent light on, he felt his eyelids closing with chemical sleep.

"Dammit," he said, sitting up. The pain in his back burned deep into the base of his spine. The outside edge of his left foot still had no feeling. Shaking his head and drawing a breath, he tried to clear his mind. He needed to consider his options. Nothing came to him. He would have to be patient, just play each moment as it arrived. The trouble was the right moment could slip by, and he might know it only after it had passed.

He closed his eyes and listened. Down the hallway, he heard pages flipping. Even sitting up, his mind began to drift off to sleep again. He opened his eyes and cursed.

Down at the lighted end of the hallway a door opened, and someone entered. A chair scraped the floor.

"You needed me?" a man asked.

"Yes sir," the first soldier said. "He's awake."

"The other two?"

"Still out."

Jeffrey stood and stepped up to the bars.

Leif and Stacy are here.

"I'll get the Commander." The door opened and shut again. The chair scraped on the floor, and then a page flipped.

Jeffrey looked to his left and saw that the hallway dead-ended about twenty feet further down. The cells were all on his side. He looked at the floor of his cell and estimated it to be about seven feet wide. There should be three more cells to his left. He looked to his right, to the soft glow of light, but could not see an end to the hallway.

Several more cells that way, possibly.

The door opened again. Footfalls began to come down the hallway. Jeffrey stood by the bars, waiting. A man walked into view, stopped at the bars, and looked Jeffrey over, his expression calm. He had the strict, yet casual posture of a commanding officer. His black hair had brushes of gray along the sides. He wore a name badge on his BDU's that read 'C. Roberts'.

"So you're him then," Roberts said.

Jeffrey stared into Roberts' eyes, measuring his reactions: a flicker in his gaze, a dilation of the pupils, anything.

Jeffrey asked, "Who would that be?"

Roberts smiled and said, "You've caused me a great deal of difficulty."

"I would like to have caused you considerably more."

Roberts looked down the hallway and then back at Jeffrey. "Of course."

Jeffrey shifted his weight and pain gripped his back. The quickness of it caught him off-guard and he winced.

Roberts smiled. "Your back troubling you, old man?"

Jeffrey offered no response to the question. Roberts shrugged.

Just then, from down the hallway, came Leif's groggy voice, "Dad? Where the hell are we?"

Jeffrey did not take his eyes off Carter, as he said, "Looks like we're in a holding area of some kind."

Roberts held up his hand. "That's enough. Be silent."

That brought up Jeffrey's ire. He gauged Roberts' distance from the bars. Jeffrey stepped up to the bars. Roberts stepped back.

Roberts said, "Easy there, brute. I'm not going to make the same mistakes you've seen in the past."

"I've got a long past, and I've seen a lot of mistakes. You sure you can cover them all?"

Anger flickered in Roberts's eyes, and then his stoic expression returned. "You do have an interesting past. Your report says you were a Hammerhead?"

Jeffrey stared at Roberts and did not answer.

"There's no need to be timid," Roberts said. "I've reviewed your file. Lots of detail. Six years as a Hammerhead. You were decorated as the longest serving member, the only survivor of the initial group."

Jeffrey stared at Roberts.

"That means you were brainwashed longer than anyone I've ever met." When Jeffrey gave him no reaction, Roberts said, "So tell me, what does it feel like having your head filled with six years of shit and then spewing it out your ears, nose, and mouth for the rest of your life?"

Jeffrey felt Roberts getting in under his skin.

Roberts' smiled broadened, and he said, "No bother though. You'll understand the truth before we put you out of your misery."

Jeffrey gripped his tongue between his molars until he felt a stabbing pain.

"You think you're angry now?" Roberts said. "Just wait until we're done clarifying your son."

Jeffrey stared at him.

Roberts shrugged. "It doesn't matter. You won't stay silent for long." He looked up the hallway. "Get them ready to be moved."

The chair scraped and the door opened.

"He's ready," Jeffrey heard the first soldier say. Someone came through the doorway, and two sets of footfalls came down the hallway. The first soldier and another stopped on either side of Roberts.

Maybe now is the time. The door will be unlocked and it will be three to one. Not good odds, especially with my back out of sorts.

Jeffrey tried to stay calm as he felt adrenaline glow down his arms.

Any moment now.

But instead of opening the cell door, both soldiers unholstered tazers and fired them at Jeffrey. He stepped back just as the electrodes caught him in the chest and shoulder. His body locked up, and he fell backward, clipping his skull on the edge of the sink. He lay on the floor, his back arching, looking up at the water droplets condensed on the sink's pipes.

The electric fire began to let go as Jeffrey heard the cell door crash open. The soldiers grabbed his feet, pulled him to the center of the cell, and flipped him face down. They yanked his hands behind his back, and Jeffrey felt the bite of handcuffs on his wrists. The soldiers ratcheted cuffs onto his ankles.

Leaving him face down on the floor, the soldiers walked out of the cell. Jeffrey rolled to his side and pushed through the pain in his back to sit up. He saw that a short chain connected the cuffs on his ankles. He heard Leif's twitching growls as he was tazed, and then the ratchet of cuffs. The soldiers returned with Leif shuffling between them, arms behind his back. One stayed with Leif and the other, the first soldier, walked over to Jeffrey and hauled him up off the floor. The pain in Jeffrey's back caused him to shout out.

Roberts walked up to Jeffrey, a slight glitter in his eyes as he searched Jeffrey's face. "Now we're making some progress."

The soldier yanked on Jeffrey's arm, pulling him along. Jeffrey had to drag his left foot. Lifting it hurt his lower back far too much. They walked out of the cell hallway into a small area that had one steel door with a wire-reinforced glass window. A metal desk sat in the corner.

Roberts opened the door and leaned his head into the hallway. "Come in here and help us."

Two more soldiers entered the room.

Roberts said to them, "Bring her up here."

The two walked past Jeffrey and down the hallway. A cell door slid open. Then Jeffrey heard a slap, and one of the soldiers said, "Wake up, girlie."

Jeffrey turned and shouted down the hallway, "You want to hit someone, hit me."

The larger of the two soldiers standing with Jeffrey and Leif grabbed his elbow, spun him around, and hit him squarely between the eyes with his baton. Jeffrey's head snapped back and the room swam. A tunnel formed around his vision and he waited for that strange sensation of the floor flipping up and hitting him. But the room stabilized, the tunnel opened up, and he locked eyes with the soldier, trying to make it seem that the impact had meant nothing.

From down the hall, he heard: "She's way under still. Give me the adrenaline hypo."

After a moment, Jeffrey heard Stacy gasping. She groaned and then–her voice foggy–asked, "Who the hell are you?"

She yelled out in pain as handcuffs clicked. Jeffrey turned again to look down the hallway. The soldier tried to turn him back, but Jeffrey crouched, pain burning through his lower back, and drove the top of his head into the soldier's nose and mouth. If he could have grabbed the soldier by the back of the neck, he would have wrecked his face for him.

The soldier stepped back, holding the bridge of his nose. Blood trickled out from under his hand.

"Dammit," Roberts said.

The soldier lifted his club, and Jeffrey squared on him.

"Stop," Roberts said to the soldier, and pointed to the door. "Go to the infirmary and get your face sorted out." He looked at the other soldier. "You, keep him," he aimed his thumb at Jeffrey, "under control."

The soldier with the bloody nose stared at Jeffrey for a moment and walked out of the room.

The last soldier took his baton from his belt just as Stacy shuffled up the hallway in cuffs and chains, flanked by the other two soldiers. Her eyes met Jeffrey's, and then she glared at the soldiers, taking stock of each one. Jeffrey saw anger in her eyes, and he was with her.

He asked her, "How are you doing?"

"Okay, now," she said, staring at the two soldiers who had brought her up. "Sons of bitches."

"Easy," Jeffrey said, "these guys aren't quite all there."

"That's enough out of you," the soldier to his right said, as he swung his baton and hit Jeffrey on the side of his thigh, across the peroneal nerve. The strike overwhelmed Jeffrey's leg with electromagnetic numbness, and it gave way. He tipped sideways and the soldiers reached out and caught him, wrenching his arms as they held him up. He willed his leg to push on the floor, and—in a moment—the flaring pain subsided enough for him to stand on his own.

Jeffrey indicated the soldier who had just hit him with a tilt of his head and said to Stacy, "This one has a fragile ego and a fragile jaw by the look of him. We'll take advantage of both soon enough."

The soldier pulled his baton back, but Roberts grabbed his arm.

"That's enough," he said. "You'll have your chance, Miller. She's coming down, and you men need to show more control. No more of this amateur crap."

They waited in silence for a few minutes. Jeffrey watched Stacy as they waited. She spent those moments looking over the soldiers, her gaze calm and measuring. Her eyes tracked from knees, to groins, and up to throats.

The door opened, and Maxine King walked in. Despite the situation, Jeffrey was immediately struck by her beauty. She had long, angular features, delicate and strong at the same time. Her golden hair flowed down, breaking in arcs over her shoulders. Jeffrey looked to Leif, who also stared at King, and then to Stacy who stared back at him with a look of disgust on her face.

"Really?" she said.

"You have all been so bothersome," Maxine said. She walked up to Jeffrey and stroked his face. He smiled at her. Roberts walked around behind Maxine, took hold of her arm, and guided her backwards.

"Please, Maxine," Roberts said. "He's dangerous, even restrained."

Jeffrey winked at Maxine.

A lascivious luster came to her eyes, and she smiled at Jeffrey, saying, "I see."

She turned to Stacy and the smile vanished. Jeffrey noticed a slight flush cross Maxine's face as she lifted her chin and drew her shoulders square. "So, what do I do with you?"

Stacy shuffled toward Maxine, saying, "Probably kill me like you should have in the first place."

A soldier grabbed Stacy's arm and yanked her back.

Maxine stepped closer to Stacy. "Yes, that is true." She ran a fingernail down the bandage on Stacy's face. "I am glad to see, for all the damage you did to my good men, that you suffered to some degree."

"Your good men? Trash terrorists?" Stacy looked around to the soldiers. "Don't you realize she's insane?" She turned to Roberts. "Do you really believe there was no war? Do you think killing all those men and women is justified?"

"It's no use," Maxine said, taking Stacy's face in her hands. She pressed her thumb on the bandage until Stacy winced. Maxine smiled. "These men know the truth. It is you who is so confused." She said to her soldiers, "Do you see how mindlessly she holds onto her beliefs?" Maxine looked back at Stacy and said with disdain, "She really believes in the lies society has fed her."

Stacy twisted her head, fighting to get away from Maxine's hands.

Maxine let Stacy's head go. "You will see the truth of it and be corrected in your thinking. The brainwashing holds very well though. Pain is the only source of freedom for you and your companions. We will set you free, and then—as you could never be fully trusted to join us—you will be put to rest."

Jeffrey wished he were thirty years younger. From where he stood, he was sure he could—even with his legs chained—jump and kick Maxine King square in the chest. But his back was too hurt for acrobatics. He looked at Leif, but Leif was just not that aggressive. He saw on Leif's face, not the consideration of fighting, but the consideration of pain. Jeffrey felt terrible that he had led them into this mess. He should not have involved Leif. He should have ditched the Kiowa and gone underground with Stacy. He pulled at the cuffs, and the metal dug into his wrists. He gave up fighting the chain, and—for the first time since his wife died—he saw nothing but a dead end.

Maxine raised her index finger and tapped the end of Stacy's nose. "Let's begin by breaking you down some." She turned and walked out, saying, "Bring them along."

The soldiers shoved Stacy out ahead of them, and a baton cracked against Jeffrey's shoulder blade. He shuffled after Maxine and Stacy. Leif followed. They entered a wide, institutional hallway constructed of the same epoxied concrete and unfinished cinderblocks. The stark lights had enough separation to give the hallway a light-dark pattern all the way down.

Maxine led them past several closed doors with the same mesh-reinforced glass windows. Soon, they approached a door, which had no window and no handle. It was only a smooth rectangle set in the block wall. She stopped and, with the back of her hand, knocked on the door. Someone inside pulled the door open, and Maxine motioned for Jeffrey to walk in.

Jeffrey stood still for a moment. He didn't like this at all. By the smug look on Maxine's face he understood that there was something very bad in that room, and his mind raced to add up what it could be. The baton cracked across the back of his head and he turned to the soldier.

"I'm keeping a count of those, and I'm gonna pay you back double for every one."

The soldier turned his head side-to-side in a slow "no" and hit Jeffrey in the hip with his baton. Jeffrey winced, and then limped into the room, his left foot dragging. White tile covered the walls and floor of the square room. The floor sloped slightly downward to a drain at the center. Spatters and smears of blood increased toward the center of the room. A stainless steel chair sat directly over the drain, bolted to the floor with chrome fittings. A bloody and beaten body, held in place with leather straps, sat in the chair. The head hung down, and blood crusted the nose, mouth, and eye sockets. Jeffrey estimated that it had once been a man of perhaps fifty to sixty. He wondered who the dead man was just as Stacy let out a piteous scream.

CHAPTER 26

Stacy tried to run toward the body, but the chains around her ankles tripped her. She twisted in mid-air, landing on her hip and shoulder. She sat up, pulled her feet under her, stood, and walked in short steps the rest of the way to the body. She fell to her knees in front of the body, and her shoulders began shaking. Then she cried in long, gasping sobs. Jeffrey looked at Maxine King and saw that she had a faint smile on her face, as if she were watching a well-performed play.

Jeffrey felt fury rising in him, and he checked it, steadying himself. In sincere disbelief, he asked Maxine, "Why?"

Maxine turned her head to him, and her smile faded to derision. "Because she willfully got in the way of the divine process."

Anger grew in Leif's face as he said, "Your insanity is the divine process? Bullshit."

"Well argued," Maxine said to Leif. "Your thought processes are obviously well developed."

Leif lunged toward Maxine, but the soldiers grabbed him and held him back. He twisted, trying to shake them off, but they lifted his arms up behind his back and his face contorted in pain.

Leif stopped struggling and then asked, "So this is your New World?" He looked to the men around him. "What happened to that man is God's will?"

Roberts walked around to face Leif. He gripped Leif's neck with his right hand. Leif tried to pull his head away, but the guards lifted his arms up, driving him forward. A guttural sound came from Leif's mouth.

Jeffrey stepped forward, but a guard pulled him back.

"You do not," Roberts said, his dark eyes scanning Leif's face, "understand the reality of the situation." Jeffrey saw the muscles in Roberts' arm flex as he gripped Leif's neck harder. His index finger and thumb dug into the sides of Leif's neck. Leif's face turned red and the widening fear in his eyes faded to emptiness. His legs went slack, but the guards kept him on his feet. Roberts released his grip, and Leif's head fell forward. After a moment, Leif lifted his head in a series of disjointed bobs. His head stabilized, and his confused eyes tracked the room.

Roberts walked over to Maxine and held his hand palm-out, presenting her. "She is the divine mother of the New World. She will bring peace and prosperity to us all."

Leif opened his mouth, but said nothing, his eyes still foggy.

Jeffrey said to Roberts, "As long as you're in her good graces. If you disagree with her, it'll be you in that chair."

Roberts and Jeffrey looked at the body in the chair. Stacy had placed her head in her father's lap, and her loud sobbing had calmed to a sniffling. Jeffrey saw that the body's left forearm was broken so badly that jagged spikes of both the radius and ulna protruded from the skin.

Roberts walked over to Stacy. "You see," he said, "we do not disagree with Maxine, and we never will." He planted his boot on Stacy's hip and shoved, knocking her to the tile floor.

She lay on her side for a moment. Then she rolled forward and pushed off the floor with the side of her head, coming up onto her knees. She sat there looking at the floor. Jeffrey saw her broken spirit in the hollowness of her eyes.

"Why don't you try that with me?" He said to Roberts.

But Roberts ignored Jeffrey. His dark eyes remained on Stacy. He grabbed her by the hair and pulled her head back. She tried to twist her head away but could not break his grip on her hair, so she turned her eyes, looking off to the side.

"Could it be this easy?" Maxine asked, and walked over to Stacy, kneeling in front of her. "Could a Special Warfare brat be this easy to break?"

Roberts released Stacy's head, and it dropped down.

Maxine now took Stacy by the hair on the right side of her head and pulled her head to the side.

Jeffrey heard Stacy mumble something to Maxine.

"What's that?" Maxine asked, leaning in.

Louder, Stacy said, "You're so pretty."

A sincere smile came to Maxine's face. "Why thank you. I didn't imagine—"

Stacy bolted forward and, as it looked to Jeffrey, kissed Maxine full on the mouth. The intimate position of the two women confused Jeffrey for a moment, until Maxine let out a muffled scream, and he saw her trying to tug her head away, pushing on Stacy's shoulders. Stacy jerked back, and Jeffrey saw a strip of Maxine's lower lip ripping away. Soldiers ran up and pulled at Stacy. She yanked herself away from Maxine and then spit the chunk of Maxine's lip back at her. Jeffrey's stomach flipped. He was not sure if it was in pride or disgust.

He looked at Maxine and saw her pearl white teeth showing through a hole where her lower lip had been. She brought her hands up and covered the half-skull smile; blood spilled through her fingers, running like wine down her white silk shirt. Her eyes darted from one face to the next, asking each what had happened.

Maxine said through her hands, the words coming wetly over her destroyed lip, "Kill her."

"You're a funny looking bitch now," Stacy screamed at Maxine, her eyes wide and spit flying from her lips like a wild horse, tied and fighting crazy.

"Kill her, now!" Maxine screamed through her hands. She turned and ran out of the room. Roberts looked down at the floor, picked up the chunk of flesh, and followed after Maxine.

As he left the room, he said over his shoulder, "You heard her."

Jeffrey's mind had not attached to the reality of what was about to happen until the first soldier walked toward Stacy. He saw Leif struggling, yanking his shoulders and shoving with his legs. A soldier swung his baton and caught Leif on the side of the neck. Leif went limp. The soldiers holding him let him fall. He struck his head on the tile floor and came to rest in a prostrate heap, unconscious.

The soldier nearest Stacy drew his baton and hefted it. Stacy spat Maxine's blood at him. The soldier dodged, the spit catching him on the shoulder.

Jeffrey twisted his shoulders, fighting the guards who held him. A baton struck his lower back. What he had before considered intense pain now bloomed into a horrendous fire, locking up his hips and legs. His legs folded under him and the soldiers, still holding him up, wrenched his arms backward as he fell to his knees. Jeffrey gritted his teeth and growled, willing himself through the pain, but now nothing he did could make his mind push through that fire. His back and legs had shut down.

The soldier in front of Stacy whipped his baton toward her skull. At the last moment she fell to her back and kicked with both heels into the soldier's knees. Jeffrey's heart leapt as he saw the soldier's knees bend backwards. The soldier fell to the ground, screaming. His baton clattered away, and he rolled onto his belly and clawed at the floor, his body making a primal attempt to get away from the pain.

"Who's next?" Stacy said, with a bloody grin.

A soldier to Jeffrey's right aimed a tazer and fired. The voltage clicked through the weapon. Stacy fell backward, and her body went rigid, only her skull and heels touching the floor. Three soldiers ran up and rained their batons down on her. The nylon clubs clacked off bone and thumped on muscle. Horror, grief, and rage all fought for room in Jeffrey's heart as tears welled up in his eyes and rolled down his face.

The soldiers beat her far longer than necessary. When they were done they stepped aside. The soldiers holding Jeffrey dragged him forward on his knees. His back felt as though someone had cut it open and driven salted nails into the exposed spine.

Stacy lay there, peaceful enough, her half-open eyes staring off over Jeffrey's shoulder. As the soldiers dragged him closer, however, he saw that the lower portion of her right eye socket and her cheekbone, where the bandage was now torn away, had been crushed into her sinus.

"You're next," one of the soldiers said, pointing his stick at Jeffrey. Jeffrey jerked at his handcuffs, but again the fire in his back stopped him. The soldiers tried to pull him to his feet, but he could not will his legs to move.

"Have it your way," the soldier said, and pushed Jeffrey backward. He landed on his back, his arms pinned beneath him. Clarified pain flashed through his body. The soldiers grabbed his feet and dragged him out of the room. As the hallway ceiling slid by, Jeffrey's only thought was gratitude that Leif had not had to watch Stacy die.

CHAPTER 27

The soldiers dragged Jeffrey into his cell, flipped him onto his belly, and left him face down, his arms still cuffed behind his back. Jeffrey lay with the side of his face on the floor trying to focus on the cool concrete on his cheek rather than the pain in his back. His head spun with endorphins, and he realized that he was hyperventilating. He took as deep a breath as the pain would allow, held it, let it out, and repeated that in measured time for awhile. As he did this, he felt sorrow build in his chest. The memory of Stacy's crushed face kept pushing into his mind. He tried to push it out, but each time it came right back in on him. His heart felt broken, and tears dripped sideways off his cheek and the bridge of his nose.

Soon, he heard Leif stirring in a cell further down the hallway.

"Stacy?" Leif called out.

Jeffrey dreaded what must come next.

Should I lie to Leif to keep him going?

Leif called out again, a higher, worried tone coming into his voice, "Stacy?"

"Take it easy, Leif," Jeffrey said.

"What happened, Dad? What did they do?"

Jeffrey wanted to lie to him. He wanted to say to him that nothing had happened, to tell Leif that Stacy was all right. He wanted to believe it himself.

Leif's voice sharpened with frustrated anger as he asked, "What happened?"

"Stace–" Jeffrey began, but he stopped, not wanting to expose his grief.

The anger left Leif's voice. "Tell me what happened."

Jeffrey took a deep breath and imagined himself going empty. He saw all the emotion running out of him. He imagined himself as a hollow shell, dark, stretching off into nothing. The choking sensation of tears faded, and he felt able to think.

"Stacy's dead, Leif," Jeffrey said. "They killed her."

"How?" Leif said, his voice breaking, "What did they do to her?"

"Knowing she is gone is enough right now."

A quiet sobbing came up from Leif's cell, and Jeffrey felt sorrow rolling up in his own heart and mind again. He remembered what it was like when he first started fighting in the war. The first few friends to die were just as painful as the second and one hundredth. But there was a dreadful shock with the first few. When experienced the first time, the reality of death and the emotions that rush in can be terrifying. Jeffrey equated it to the first time he parachuted out of a plane and felt the sensory horror of weightlessness, unexpected and overwhelming.

Later.

He brought himself back to the vision of himself as a hollow core, cold and dark. After a moment, the visualization brought him emptiness, and he said, "Leif, I know this is a terrible moment for you, but you need to think about the decision before you."

The grief in Leif's voice choked his words. "What decision?"

"You can decide to fight, or to grieve. You can't do both at the same time. You can grieve later. Unfortunately, that will always be there for you. But you can't fight later."

Only the sound of Leif's crying came up the hallway.

"What's your decision?" Jeffrey asked. "You have to make it right now."

"I don't—" tears interrupted him, "know how to fight."

Jeffrey said, "I don't know what to do yet either, but the fight starts in your heart, in the decision to move ahead."

"I don't want to give in."

"Good."

Silence surrounded Jeffrey. After a moment, he heard grunting and scraping, then the clatter of a bed frame and a shout of pain. Another moment of silence, and Leif said, "I can't get my hands free. Maybe I can break these cuffs off." Jeffrey heard a loud clank, then another, and another. The door down the hallway opened and slammed against the wall. Heavy footfalls came down the cell passageway, and a soldier walked into view and stared at Jeffrey. He then walked farther down the passageway.

"What the hell are you doing?" the soldier asked.

A loud clank rang out.

"Stop that, right now."

Another clank echoed up the passageway, then Jeffrey heard the brush of a holster and the click of a tazer. Leif growled as the tazing locked up his body.

"You try to break those cuffs and I spark you again. Got it?"

Leif said, "Yes," and the clank rang out again. Even though Jeffrey was worried for his son, he smiled. The click of the tazer sounded again, followed by Leif's grunting.

"Had enough?" the soldier said. Jeffrey heard the click of a new cartridge being loaded onto the tazer.

"For now."

"Good."

"Great."

There was a pause and Jeffrey imagined the soldier, furious at his inability to cow Leif, aiming the tazer and fingering the trigger. Jeffrey expected, at any moment, to hear the spark again, but instead he heard the brush of the tazer going into its holster. Footfalls sounded, and the soldier came into view in front of Jeffrey's cell door.

The soldier pointed at him. "What about you? You want a spark?"

"Why, no thank you."

"Now, there's someone smart enough to know who's in charge."

"You come in here, take these cuffs off, and put down that tazer. We'll see who's in charge."

The soldier scowled at Jeffrey. For a moment, Jeffrey thought the soldier would come into the cell. But the soldier gave a dismissive sweep of his hand, and walked back up the hallway. The chair in the front room scraped on the floor, and the soldier's ass thumped into the chair.

Jeffrey lay with the side of his face on the floor for some time. His eyelids grew heavy, and he closed them. It seemed that he opened them only a moment later. He moved his lips, and his dry tongue stuck to the roof of his mouth. As the confusion of awakening subsided, he wondered how long he had been asleep. His hands tingled with numbness. He rolled to his right side to allow his hands to get blood, and his back spiked at him. He rolled the rest of the way onto his back and then, through searing pain, sat upright. He tapped his left heel on the ground: totally numb.

Then he heard a distant thump.

The soldier at the desk said, "What the hell?" and his chair scraped back. Jeffrey heard the door open. Someone walked into the room. The soldier asked, "Who are you? Do you have authorization to be down here?"

"No."

Something whipped the air, followed by a soggy crack. A body hit the floor. Now silence. Jeffrey closed his eyes, listening into the stillness. He heard the door open and metal clanked. Boot rubber squeaked on the floor. Footsteps left the room, but the door did not close. The soft sound of fabric dragging along the floor entered the room. A thump like a sack of wet sand being set down followed. He heard the footsteps go back out of the room. The fabric dragging repeated and then the dropping thump. After another silence, a chair scraped along the floor, and the door clicked shut.

Jeffrey heard footsteps coming down the passageway. A young man, a kid really, came into view at Jeffrey's cell door. He had brown hair combed straight back and wore military-issue, black-rimmed glasses. His BDU's fit loosely on his thin frame. Jeffrey felt as though he knew the young man's face but could not lock down why.

The young man took a small, pink object out of his pocket, fumbled with it, and then pressed it on the thumbprint reader. The lock clacked. He slid the door open and entered the cell.

Jeffrey shifted his body to keep his legs between him and the young man.

"No," the young man said, "don't hassle me. Move so I can undo your cuffs."

Jeffrey leaned back and rolled to his left side to expose the cuffs. The young man fumbled at Jeffrey's wrists. With a click, the cuffs came loose. Jeffrey lay on his back and rubbed his wrists. The young man twisted at the cuffs on Jeffrey's ankles. It took a moment for him to get the key to turn.

Jeffrey asked, "Who are you?"

"You don't know me," the young man said, "but you've met my brother."

"You'll have to refresh my memory."

The young man unlocked the last cuff on Jeffrey's ankle, saying, "When there's time."

Jeffrey noticed sweat on the young man's forehead. The young man stood and took the pink object from his pocket: a severed thumb. His hand trembled slightly. He left the cell, walking down the hallway. Jeffrey heard a lock clack and a cell door slide to its stops.

"What the hell do you want?" Leif asked.

"Don't struggle," the young man said, "I'm here to help." Something hit the cot with a clang. The young man had frustration in his voice, as he said, "Stop."

Jeffrey rolled over onto his hands and knees, and then crawled to the bars. He pulled himself up to standing. The fire in his back ran down his right leg. His left still had no sensation. He tried a few steps and could walk as long as he only dragged his feet. With each step, an electric jolt ran down his right leg. He heard the sound of chains falling to the floor, and then the young man came back up the corridor followed by Leif.

"Lift up the back of your shirt," the young man said, taking a syringe from his pocket.

"Who the hell *are* you?" Jeffrey asked, again.

"We need to hurry."

"You're not getting anywhere near me with that needle until you explain yourself. We clear?"

The young man looked at Leif, and Leif nodded agreement.

"You may have unlocked our cuffs," Jeffrey said, "but this could just be a tactic, the old Mutt and Jeff mind bend."

"Ah." The young man's face brightened as he held up his index finger. He motioned with his hand. "Follow me." He walked away from them, down the hallway.

Jeffrey began shuffling after him, holding the wall. Leif grabbed Jeffrey's arm and helped him walk. As they came into the area with the metal desk, Jeffrey squinted through the bright light and saw a spray of blood on the wall, and then three bodies, each with a caved in area on its temple. On the desk lay a collapsible baton with a steel ball at the end, wet with blood.

"Yeah," was all Jeffrey could think to say.

"Yep," the young man said, smoothing back his hair. "They went down pretty easy. They sure didn't suspect me." He grasped the rim of his glasses and adjusted them as if he had just completed a complex physics problem. Jeffrey shuffled over to one of the bodies. With some effort and intense pain, he lifted his foot and stepped with his full weight on the folded hand. The bones cracked.

Definitely dead or, at the least, dying.

"They'll have more soldiers here soon," Leif said. He pointed at a broad-lensed camera mounted in the corner, up where the wall met the ceiling.

"Oh, don't worry," the young man said, "the guys who monitor those cameras were playing cards the last time I walked by the security booth. We still need to hurry though."

"Doesn't it bother you at all that you just killed three men?" Jeffrey asked, staring at the kid's face, searching for his reaction to the question.

The young man looked at each body. He laughed and said, "I suppose it should. I've never so much as hit someone before, but it had to be done. Doesn't bother me though. I back my brother up one hundred percent. He said to help you, so I'm helping you. I suppose after what happened to him, every one of these bastards can die for all I care."

Frustrated anger showed in Jeffrey's voice as he asked one more time, "Who—the—hell—is your brother?"

"We really have to get going," the young man said, bringing out the syringe from his thigh pocket again. "You'll need this." He walked toward Jeffrey.

Jeffrey let him get close and then grabbed his wrist. He said, his voice growling in anger, "Who are you—who's your brother—and what's in that hypo?"

The young man tugged at his arm, and Jeffrey tightened his grip. The young man looked at the door and then back to Jeffrey.

"Okay, but then we get the hell out of here, right?"

"Exactly," Jeffrey said, and let go of the young man's wrist.

"My name's Kyle Morgan. My brother's Brennan Morgan. You tried to kill him. At least I thought you did, until I got a chance to talk to him. He told me what had happened, and how—laying in the freighter's wrecked bridge waiting to die—he'd had a revelation: the cause was wrong." Kyle Morgan picked up the collapsible baton, wiped it on his thigh and then slammed it end-down on the desk, shoving it back in on itself. He slid it into a thigh pocket.

"I was angry with him at first," he continued. "But I followed my brother into this, and when he talked me through his thought process, I realized he was right. Maxine King has to be stopped."

Jeffrey held up his hands. "I don't follow any of this. I don't know your brother. I've never met a Brennan Morgan, and I know I've never met you." Then Kyle Morgan looked back at the door. As he turned his head, Jeffrey saw the resemblance. Kyle's brother had turned the same way moments before he had been shot.

Jeffrey said, "Your brother was the first gunship's commander, the one who was shot by his own man. Shaggy blonde hair and a scar on his face, right?"

"Yeah, that's him," Kyle said. "You could have killed him, but you didn't. Instead, you gave him pain meds."

"You realize I would have killed him, given the need."

"No, that's not the point," Kyle said, looking back at the door. "Look, we have to get going now." He held up the syringe.

"Last thing," Jeffrey said. "What's in the syringe?"

"It's a local anesthetic and an anti-inflammatory mix," Kyle said. "That's what took me so long to get down here. I had to get this ready."

"You know about this stuff?" Jeffrey asked, unsure he wanted this kid to inject him with anything.

"I'm a medic. Brennan wanted me to join up, but I'm a conscientious objector myself. I'm more into helping."

"I would argue," Leif said, motioning toward the three bodies, "that you have a bit more self-discovery to do."

"Oh," Kyle looked over the bodies as he adjusted his glasses, "I suppose if I'm properly motivated…"

"Okay," Jeffrey said, "I don't have any other options, so let's do this."

Kyle grinned like a kid who had just been given permission to knock a hole in a wall. He walked around behind Jeffrey. Jeffrey felt the back of his shirt being lifted followed by a sharp pain in his lower back as the needle slid home. The spike of pain released, and then Jeffrey felt another spike.

"I'm giving you four injections, two on either side. This will block out a lot of the nerve impulses. You won't feel as much pain, but don't be fooled, your back is still messed up, so take it easy. You could end up crippling yourself. These injections are taking away an important message your body is giving you."

The pain in Jeffrey's back melted away, and he was left with only the numb feeling down his left leg. He took a step and the electric tingle ran down his right leg, but not painfully so.

"Better?" Kyle asked.

"Definitely."

"Great. Now I have to get you out of here."

Jeffrey reached down and pulled a tazer and baton off one of the bodies. Leif followed his example. Jeffrey took the third soldier's tazer and handed it to Kyle.

"We're not leaving," Jeffrey said. "You say you want to help?"

"My brother said to."

"Then help me find Maxine King."

CHAPTER 28

Maxine King slept in a drugged haze. As she rolled to one side, the bandage on her face crinkled. The stitched-in flesh shifted and pain, overreaching the drugs, stabbed deep into her skull. She woke with a moan. She tried to focus her eyes on the dark room, but could not. She closed her eyes and drifted. She remembered the doctor's face, too intimately close, as he stabbed her with anesthetic. He pressed the hooked needle into her lip with a dull pressure and then pulled it away from her, tugging the suture tight. He brought out a black tube with a cord and told her he was reattaching blood vessels. The smoke made her stomach clench.

She woke again and cursed through the bandages around her mouth. She could not get the doctor out of her head. Each time she closed her eyes it was the same. She looked at the clock next to her bed. Its green numbers blurred. She looked back into the unfocused darkness and felt she was not alone in the room. Out of the darkness, a large figure walked up to the bed and leaned over her. She concentrated on the blurred face, brought it into focus, and saw that it was Holt. She tried to call out for a soldier. As she opened her mouth, searing pain lit up her face. The darkness of the room smudged into violet watercolors. She let herself sink into the mattress. Her eyes closed, and the doctor was back in front of her, pulling the thread through her lip. The thread went taught and tugged at her numb face.

The doctor leaned in close again and said in a whisper, "You're a stupid bitch for letting her get that close to you."

Fury boiled up in her, trying to surface through the slick of drugs. However, she remembered the doctor was only a dream and calmed herself, nodding agreement.

"The most important thing is…," the doctor said.

Maxine focused on the doctor's face as he spoke, but when he opened his mouth to continue, a faint alarm came out. Maxine's eyes fluttered open to darkness. The door to her room opened, white light shocked her eyes, and the alarm blared. She pressed her hands over her drugged ears and closed her eyes. The doctor pulled at the thread again and spoke, but she could not hear him with her hands over her ears. She pulled her hands away, and the doctor said, "Maxine, I'm sorry, there's been an alarm, and…"

She opened her eyes and found Carter Roberts leaning over her. The door to her room had closed, muffling the alarm. She tried with some success to focus on Carter's face.

"We just need to make sure you're safe."

"An alarm?" she asked, her throat dry. "What's happened?"

"Nothing," Carter said, laying his hand on her forehead.

Carter has been such a good friend to me for so many years, so faithful. She felt safe with him beside her.

"We just need to check to make sure everything is secure, and then we'll be on our way." People moved through the room, their flashlights sweeping the walls.

She tried to speak again, but pain lanced through her lower jaw and up into her sinus. She pointed at the lights.

"They're doing a quick sweep of your room," Carter said, "just as a precaution."

"Why…" She wanted to ask him why a sweep was necessary but became confused.

Why are all these soldiers in my room?

She could not remember what Carter had said, and that frustrated her. She shoved Carter's hand off her forehead. Carter turned and walked away. The door opened, and the splitting light filled the room again. The alarm blared. The door shut, and everything became muffled. The loneliness of the room wrapped around her, and the pain killers drew her under. The doctor pulled the thread away from her face again and, as the thread went taught, tugged at the flesh.

"You will unite the world," the doctor said, "be its mother."

Why is this fool reminding me of this? Of course I will unite the world.

God had given her visions of the truth and shown her that she would be the one to create the next social revolution: peace and prosperity burned into the human race through nuclear fire. Thinking of the bombs again, she imagined the ships exploding, sweeping power from the warmongers' hands. She would hold military sovereignty and would use it to bring peace. These thoughts calmed her, and she slipped into a vast emptiness.

...

She woke at dawn. The drugs had receded enough to leave her with a stiff pain in her face, but she could focus her eyes and think clearly. She tried to piece together her disjointed memories from the night before.

Had Carter really come in here?

She thought of the dreams and became irritated. She should have more self-control. She had to be strong; she had a revolution to champion. Sitting up, she slid her feet to the carpet. She was fine. She stood up, walked to the door, opened it, and looked out. Two soldiers holding rifles looked over at her.

What in God's name had happened last night?

She closed the door and walked to the smooth, black panel of the intercom desk. She touched the panel, and displays imbedded in the obsidian surface turned on. She muted the video feed and dialed Roberts.

When he answered, she cut him off. Talking brought a tearing pain to her lower lip and jaw. The pain, coupled with the bandaging on her face, muddied her speech. "Mr. Roberts, what is going on?"

"Ma'am?"

"Why do I have guards with rifles at the door to my bedchamber?"

He did not answer. She heard him give a muffled order to someone.

"Mr. Roberts?"

"There's been a small problem," Carter Roberts said. "We'll have it in hand soon."

"What has happened?"

"Until we have it in hand, you should stay there."

"What the hell has happened?" She opened her mouth too far and winced.

"Holt and his son escaped last night."

Fear rushed through Maxine as if cold water had been poured down the tube of her spine. She considered the vision of Holt bending over her in the night.

He hadn't really been here. He would have attacked me. The vision merely foretold of his escape.

"Carter?"

"Yes, ma'am?"

"Did you come into my bedchamber last night?"

"Yes, after we were notified of the escape, we came in with a security detail and searched your bedchamber thoroughly."

"You found nothing?"

"You are safe there. We swept the area and then posted guards, two at the door and two at the end of the hallway."

"Thank you, Carter."

"Yes, ma'am. You are welcome, ma'am."

She tapped 'end call' on the screen and then placed her palms on the smooth surface of the desk, bracing herself against the burning in her face. As the clarity in her mind increased, so did the pain from her injury. She walked back to her bed and took the orange vial of pills from her night stand. She remembered the doctor prescribing them.

The label read: Take one pill by mouth every four hours, as needed for pain.

She sat on the edge of the bed and shook two of the pills into the palm of her hand. Then she slid the pills, one at a time, through her parted teeth. Taking a glass with a straw from the nightstand, she put the straw between her lips. She tried to sip at the straw and her lower lip flared with pain. Gripping her sheets with her free hand, she waited for the pain to pass. When it had diminished, she used her tongue against the roof of her mouth to trap and seal the straw, and sipped at the water. She set the glass down and swallowed the water.

She lay back on the bed and looked up at the vaulted ceiling. The pain in her face continued to grow in intensity. Tears began forming in her eyes as she wondered how much worse it would become. Then, a luxurious easiness spread over her. It started between her shoulder blades and melted up into her neck. When it reached her face, the pain diffused and faded away. The walls shifted to a cool, deep blue and seemed to lift away from her. The sunlight, coming through the garden windows, flowed with individual photons. She smiled, and a distant pressure reminded her to keep her face still. She inhaled. The air sliding through her teeth and into her nostrils felt like silk. Her eyes rolled back in her head, and stars turned above her in sparkling, blue hues.

From far away, she heard the click of a door. She opened her eyes. The ceiling spun back from the darkness of the stars, and she looked toward the garden. The door hung open, and the blue sky over the trees shimmered violet. She closed her eyes.

"You are a very beautiful woman," a voice said. The pitch of the voice ran along her spine with a brilliant green vibration, and the small of her back tingled. She smiled, feeling dull pressure in her lip.

"But not that smart."

What?

She opened her eyes and found Jeffrey Holt sitting on the bed beside her, the morning light glowing around his shoulders and head.

"Oh, the dream man is back," she said, feeling the distant ache in her mouth.

"I had no idea you felt that way."

"I do. You are a strange part of my mind, aren't you? Trying to scare me." She sat up, supporting herself on her elbows, and observed the aura surrounding this vision of Holt.

"Why are you here?"

"I'm going to convince you to stop those nukes."

He lifted a baton from his lap and smacked it in his palm. With each smack a cascade of stardust fell out of his hand.

What could this mean? Why am I envisioning him here now?

Jeffrey's son walked up beside him and she chuckled, saying, "You as well?"

Then a third man, who wore glasses, walked up.

The man said, "We have to hurry. The room's soundproofed, but someone could come at any moment. I locked the door, but it would be easy enough to kick in."

She squinted her eyes to better focus on the man's face. She did not know him. Then she looked at Jeffrey and his son, and she thought for a moment that they were real.

But I am safe here. Carter said so. Why is this vision of the third man coming to me?

She studied his face. Then she looked over all three men and noticed that they wore black uniforms, the same style Carter issued to her soldiers.

What could that mean?

"She's so drugged up she won't feel a thing," Holt's son said.

"Dammit," Holt said, "look at her. She isn't even afraid."

"Why should I be afraid of you?" she asked Holt. "You can't stop that which is destined to be."

Holt raised the baton and brought it down on her shin. She heard a resonant thump, but only felt a dull sensation pressing into her leg, as if something soft and heavy had been set there. She studied their faces, intent on understanding the vision.

258

"You see?" Holt said. "Nothing."

That's it! I am receiving a confirmation that God will not let me fail. Holt, the last symbol of resistance, cannot hurt me; he cannot stop me.

She felt the joy of impending victory rise up again.

"That's not a problem," the man wearing glasses said, as he inspected the vial by her bed. "I've got a counter-agent to this painkiller. Jesus, how much of this did you take, woman?" She held up two fingers in response.

"No wonder," the man wearing glasses said. He took a bag out, unzipped it, and reached in. Glass vials clicked against each other as he shifted his hand through the bag. The tinkling glass echoed through Maxine's mind, crystalline. Her eyes fluttered closed and the stars, more intense this time, flew around her. Her heart filled with the joy of success and perfect wellbeing. She felt pressure on her arm. Opening her eyes, she looked down. The man wearing glasses had injected her with something.

A cold sensation began to flow up her arm. It felt wonderful, as if someone had poured deep-blue water from a glacial lake into her bloodstream. The coolness drifted into her chest and she felt her heart pulsing it into the rest of her body. Then the wonderful world clarified into a horrific pain in her face and shin. Her eyes focused along with her mind. She cried out at the sudden rush of pain, and her hands came to her face as she felt the stitches pull at the skin. Tears warped her vision and then spilled, in heated trails, down her cheeks.

She looked back at the three men and then at the pulsing, heavy ache in her leg. There, a contusion already showed on the flat of her shin. She looked over Holt's shoulder, toward the door. It was so far away. She yelped out a scream, but the intensity of the pain caused her to swallow back the sound. She coughed, which brought even more pain.

She had to get away, had to get to her guards. She rolled away from them to the left side of the bed and fell to the floor. She scrambled to her feet and ran, as best as she could, for the garden door. A tremendous blow smacked her skull and the carpet flipped up and hit her. Holt's baton landed next to her. Her head spun and nausea soured her guts. She came up onto her hands and knees. The thought of vomiting into her stitched mouth made her stomach turn even more, and it came up. She tried to open her mouth, but pain stopped her. The vomit filled her mouth and sprayed between her partially separated teeth. It filled her nose and shot out both nostrils, spraying the carpet in front of her. She felt warmth speckling her hands and forearms.

She gagged and coughed. The rest of the vomit drooled through her teeth as the stomach acid brought blazing pain to her lower lip. She spit the remaining chunks out as best she could.

"Look at her," Holt said. "She's a train wreck."

She looked over her shoulder. The three men had walked around the bed and now stood behind her.

Holt's son said, "I think we should give her what she gave Stacy." In his eyes, she saw devotion to the idea.

"No, let's finish this the right way," Holt said. "There are more important matters at hand than revenge for Stacy's death."

"What?" The man wearing glasses said, as he zipped up his medicine kit. "Your friend you mean?"

"Yes, Maxine here ordered her beaten to death and–" Holt began, but the man with glasses interrupted.

"Oh, she's not dead, at least not the last time I saw her."

"What?" Holt grabbed the man's arm. Maxine didn't hesitate. She began crawling toward the garden door.

Her focus on the open door distracted her from the pain in her face. Behind her, she heard the man wearing glasses say, "I'm sorry, this whole time... with everything else going on, I didn't think to tell you."

Weakness trembled in her arms as she pulled herself along the carpeting. She saw the exterior garden entrance across the grass. If she could get to the other side of the garden, get through that door, she would surely find some of her soldiers.

The man said, "I was in the hallway when you were dragged out. I blended in with the other soldiers. They called for a body bag and a gurney. When it arrived, I walked in right behind it and then helped them push the gurney to the infirmary. The other soldiers just left. They thought she was dead."

Maxine had crossed over half the distance to the garden door.

Just a few more feet, and then I'll get up and run.

"They thought she wasn't breathing, but she was, shallowly. To survive a beating like that, well... there's no debating how strong she is. I started emergency care on her–pulse, blood pressure–and when the duty nurse came in, he began assisting me without question. A doctor arrived and she and the nurse took over, stabilizing her. Due to the amount of head trauma, the doctor sedated her with a propofol IV drip, effectively inducing a coma."

"She's a mess right now, but they're looking after her. She could end up in a vegetative state due to those skull fractures. I've seen that before in vehicle accidents. I'm guessing there's bone fragments in...," but he trailed off, and then said, "She's going need some pretty serious help, and soon."

Maxine heard Holt say, "Why the hell didn't you tell us this before? We have to get this moving."

I'm close enough now, but they will be on me the moment I run. They are probably faster, but I have a good lead now.

She braced her arms and legs on the floor and then lunged forward. Her nightgown did not move with her, but caught on something. Some threads in the shoulders ripped, but the garment held. Her bare feet slipped on the carpeting, and she landed on her elbows. She looked down. A boot, with dirt in the tread, pinned the hemline of her nightgown to the floor. She looked up to find Holt's son staring down at her.

Holt walked over to her, grabbed her arms, and yanked her to her feet.

"You're going to get Sam Cantwell on the intercom for me."

"No."

"This isn't a debate. You'll do it." He pushed her ahead of him to the console. He touched the console, and the screen lit up with the United Aerospace logo. Then the screen darkened and "Locked—Enter Passcode" appeared.

Maxine said through her bandages, "In a few hours, the entire military fleet will be destroyed. In a few minutes, that door will be broken down. You will be traitors in the New World."

Holt sighed just as someone knocked on the door. Maxine tried to yell out, but Holt's son slapped his hand over her mouth, bandages and all. The pain was transcendental. Her shout, pinned in her mouth, boiled out her eyes as tears. She wanted to fall to the floor, to let all of her muscles go slack, to fall away from the pain in her face, but Holt's son held her up.

The intercom beside the door flicked to life, and Carter's voice said, "Maxine? Are you up?" Another knock at the door. "Maxine? Is everything all right?"

Holt walked toward the door and motioned for his son to follow with Maxine. When they reached the door, Holt turned to face her. He took out a black knife, unfolded it, and touched the tip of the blade to Maxine's lower eyelid. She felt the blade bite into the skin. The cut burned with the salt from her tears.

Holt leaned in on her. "If you struggle, I could slip."

Maxine held her head still.

"Now, Leif is going to let you talk, but if you yell, I blind you. Got it?"

With the blade resting on her eye socket, she nodded ever so slightly. Holt motioned to his son, and he released his grip on her mouth. Holt pressed the intercom switch by the door and then made a circular "get talking" motion with his hand.

She said, "Yes. I'm fine." Holt released the intercom switch.

The door handle dipped down, and Holt cursed under his breath. The door stopped against the lock.

The intercom clicked again. "Maxine, open the door."

Holt turned to Maxine. "Tell him to let you have a few–" but the lock on the door disengaged, and it opened.

As it opened, Holt took two quick steps to stand behind it. Maxine saw Holt fold his knife and pocket it. Carter walked in and Holt shut the door with a gentle click. Carter's head turned just as Holt's fist slammed into his jaw. Carter fell to his knees and began to tip over. Holt grabbed him and covered his mouth with the palm of his hand. Holt turned Carter toward Maxine. Carter's glazed eyes drifted for a moment. Then they focused, and he looked straight at her. He began to struggle, grabbing Holt's arms and wrenching on them. But he could not break free.

Holt leaned down to his ear. "If you keep struggling, and make too much noise, you both die."

Carter stopped fighting Holt, and Holt took his hand off Carter's mouth. Carter looked at Maxine, concern in his eyes. Maxine thought she must look terrible to him.

Worry for her showed through in his tone as he asked, "What have you done to her?"

Holt's son said, "Nothing she hasn't fully earned."

Holt pushed Carter over to the intercom desk. He took out a pair of handcuffs and restrained Carter's hands behind his back.

"Now, one of you, I don't care who, is going to set up a channel to Admiral Sam Cantwell, or someone is going to start losing skin."

CHAPTER 29

As Jeffrey stared at Maxine King, his anger faded to disappointment. With her face bandaged, eyes red, and shoulders bent forward in defeat, she just wasn't the same arrogant witch. Jeffrey had wanted revenge, but now only felt sorrow that he had been unable to prevent Stacy's beating.

Put it aside. Right now I have to stay focused on the orbiting ships. The clock hasn't run out on those men and women.

Jeffrey pushed Roberts to his knees and sat in the chair beside him. The console had gone dark, so he touched it, and "Locked—Enter Passcode" re-appeared.

Jeffrey looked at Roberts. "Enter the code."

Roberts' eyes tracked from the screen to Jeffrey, but he said nothing.

"Not going to help me?"

"No."

Jeffrey pointed at Maxine King. "You're going to let people die because of that woman's delusion? She's a little insane looking to me."

Roberts looked over to Maxine. "She will always be beautiful to me."

Leif said, "You people aren't all there, you know that?"

"I'll get the code one way or another," Jeffrey said. "Just enter it now and save you and her the trouble."

Roberts turned and glared at Jeffrey. Jeffrey met his glare, waiting for Roberts to speak, but Roberts said nothing.

Jeffrey felt anger rising up in his chest, and blurring to rage.

I've had my limit of these two.

He drew air deep into his lungs and let it go, his chest depressurizing. But the frustrated anger stayed with him. His right hand gripped into a fist. He breathed again.

Anger makes a poor companion. You'll adrenalize and make stupid mistakes.

Roberts continued giving him a blank stare.

Rage flared up beyond Jeffrey's self-control. He grabbed Roberts by the back of the neck, digging his fingertips into the nerve bundles. Roberts, probably a military man himself at some point in his past, put his hands on the desk and pushed back on Jeffrey's grip. Jeffrey let Roberts push back a few inches and then shoved him forward, slamming him face-first into the edge of the communication desk. Then he pulled Roberts back. Blood coursed from the ruined bridge of Roberts' nose.

"You want more?" Jeffrey said, digging his fingers into Roberts' neck harder, wanting to crush the vertebrae to powder. "Tell me the passcode. Now."

Roberts' eyes lolled in their sockets and then focused on Jeffrey. He spit out some blood. "Nothing you do can make me help you."

Jeffrey released Robert's neck and looked at Maxine. He stood and said to Kyle Morgan, "Make sure he stays on his knees."

Jeffrey motioned for Leif to bring Maxine to him. Leif shoved her forward. Jeffrey waited until she was close, and then–in a quiet, calm voice–he said, "Do you want to tell me the passcode?"

She opened her bandaged mouth slightly and spit on Jeffrey's chest. Roberts chuckled behind him. Jeffrey looked over his shoulder and then back at Maxine.

"So be it," he said. He took the knife from his pocket and clacked it open, one-handed.

He said to Leif, "Hold out one of her index fingers."

"What are you going to do?" Maxine said through her teeth. Jeffrey smiled at her, hoping to make her believe that he was sadistic enough to enjoy what was about to happen.

"Nothing," he said, "if you tell me the passcode."

She closed her eyes. "This is a test from God. I will prevail. He has shown me."

"You know what I think?" Jeffrey said, touching the flat of the blade to her cheek. "I think God prefers people like Stacy Zack."

Maxine's eyes opened, and Jeffrey saw fury in them.

Jeffrey gripped the tip of her silver fingernail between his thumb and index finger. Maxine tried to pull her hand away. Leif held her still. Jeffrey set the edge of the blade up under her fingernail and sliced slightly into the skin. Maxine screamed and tugged at her arm.

"Last chance."

"Oh dear God," Maxine said through her teeth, "help me." Her whole body shook, and she said, "Carter, I can't be ruined, don't let them, tell them the passcode. I can't."

"Not now, Maxine," Roberts said. With his hands still cuffed behind his back, he leaned his shoulder into the desk, stood, and turned toward her. Kyle grabbed his shoulder and Roberts pulled away from him. "You can't give up now." He spit blood onto the carpet. "I know you're afraid, but take strength in your vision."

"They'll kill me," she said.

"You cannot die," Roberts said, his voice now soothing. "You're the mother of the New World. It has been decided by God. We will change the face of human civilization together. You have to remain strong."

Jeffrey said, "Enough," and nodded to Kyle.

Kyle grabbed Roberts by the upper arm and tried to pull him down to his knees, but Roberts turned and drove his shoulder into Kyle, knocking him to the floor. Kyle scrambled to his feet.

"The baton to the side of the knee perhaps?" Jeffrey said.

Kyle pulled his baton from his belt, and swung it at Roberts' left knee. Roberts hopped back, and Kyle missed.

"Dammit," Jeffrey said, stepping around from behind Maxine. Roberts turned toward Jeffrey just as Jeffrey's hand, palm open, caught Roberts under the chin. The strike lifted Roberts off his feet, and he landed on his back with a punt of breath.

"You get up again," Jeffrey said, "and you'll regret it."

Roberts rolled to his side, groaning.

Jeffrey walked around behind Maxine and grabbed the tip of her fingernail. In one sliding sweep, he sliced the nail and nail bed from her finger. Maxine's eyes went wide, and her mouth came open. Chest fluttering, she seemed unable to draw a breath. Her face tinted red, and her shoulders trembled. Finally, she sucked in air and screamed.

"Tear a stitch?" Jeffrey held out the nail with the meaty underside up. "I can do all ten. Then I'll begin cutting off the finger joints themselves. We'll cauterize the stubs with an open flame to keep you from bleeding out."

Maxine trembled now in the involuntary manner of the hypothermic. She slouched over and, as tears ran from her eyes, twisted her head from side to side. She looked at Jeffrey, and her eyes begged him to stop.

Jeffrey tossed the fingernail to the carpet. "Get her thumb out." Then he said to Maxine, "Did God tell you what sort of condition you'd be in as the mother of the New World?"

Leif's fingers wrapped around her thumb, and Jeffrey grabbed the tip of the nail. He placed the blade under the nail, again cutting the skin just a bit. A bead of blood welled up from the cut.

Maxine winced, looked at the desk, and—her words muffled by the bandaging—said, "Communications console, Maxine King zero-zero-eight, open channel, contact Admiral Sam Cantwell."

The "locked" image darkened. Then the desk illuminated with the United Aerospace insignia. A professional female voice said, "Voice recognition not confirmed, please re-state."

"You cowardly bitch," Roberts shouted at her. "How dare you give in. Don't you know what this will mean?"

Maxine glanced at Roberts and then stared at the desk. Kyle flicked at a syringe, jabbed it into the side of Roberts' neck, and Maxine's last line of defense folded over, unconscious on the floor.

Jeffrey cut deeper into the tip of her thumb, and Maxine let out a trilling shriek as she tried to yank her hand free. Jeffrey and Leif held her in place. She looked at Jeffrey, her eyes terrified. "Please stop."

"Unlock the console," Jeffrey said, "and I'll stop."

She nodded and said with slow, careful words, "Communications console, Maxine King zero-zero-eight, open channel, contact Admiral Sam Cantwell."

"Verified," the female voice said. "Raising contact Admiral Sam Cantwell."

Maxine lowered her head.

Jeffrey said to Kyle, "Bandage her finger."

From the console, an older, male voice said with uncharacteristic shock, "Hello? Maxine?"

Jeffrey looked at the screen and saw Sam Cantwell's weathered face. The concern in Cantwell's faded-blue eyes darkened to scowling animosity when he saw Jeffrey.

"Holt? What the hell is going on? Why does this call show as coming from Maxine King's residence?"

CHAPTER 30

"Admiral Cantwell, how are you today?"

"Cut the crap, Holt. I've been briefed on what you've done over the last few days. What the hell's gone wrong with you? Did you have some kind of post-traumatic reaction when United Aerospace came to inspect the site? They show up for a routine engineering inspection and you start killing them. You need to stand down and turn yourself in."

Jeffrey motioned for Leif to bring Maxine King to him. He pointed to the screen and said to Maxine, "Tell him."

"Sam," Maxine said with deference, "Jeffrey Holt thinks that I am out to destroy the world's military."

Her audacity shocked Jeffrey. He looked at the fingernail on the carpet.

"Jesus Holy Christ, Holt," Cantwell said, leaning in to look at Maxine. "What have you done to her?"

"Sir," Jeffrey said, "she thinks the war never happened. She has fostered a cult within her staff and has a standing army ready to take power once she has destroyed the fleet."

Admiral Cantwell stared at Jeffrey with his mouth slightly open.

"Look, sir," Jeffrey said, "I know this sounds insane, but…"

"That's enough, Holt," Cantwell said. "This doesn't just sound insane, it is insane. You're having some kind of post-traumatic stress reaction. Now I realize that you…"

"They tried to kill Stacy Zack and did kill the rest of her team."

"Who the hell is Stacy Zack?" Cantwell said, and then shook his head. "It doesn't matter. You need to stand down. Let Maxine go and let her security take over."

Cantwell pressed a switch on the desk in front of him and leaned into a microphone.

"Miramar Base commander?"

A muffled voice responded.

"Send a force to Maxine King's residence to assist her security forces in dealing with a hostage situation."

The muffled voice said something.

Cantwell said, "Just get some soldiers moving now. I'll keep you informed. And let King's security forces know you are coming."

"Sam," Jeffrey said, "if anyone comes through that door, Maxine dies. Got it?" At this point, Jeffrey did not know if he was bluffing or if he really would kill Maxine.

Cantwell scowled. He pressed the button on the desk and said into the microphone, "Belay my order to notify her security forces until the situation can be coordinated, but get your troops en-route now."

Cantwell looked up from the desk. "That's the most I can do for you, Jeffrey. If you surrender peacefully, you won't be harmed." He looked at Maxine. The anger in his eyes shifted to concern. He looked back at Jeffrey. "Jeffrey, you're not well. Does that strike you as a possibility?"

Jeffrey looked at Leif.

Had this all been a breakdown?

He tried to think back to the beginning.

I'm sure I reacted correctly. It's all been real. Maxine admitted it. Freisman admitted it. The bodies were real enough. So was Stacy. But, in the bridge of the freighter, I shot first...

Jeffrey looked back at Cantwell. "Look Sam, we've known each other a long time. So, I need you to trust me—"

"Jeffrey, you have to stand down now—"

"No," Jeffrey shouted at the screen. "You have to listen to me. If you won't do it, I'll use Maxine here to make you listen to me."

"Jeffrey... you're not well," Cantwell said.

Jeffrey gripped Maxine by her hair and pushed her close to the camera. Then he held the knife next to her face. He couldn't just make her confess now. Cantwell would only see that as the pressure of coercion. Given enough pain, she would claim to be the King of Morocco.

"You're going to do one small thing for me," Jeffrey said to Cantwell. "Then we keep talking."

Cantwell gave a small nod.

"Have your technicians check your fusion reactors. If I'm crazy, you won't find anything out of order. Scan for plutonium, or whatever you do. Maxine here has had her technicians plant nukes in your reactor cores while servicing each ship. According to her, they'll go off in the next few hours, splitting your ship and all the other ships in the fleet inside out. Stacy Zack and her team stumbled onto one of those devices during a training exercise. That's why Maxine wanted her dead."

"Jeffrey," Cantwell said, his tone now pleading, "be reasonable. Does that sound likely at all?"

"I'm not asking you, Cantwell. I'm telling you," Jeffrey dipped the tip of the blade into Maxine's cheek and she screamed through her teeth.

"Jeffrey, Maxine King is a great supporter of the military—"

"Do it. Now."

Cantwell held up his hands. "Okay, I'll have a crew check our reactors right now. If we find nothing, will you at least consider the option that you need to give yourself up and get help?"

"Sure," Jeffrey said. "Yes." But he didn't mean it in the slightest.

If they don't find a nuke on Cantwell's ship, does that mean he's involved? Or does that mean I'm wrong? Might Cantwell's ship not be rigged? If there's no device...

Jeffrey looked over his shoulder at Kyle and Leif. Then he looked back at the screen.

I have no backup plan. I'm trapped in Maxine's mansion, surrounded by her private army, and only have two men... I also have to consider one barely alive woman I can't leave behind.

"Good," Cantwell said. He turned his back on the camera, called an officer over to him, and issued some orders to her that Jeffrey could not make out.

I hope he's not just humoring me. He really appears to think that I've gone insane. If that's true, perhaps he isn't involved with Maxine. But he's a politician as much as a military man. His career has depended on his ability to cover his intentions and reactions.

Cantwell sat on the side of the screen not looking at Holt. A man walked up to Cantwell with a clipboard. Cantwell waved him away with a snap of his hand.

Minutes passed, and Jeffrey became more and more nervous.

Are they checking the ship, or stalling for time?

He looked over his shoulder at the door and felt the hairs on his neck prickle as he thought of the door being kicked in. With a warning from Cantwell, which might have already been given, Maxine's security forces would be on them. Then it was do or die.

"No games, Sam," Jeffrey said. "No games, or Maxine will suffer, understood?"

Cantwell's eyes flicked up to the screen. "I'm just waiting for a report back. You'll have my full cooperation until then. I can offer you at least that much." Cantwell looked at Maxine and concern again came to his eyes. "Darling, are you all right?"

"Darling?" Jeffrey looked at Maxine. "Are you sleeping with Sam Cantwell too?"

She said nothing, just whimpered a bit.

Jeffrey looked at Cantwell who flushed red and stared at Jeffrey, daring him.

"That's quite a slip of words, Admiral. Something you want to say?"

Cantwell's wife's a congresswoman. An affair would ruin him... If he really does have an affair going with Maxine King, then this is a dead end.

Sam Cantwell said nothing, and Jeffrey felt his last shred of hope slip away.

Jeffrey looked over his shoulder. "Kyle, get Roberts' side arm and cover that door. I have a feeling we're going to have some company soon." He pushed Maxine over to Leif.

"Get her between you and the door. If you see something get thrown into the room, close your eyes. They'll probably come in behind a flash grenade. Once the flash is over, keep her between you and anyone who comes in the door."

Jeffrey looked at the screen and saw Cantwell now had his back to the camera. He talked with the officer he had earlier given orders to. As she spoke, she jabbed her finger toward the floor of the bridge. Jeffrey could not make out her words but saw urgency in her eyes.

Cantwell turned and looked at Maxine. "How could you… even *consider* this as the right way?"

"There is no time, Sam. I am sorry that you and your crew will die, but it is the divine—" Maxine began, but fell silent when Cantwell waved her comment aside.

He pressed his thumb on the desk, and a panel opened. He slapped his palm on a button and said into a microphone, "This is a red alert. All hands to stations."

Maxine turned to Holt. "There is not enough time to evacuate the ships."

On the wall behind Cantwell, red lights began rolling in caged housings. He entered something into the console on the desk and leaned in on the microphone again.

"Send an emergency message to all ships' commanders." He paused and then said, "This is Admiral Sam Cantwell. We have a situation. It is possible that nuclear devices have been planted on U.S. Navy ships. Send teams to inspect all fusion reactors. Do not attempt to disarm the devices as the example we have has a detonation time of less than fifteen minutes. Follow emergency reactor ejection for the rigged cores. Make all other actions secondary to this task. Complete reactor surveys, and then follow up with sweeps of the entire ship.

Report on status immediately. Note: this is not a drill. Again, this is a live situation, not a drill. End message."

Cantwell looked back up to Jeffrey, "I owe you an apology, Holt, but I don't have time for it now."

"They can't eject the cores," Maxine said, her eyes pleading for it to be true. She looked at Cantwell. "You can't eject the cores, there's no mechanism for that."

Cantwell stared at Maxine and said, "Yes, we can. We make some changes to our reactor cores after delivery, classified of course. In this case, it appears those changes actually stayed classified."

A wave of relief ran through Jeffrey. He wanted to say something, but could not think what it might be. He felt tired, and old. Then he thought of what he needed to say. "I do need one more thing before you go, sir."

"Yes, what's that?"

"Your troops coming here, don't forget to re-clarify who they are coming for."

Cantwell nodded. "Yes, of course." He tapped the desk in front of him, then leaned in on the microphone. "Miramar Base commander,"

There was a muffled response.

Cantwell said, "Inform troops en route to Maxine King's residence that she is being held in custody by three men. One Jeffrey Holt is in command of that group. Assist Mr. Holt in securing Maxine King. Send additional troops now in a number great enough to take King's local security force into custody. Secure all weapons systems, including vehicles and aircraft."

Jeffrey heard more muffled comments.

"I appreciate your concerns, ma'am. I will give you more detail later."

Sam Cantwell looked back at Jeffrey, his expression now grave. "I'm sorry Jeffrey—"

Jeffrey interrupted him. "I could care less at this point."

"Understood." Cantwell looked at Maxine and said, "I don't understand. How could you?"

Anger came to her tear-streaked eyes. She said through her teeth, "You know the war was faked. Everything you are is a lie. You know what the government did to you. Any fool can see that this must happen."

Cantwell shook his head, "Any fool might see that, but it isn't going to happen, Maxine. As we speak, your nuclear devices are being jettisoned into space and destroyed by fighters. Other nations' ships you have contracts with are being notified as well."

"It can't be over," she said. "God told me."

"I can't help you with that," Cantwell said, and pressed a switch on the desk. The screen went to the blue and white United Aerospace logo.

Maxine King looked at Jeffrey, then at Kyle, and then to her unconscious Roberts. "It can't be over," she said, and her legs gave out. Leif set her down on the floor. She sat with her legs askew and looked up at Jeffrey, confused. "You can't stop me."

Jeffrey looked at the door. "We need to get to Stacy."

Kyle said, "What we need to do is wait here for support troops. We're still in the center of the hive, and no one out there knows they're on the losing side. Not yet." He walked over to Jeffrey and put his hand on Jeffrey's shoulder. "Our being with her will have nothing to do with her living or dying at this point. If she is tough enough, she'll make it. If not, our being there won't stop her dying."

EPILOGUE

Jeffrey looked over the project plan on his computer screen and then typed into the current calendar day: "Demolition of the forward cabin of the Jules Verne freighter has been completed as of today. Work will begin on the port engine nacelle Monday." At the top of the calendar, bright-yellow text read: "Project currently overdue three months, one week, and two days."

He leaned back in his chair.

I hate being this far behind in my project schedule. If the damn bean counters would just let me reset the clock.

But the project managers had told him a reset would interfere with the landing schedule.

"Try to make up as much time as you can," the office had said.

He stood up and stretched. The work the doctors had done on his back still amazed him. His two new titanium lumbars had him up and walking in a few weeks. His back felt twenty years old, but the dull ache from his knees reminded him of his age. He pushed on his back again, remembering the pain he had been in when Kyle Morgan's injection had worn off. His spine had felt as though it was shattered glass, cutting into the muscle. He remembered soldiers lifting him onto a stretcher and carrying him to a waiting transport. A medic, wearing BDU's with a red cross on her chest, walked beside him. She held up an IV bag with one hand. When she released the clamp with the other hand, Jeffrey's vision blurred, and he faded into wonderful nothingness.

The day after Jeffrey came out of surgery, Leif visited him at Miramar. He told Jeffrey that the military had taken Maxine to a maximum-security hospital. Leif mentioned Carter Robert's imprisonment, but Jeffrey waved that away. He only wanted to know one thing: how was Stacy? Leif told him that she had been transported to the East Coast. Leading neurosurgeons had repaired her skull, but when the doctors shut off the propofol drip she had stayed in a coma. There was nothing left to do but wait and see how she responded. The doctors had no idea if she would regain consciousness, or what state her mind would be in if she did. Leif knew nothing beyond that.

A few days later, Sam Cantwell had visited. He entered the room, not as his usual self, striding in and taking over the space, but slowly, almost apologetically. He nodded at Jeffrey and then sat in the chair beside the bed in silence. He leaned forward with his elbows on his knees and stared at the floor, hunched and somehow beaten. At first, Jeffrey did not know what to say, so he began by retelling Cantwell everything that had happened from the first to the last.

When he had finished, Cantwell looked up at him with tired eyes. "I'm sorry I doubted you, Jeffrey."

"This is bigger than losing reactors, isn't it?"

Cantwell sighed and put his head in his hands.

"Did you know her plan for the fleet?"

"No, of course not," Cantwell said without defense. "I'd have stopped her if I had. She knew me well enough to know how to play that card. She told me just enough to gain the access she needed and nothing more."

"Did you think Maxine was right about the war?"

"In the end, I believed her," Cantwell said, as he leaned back in his chair and looked at the ceiling. "She was compelling. I fought in the war, or at least I think I did." He looked back at Jeffrey. "The war seemed so unreal anyway; it just made sense to me. I suppose, after all these years, part of me really hoped it had all been an implanted lie. That meant none of it was real. The memories have haunted me so many years..."

Jeffrey could only nod at this. He knew of a way to set the issue to rest, but he considered that Cantwell might not want to know. Jeffrey also felt tempted by the possibility that a lifetime of nightmares and sorrow never actually happened. However, he had to know one way or the other. Those memories had shaped his life so much that, if they were implants, his entire self had become a fabrication.

Cantwell said, "I don't know what to believe anymore, Jeffrey. I do know that my carelessness nearly killed thousands of service men and women." He looked up at Jeffrey and then back to the floor. Jeffrey saw that the fire had gone out of Cantwell. His honor and purpose had collapsed, and all that remained sitting with Jeffrey in that hospital room was an old man.

"I'm preparing my resignation," Cantwell said.

"Don't be an asshole."

Cantwell lifted his head and looked at Jeffrey.

"The Navy needs you, Sam. There are too many officers serving who only have theory in their heads. You know that if another invasion occurred, we'd be lost without experienced leaders."

Jeffrey thought he saw a glint of the former soldier in the man's eyes.

"What right do you have to say that to me after hiding in a scrap yard for 40 years?"

Jeffrey shook his head, saying, "I'm no politician, Sam. I'm no use outside of war. But I'll make you a deal. If you stick with it, I'll be the first person to walk into your office if there's ever another invasion."

Cantwell stared at the floor for a moment and then nodded. "I'll have to think about it." He looked at Jeffrey. "I can't tell you how much..." he trailed off and then shrugged, saying, "You've saved so many lives, Jeffrey."

"There's only one life hanging in the balance right now that I care about."

"Yes. I think she'll pull through, if she's as tough as you've said."

"I don't need hope, Sam. I need her to be okay."

Cantwell nodded and then said, "Still, we're all in your debt. If there's ever anything we can do for you, just let us know."

Jeffrey had intended what he'd said next to be a joke, something to lighten the mood. He hadn't understood that when Cantwell had said "anything" he'd meant it.

Jeffrey made his request, and Cantwell gave a curt nod, stood, said, "I'll get right on it," and walked out of the room. Jeffrey sat in shocked silence for some time after.

Jeffrey smiled at the memory as he walked over to the cabinet. He took off his new Gorilla control jumpsuit. The suit's metal rings clicked on the cabinet as he hung it up. He put on his dungarees and a blue t-shirt. He laced up his scarred boots, and walked to the door.

Pulling open the door, he stepped out of the bunker and into the warm autumn air. He looked at the landing pad. There, throwing a long shadow across the desert floor, sat the result of Cantwell's promise: a new Kiowa gunship, its nose cannon and missile pods removed. Jeffrey walked around behind the gunship and pressed his thumb on the locking pad. A bar of green light scanned it. He pressed the switch next to the pad, and the Kiowa's ramp lowered to the tarmac. He walked inside and pressed another switch. The interior dimmed as the ramp lifted and thumped closed. He moved into the cockpit, settled into the pilot's seat, and strapped himself in. The Kiowa's interior still held the faint ozone scent of new electronics and fresh welds.

With a practiced run of fingers, he brought the systems up and fired the engines. He left the flight helmet attached to its holder. The engines warmed. Even after the indicators turned green, he waited a few moments. The military had agreed to maintain the ship for him, including unlimited access to fuel, but he did not want to be ungracious in its treatment.

He pulled the stick back, lifting the gunship fifty feet above the roof of the concrete bunker. Then he flew out over the folded Gorilla and the orderly stacks of material. As he came to the end of the stacks, he pulled the nose of the ship back, aimed it at the mountain ridge, and throttled on, shooting out of the small valley. He leaned the gunship left and looked down on the Jules Verne. The footprints of the Gorilla lay all around the crash site. Where sections of wreckage had landed, now only circles of footprints surrounded empty craters. The main body of the freighter lay out on the lakebed like a decapitated beast, ending in a flat bulkhead just past the engines.

Jeffrey dropped the right wing down, turning the gunship due west. He leveled off and slid the throttle forward to its stops, heading for Ramona, California.

...

As he approached inhabited areas, he throttled back and kept the gunship just below the speed of sound. When he arrived at the Ramona airport, the surrounding mountains threw long shadows out across the runway. He turned the ship in and set down on the tarmac. Unstrapping himself, he walked into the darkness of the troop area, his boots thumping on the metal decking. He pressed the switch, and the ramp opened, hissing as it lowered. He stepped out on it, riding it down to the blacktop.

He did not see Leif's car in the parking area, and he scanned the road. Finally, he caught sight of the car coming up between two hangars. Jeffrey stepped off the ramp and walked across the tarmac. As he walked around the chain link fence to the parking area, Leif's car pulled into a parking space. The driver's door opened, and Leif got out. Leif had the same thin frame and loose t-shirt. Yet, he had changed, grown bolder. When they made eye contact—instead of glancing away—he stared longer, searching his father's face.

"Where is she?" Jeffrey asked.

"It's good to see you too," Leif said. "At least I know where your allegiance is."

Jeffrey opened his mouth to reply, but the passenger door of the car opened and a cane came up out of the car, clanking on the window frame.

Jeffrey moved around Leif, but Leif grabbed his arm and said in a quiet voice, "Let her alone, she wants to do things herself."

Jeffrey nodded.

Stacy gripped the window frame with one hand, pressed on the cane with the other, and stood up out of the car. As she came around the car, Jeffrey noticed that she had even less of a limp than the last time he had seen her. Her hair had grown longer as well, almost to the length it had been when they first met.

He walked over to her and said, "You shouldn't be pushing yourself."

She propped the cane on her hip and wrapped her arms around him. Jeffrey gripped her in his embrace and kissed the top of her head. He loved her as if he had known her from the day she was born. The aliveness of her, her warmth, welled tears in his eyes. It had been this way each time he had seen her during her recovery. The first several times, he couldn't touch her hand or arm without breaking down entirely. But lately he had done better.

Stacy let him go and, looking up at him, smiled.

He took hold of her chin and tilted her head. The surgeons had shown their skill, rebuilding the bone structure and removing all the scars but one, which ran across her cheek. Aside from the one scar and her limp, she showed no signs of what she had been through. That included her attitude, which had been fiercely positive from the moment she regained consciousness. Yet, her smile did not shine in her eyes.

Jeffrey had watched the grief from the loss of her father darken each moment of her recovery.

It may be difficult for her to believe right now, but it will get easier.

"How's your mother holding up?"

"She's okay... not very good really. Losing him has been really hard on her."

Jeffrey could only nod at that.

He touched her cheekbone. "Why don't you let them remove that last scar?"

She pushed his hand away. "What? The one you gave me with your crappy stitching? Never. It's mine."

He touched the scar again, and tears overwhelmed him. He lifted the collar of his t-shirt and pressed it into his eyes.

"Oh my God, Jeffrey," she said, in a mocking but tender way, "you've got to get over this. It's water under the bridge. I'm okay now."

"I know," Jeffrey said, his voice still a bit unstable, "I know."

Leif pulled two suitcases from the trunk of the car, set them down beside Jeffrey, and pushed the trunk closed. Jeffrey picked up the bags.

"Dad, leave me something to carry."

Jeffrey smiled and said, "I've got a metal spine, kid. Back off. Help Stacy."

"I can get there myself," Stacy said, and began limping toward the gate.

"Sure you can," Jeffrey said, "but I'm not going to wait all night watching you hobble your short self all the way over there."

Leif came up to her and took hold of her arm. She scowled at him.

"You heard the man," Leif said. "He's old and short on time."

"Not exactly how I put it," Jeffrey said, as he pushed open the gate and walked out onto the tarmac, toward the gunship.

...

When Jeffrey had himself settled into the pilot's seat, he asked, "You folks strapped in?"

"We're almost ready," Stacy said from the back. "What's in this crate back here?"

"A boat," Jeffrey said.

"A boat?"

"Make sure to strap in tight," Jeffrey said over his shoulder. "I feel like having some fun tonight."

"Be nice," Stacy said. "I would like to live through a weekend camping trip."

Jeffrey smiled and said, "Have a little faith." Pulling the gunship off the tarmac smooth but fast, he shoved the throttle on, leaving the airport in a wall of thunder that shook the hangars.

...

The three-pronged volcano rose up out of the South Pacific. At the volcano's base, the water in the cove glittered with moonlight. The sounds of breaking surf and wind flowing through the palm and sandalwood trees had been uninterrupted for many years. From high up, strobing red and green lights approached the island. Landing lights burst from between the red and green lights and illuminated the beach, throwing unnatural shadows into the forest. The roar of jet engines overwhelmed all other sounds. The lights spun above the beach, and the gunship made its final descent, touching down. The brilliant-white landing lights and strobing marker lights shut off, leaving the beach in darkness. As the engines spun down, the sounds of the surf and breeze returned. The gunship's rear ramp opened, spilling light across the beach.

As the ramp descended, Leif walked out onto it, riding it down. Stacy followed him with her cane. Jeffrey stood in the opening, waiting for Stacy to make her way to the sand. Then he switched off the interior lights. As his eyes began adjusting to the moonlight, he walked down the ramp. He sat on the end of the ramp, unlaced his boots, pulled them off, and removed his socks. Setting them aside, he stood and wandered out onto the beach, the cool sand contouring to his feet. Along the eastern horizon, the afterburn of the sun still hung in a violet swath.

"The sun didn't set that long ago here, but we were in the air four hours," Stacy said.

"Yep," Jeffrey said.

"You're proud of your little gunship aren't you?"

"My only regret is that it isn't the one that kept us alive."

In the distance, thundering waves broke along a reef, their tumbling crests streaked with white foam.

"Well," Jeffrey said, clapping his hands together, "we should get some sleep. A big day tomorrow."

"I don't know about you," Stacy said, stabbing her cane into the sand, "but tomorrow I'm going sit on this beach, in the shade of that palm tree over there, and forget about the world."

...

Stacy woke the next morning just past dawn. Jeffrey's tent hung open, empty. She found Leif standing on the beach looking out across the water. Over his shoulder, she saw an inflatable, black Zodiac spraying a rooster tail as it hopped over the distant breakers. She could still make out Jeffrey's gray-white hair at that distance.

"What do you suppose he's up to?" she asked Leif.

"I have no idea."

...

After Jeffrey pulled beyond the reef, the ocean went into a smooth roll, and the Zodiac ran out across the water fast. The air, still cool from the night, coursed over him, lifting his shirt up in a dancing flutter. He cut the motor, and the boat slowed and sat down in the water. As it came to a stop, it rose and fell with the calm ocean. The rising sun sparked out above the volcano in a clear blade of light. Jeffrey inhaled the air, purified by ocean storms.

He reached out and grasped a yellow, plastic case and dragged it to him. Releasing two catches, he flipped the lid over on its hinge. He clacked a knob and the monochrome-copper screen lit up with an image of the ocean floor. Forty feet down, coral mottled the sandy floor. Jeffrey set the sensor to pick up on dense traces of carbon fiber as well as titanium. The image went dark, nothing found. He twisted the motor's throttle, and the boat moved forward.

He crisscrossed the ocean like this for several hours, staring at the screen and seeing nothing. The sun climbed up in the sky. As the heat of the day came on, he shut off the throttle and let the boat stop. Then he sat on the side and allowed himself to fall backward into the water. The bathtub-warm ocean wrapped around him and, when he pulled himself back into the boat, the breeze cooled his wet shirt and skin.

He looked at the monitor. Nothing. This is where it should be, but he couldn't be positive. He remembered coming in at a steep angle and watching it strike the water to the southwest of the island as he hung from his parachute cords. It had to be out here; it should be right under him.

He pulled farther away from the island and the sandy bottom rose up at him, now twenty feet deep. As he turned the boat away from the rising sand, something on the screen caught his eye, a shimmer of light. Had it been the sun, or his tired eyes? His neck ached from bending over the scanner, and his hand tingled with numbness from the buzzing outboard motor. He had already swapped out the battery pack with his spare, and now its indicator tilted toward empty. He would have to return to the beach soon.

He turned the Zodiac and came back around. Traces of something illuminated the screen. He shut the motor off and leaned over the screen, holding his hands up to block the sun.

Scattered traces of carbon fiber.

He felt excitement course through him. He throttled the motor, head still down, and aimed the Zodiac in a tight circle, each lap larger than the first. He saw the pattern now, a trail of carbon fiber moving east. He turned the Zodiac to follow the trail, and a large delta shape of titanium came onto the screen.

Can that really be it?

As he came closer, he turned the magnification up. Sure enough, the skeletal outline of a Phantom-class fighter glowed on the screen. Jeffrey could even see the bladelike forward canards extending from the nose.

He came right over the shape of the fighter and shut off the motor. Looking over the side of the boat, he saw coral and sand warping under thirty feet of water. He threw out a black-coated, steel anchor. The Zodiac floated in the current for a moment, and then the anchor line pulled tight.

He took off his shirt, exposing the grinning hammerhead on his shoulder and the wealth of scars across his torso. He tugged diving fins onto his feet and strapped on a buoyancy-compensator vest with a thin backpack re-breather. He put on his mask, checked the regulator, fitted the mouthpiece, took a few breaths and then, pressing his mask to his face, slipped backwards off the rubber side of the Zodiac.

He sank down, watching the bottom of the Zodiac tilting above him. The surface of the water fractured the sun in a brilliant kaleidoscope. He turned over. Below him, tendrils of bending sunlight ran across the ocean floor. He swam down to where the anchor rested in a coral outcrop. He swam around the coral. This was not it.

He looked around and saw, about fifty feet away, where another coral outcrop had the shape of a long diamond. The frame of a windscreen extended from the berm of pink coral like a hand from a grave. He kicked his fins and drifted toward the outcrop. As his shadow passed over the windscreen spars, several silver fish darted away.

He drifted over the open hole of the cockpit and saw that coral had overgrown the instrument panel. Taking a pick from his belt, he pried at the coral, breaking several sections away. Detritus floated up in a cloud and then settled away, exposing a tarnished silver chain hanging off the encrusted knob for the landing lights. He pulled on the chain and it snapped. He let the broken section of chain go, and it dropped down into the darker region of the cockpit. Hooking the end of his pick under the coral, he pried a lump off.

He put the lump of coral into a mesh collection bag and swam up to the surface, tossed the bag into the boat, and pulled himself up and in. Taking off his mask, he tossed it to the bottom of the boat and spit out his mouthpiece. With fins and re-breather backpack still on, he opened the bag and removed the lump of coral. He took out his pick and tapped and pried at the lump. It cracked away exposing a golden coin with a square hole in the center. The exposed side had four Chinese characters on it. He turned the coin over. There he saw a curled dragon.

Having it back in his hand shook him, but not in the way he had expected. It brought him back to the night his future wife had handed him a wooden box as they sat on the hood of his car. Jeffrey opened the box and found the coin.

"What's this for?" he asked, taking it from its mount and turning the coin over in his hand.

"Good luck," she said, and kissed him on the cheek.

"I don't need luck," he said in his youthful arrogance.

"That's why I chose this," she said, as she took the coin from his hand. She turned it over and ran her finger over the dragon. "This is who you pretend to be," she said with a smile, "but," and she turned the coin over to the four characters, "this is who you really are."

"What are those?"

She put the coin back in his hand, took hold of his head, and drew him toward her. She kissed the bridge of his nose and said, "Those are the four elements. You can pretend to be tough and angry, but I know you better. You're a very complex and wonderful man, Mr. Holt, full of all different kinds of possibilities, and I love that about you."

Sitting in the boat, rocking with the ocean, Jeffrey felt sorrow burn through his chest. His stomach fluttered. Tears filled his eyes, blurring his vision. Then, when the tears ran down his face, the coin came back into focus. He breathed in, and the breath caught in his belly. He looked away from the coin, back toward the island.

"You're gold to me Jeffrey Holt," she had said to him. "You make sure you make it home."

He had promised her he would, and felt he had lied when he said it. But, despite everything, he had kept the promise.

Now, so many years later, she could not do the same for him. When she died, he had been furious with the world, felt cheated.

The impulse to toss the coin back in the water overwhelmed him for a moment. Gripping the coin, he let the feeling pass. He did not want to escape the memory of her; he simply wished the pain of losing her wasn't so indelible. Then, as now, his grief subsided somewhat, allowing him to move on.

He opened his hand, looked at the coin, and sighed. He brought himself back to the purpose of the wreck, and what the coin confirmed. There had been no lies, no false memories implanted. All the battles, his scars, and the memories of his close friends screaming to death over the com had been real.

He slipped the coin into his pocket and looked into the water, down to the blurred forms of coral. There lay the physical evidence of one of the many moments death had scraped its claws down his back. He did not want to turn away. He felt closer to the younger man he had been and closer to her.

He pulled his gaze away, looking to the island. Through the spray of the breakers, he could see two figures on the strip of beach. Yanking on the rope, he unseated the anchor, drew it in, and sat in the back of the boat as it drifted away from the crash site.

He scrubbed his fingertips in his white beard, then reached back, and twisted the motor's throttle. As the Zodiac leapt out toward the island, he offered no final glance at the wreck. His eyes remained on the beach. There the two small figures stood close to one another. He contemplated what their futures might bring, but then considered that it didn't matter. Right now, those two were alive and well. In that, Jeffrey Holt found a deep sense of peace.

THE END

Author Jason Andrew Bond grew up in Oregon and currently lives in Washington State with his wife and son. He holds a Bachelor of Arts in English Literature from the University of Oregon and an MBA from the University of Colorado. Writing has been a lifetime dream, which–after many years lying dormant–has taken form in *Hammerhead*, his first novel. He is currently in the process of editing his second novel, and has begun to break ground on his third. Outside of writing and his family, martial arts is an important part of his life. At 18 years of age he entered an Aikido dojo for the first time, and has since trained in Jeet Kune Do, Tae Kwon Do, Shudokan Karate, Goshin Jutsu, and Brazillian Jiu-Jitsu.

For more about the author, future novels, and events, please visit:
www.JasonAndrewBond.com